THE GIRL

WHO

RESET THE

LIGHTNING BRAIN

A NOVEL

Best Selling Book Series in India

CLIFF RATZA

THE GIRL WHO RESET THE LIGHTNING BRAIN

A NOVEL

CLIFF RATZA

The Girl Who Reset the Lightning Brain

Copyright ©2025 by Clifford Ratza

All rights reserved. No parts of this book may be used or reproduced by any means, graphic, electronic, or mechanical, including photocopying, recording, taping, or by any information storage retrieval system, without the written permission of the publisher except in the case of brief quotations embodied in critical articles and reviews.

ISBN: 978-1-967375-90-5 Paperback)

ISBN: 978-1-967375-91-2 (E-book)

Library of Congress Control Number: 2025921199

Printed in the United States of America

Published by:

info@thequippyquill.com
(302) 295-2278

About the Book

The Girl Who Reset the Lightning Brain–our first book in the Reset Series–starts at a University of Texas at Austin's athletics center; Electra has just reset the record for its fitness test.

After an eighteen-month absence caused by a fire that destroyed her house and almost incinerated her, Electra is now ready to re-enter the "multiverse arena" of her life that she must now reset. She needed the absence to recalibrate herself, physically and mentally, and to readjust her personal and professional worlds after a supra-international conspiracy tried to terminate her.

And she has a new identity–Native American Indian ethnicity attached to the name Professor Electra Alisha Kirchner–for whom Indira the Singularity has created all documentation necessary to cover her early thirties, newly appointed adjunct professor position specializing in Space Medicine at U.T. Austin's Astrophysics Program.

The old Irani-Alisha-Electra trio is officially dead, even though forensics investigators found no remains in the rubble of the fire. Electra changes identities to remain in the shadows while redirecting her priorities and protecting her clone siblings and friends from potential danger due to association.

Electra combines some of the old with all that is new to engage in a lifestyle that will equip her to deal with adversaries old and new, who don't know that the lightning brain is alive and well. World climates–Environmental, Health, Social, Technological, Political, and Economic–are heating up and Electra plans to cool some of them down, getting as much help as Indira sees fit to give. So, follow the action-adventure trail starting on page one and leading to far-flung venues where all the events will climax at another unguessable ending.

The book's theme should resonate with all of us: no matter how exceptional the person, anyone can become a victim in a world that can't handle the truth, and each of us must handle the complexities of being "merely human" while applying our talents to whatever we want and developing our skills to whatever level suits us best by following an optimistic, pragmatic philosophy.

Readers should enjoy the book on whatever level they wish:

- Gripping action-packed thriller
- Glimpses into a plausible near-term future
- Insights for dealing with the "human condition"
- Illustrative worldview philosophy
- Fast-paced, suspense-filled, emotive narrative and imagery
- Introduction to topics every reader wants to know
- Interesting talking points going beyond sound-bites

So, get ready to enjoy what you are about to read as our nuanced characters confront life's contingencies. And just like for each of us, their actions might not always take them into the arenas they had planned for. But perhaps there is one outcome we can guarantee: your reading pleasure here and in upcoming books.

Main Characters

Protagonist

- Electra Kirchner (previously known as the Irani-Alisha-Electra trio and now the Electra-Alisha duo. Alisha is her official middle name as well as her alter-ego's).

Supporting Main Characters

- Indira (the Singularity) and Jason (the sub-Singularity). Electra's AI-empowered neural network software created Indira, the self-aware Singularity, over twenty years ago, who in turn created Jason. Both continue evolving.
- Evita (Eve) Cortez. Electra's favorite clone child. Renee, the Rainforest Girl, was brought back from the Amazon Rainforest by Electra, who named her Renee.

Supporting Secondary Characters

- Alonzo Cortez. Eve's identical twin clone brother.
- Monet Banda. Alonzo's Zimbabwean co-friend.
- Nari and Nila Bose. Another set of Electra's identical twin clones.
- The two sets of "orphan" twins, unaware of being clones, had been raised by Su-Lin Song Chou.
- Sanjay Kumar. Nila's Oriental Indian husband. They live in Mumbai.
- Professor Steven Plannert. Professor at George Washington University (GWU) and head of its Environmental Scanning Committee.
- Jonathan Segal. A professor at GWU's Environmental Sciences Department.

Minor Characters

- Indy-M and Jason-M. Androids. Lifelike robots loaded with Indira's advanced neural-net software.
- Odell Boyken. Electra's minority business partner in CFS Holistic Healthcare.
- Amahl and Zara Karim. A brother-sister pair of adolescents Irani rescued while on a mission to Isilabad.
- Xinqian (Xing) Hung. "Gang of Three Plus One" leader reporting to the "Bigger Brother Conspiracy."
- Newton (Newt) Kinslinger. President of the United States. Britt Starling. Commander of NASA's first Manned Mission to Mars. Boomer Gowon. Mars Mission First Officer reporting to Commander Starling.
- Miles and Shanna Drummond. A black brother-sister pair living in Austin, TX and being raised by a single-parent father (Marcel) - a studio musician.
- Darla Tinibu. Zimbabwean "power broker" whom Monet works for. Jiang (Jan) Brewer and Wen (Wendy) Tong. Sociopolitical analysts/consultants living in Beijing and reporting to Eve.
- Rick (RT) Tabasko, Parson (PH) Holsum, and Lucian (Mr. LP) Perteau. Electra's entrepreneurial-minded business partners.

Dedication

I am eternally grateful to my parents, Clyde and Betty Ratza, for all they gave and did for me. Mother was reader par excellence, and I believe she would have enjoyed reading and sharing my novels with Father, so I always begin book dedications by mentioning my "Royal Pair."

And I thank my sister, Claudia, for sharing and showing me the beauty of prose and poetry. Thanks also to Robert Williams and his entire Quippy Quill Productions Team. Their collective efforts brought to life this first book in its sequel series.

The Girl Who Reset the Lightning Brain is also dedicated to readers looking for a continuing action-adventure saga that shows a condition all of us share: we are always becoming as we adjust to events that may carry us into arenas far different than our wishes. And although Electra and her multiple personalities might not always reach expectations, a poem from Indira offers each of us a measure of whimsical pleasure while preparing for what may come.

The Arena

Did the arena survived in the ring,
Managed to battle to standstill or draw.
Did all I could to prepare what's to come,
Though seldom came victory because no one foresaw.
Everyone has to spend time center-stage,
Some will achieve results better than I.
Steel your emotions and look for an edge,
Give it best effort you simply must try.
Sooner or later you're on the way out,
Chance will decide when the battle is done.
No matter the record you're granted reprieve,
Exchange weathered gloves for a place in the Sun.
Unchained from the past so enjoy your today,
And ignore for the nonce what is coming your way.

I hope my latest novel keeps you fully engaged to the very end, as it shows our characters always doing their best whenever entering new arenas. Thank you for joining their journey.

Contents

Chapter 1
November 2166
"Re-entering the Arena"

"You can start cycling down, Ms. Kirchner. You've just reset our athletic center's fitness record."

Electra forced herself to reduce the cadence of the elliptical trainer after hearing the words just yelled from the fitness instructor who was recording her performance.

The endorphins I'm generating are giving me a runner's high that'll push me even higher if I don't cool my obsessive-compulsive drive, so I better do it now.

Electra stepped off the machine five minutes later, soaking in the scent of a freshly laundered towel as well as congratulations from the instructor.

"You've got the highest totals in each category–pushups, pullups, dips, and sit-ups. And the resistance-adjusted distance you covered in thirty minutes exceeds even the men's. I'll have to check, but you might be better than any of our university athletes. What's your secret?"

Electra stopped wiping away perspiration long enough to answer.

"Perhaps some of my Navajo DNA contributes. American Indians are known for strength and endurance."

"Maybe so, but you still have to convert all that potential into kinetic performance."

"Well, I do have a singular personal trainer who always keeps me motivated."

"Well, whatever your trainer says certainly works. Why don't you enter the regional fitness club competition? I can't imagine anyone beating you."

"Thanks for the offer. I'll let you know after I talk with her..."

After returning to her Austin townhome and then snacking on a peanut butter-covered banana, Electra invoked at her workstation Indira's GUI; fifteen minutes later, Electra continued sipping a Coca-Cola while Indira's voice continued matching her thoughtful expression, which usually accompanied their weekly review meetings.

"I could not observe much of your performance. Your center's surveillance coverage is spotty, so please tell me how you did."

Electra took another sip before putting down her Coke and putting on an expression that matched Indira's emerging smile.

"I reset the scoring record, and the fitness instructor wants me to enter a regional club competition. I think I know what you'll say, but please tell me anyway."

Indira did so without delay.

"First, I'm pleased that you're smiling but not gloating. The combination of your yearlong training regimen and my adjusting your DNA-regulated hormonal and aging systems have given you the fitness level of an elite early-thirties athlete. And I don't recommend entering more competitions. You must still remain in the shadows even when re-entering the arenas of your choice. But why this compulsion to maintain such an exceptional fitness level?"

"You should understand cognitively and emotionally, but not physically because you inhabit Cyberspace. Perhaps you will if you, uh, I mean we, ever upload you into an android. Is that your intention?"

"Not for the time being. So please, tell me why?"

"Unlike cognitive and emotional personas, the physical is much more susceptible to physiological decline. And for me, the desire for physical excellence is a combination of lifestyle and the thrill of an endorphin high I get when performing at an exceptional level. And now that you've reset my performance scale, my daily routine will keep its decline to a minimum."

"Now I understand. So, now that you are satisfied with your fitness level, what are your immediate intentions?"

"Well thanks to you, I can now reactivate two careers that might lead to others. The old me, the Irani-Alisha-Electra trio, is officially dead, burned to a crisp when the Bigger Brother conspiracy destroyed my DC-area house.

"But you hacked into all necessary academic and government files to create the new me–Professor Electra Alisha Kirchner–a recently appointed adjunct specializing in Space Medicine at UT Austin's astrophysics program. My new hairstyle, cosmetics, and wardrobe complete the makeover. And you put all my assets in a trust fund you control via your AAM Investment Services business that gives me enough money. I can use all the above for cover when contacting people from my previous life."

Indira's nod said she agreed before adding,

"And the minor cosmetic surgery peeled away enough years and changed enough features so your assumed Navajo heritage shows. Native American and Oriental Indian skin color and facial structures are similar. No one will ever discover the real you unless they do DNA matching, but that will never happen because only we have samples."

Electra's smile morphed into a question when she said,

"The embedded chip upgrade and lightning brain reset you did with the Brain Probe—I don't feel any different most of the time, but how different am I now?"

"Your chips are as good as those used by DOD or NASA. And your cognitive and emotional personas have improved because your hormonal and neurochemical systems are more youthful, matching your early thirties official age. And they force-multiply your now-exceptional fitness level, which increases the production of both neural and bone marrow stem cells along with the enzyme telomerase, which lengthens the telomere protective cap on your chromosomes. But don't advertise any of this."

Electra's smile returned with her cheery-sounding words.

"Don't worry, I'm a pro at staying in the shadows while getting to where I want to be. And that means reconnecting with my four clone siblings as well as Jonathan Segal via Professor Plannert."

"And don't forget that by posing as your executor, I have monitored your siblings via Eve and have maintained some continuity for you. I have made all the fiduciary adjustments you wished."

"Thank you for that. And you've also helped Eve reset herself after my untimely disappearance. She'll be my first clone child to know who I am when she's ready, but that won't happen soon. However, I'm ready to reenter my arenas, allowing me to take over from the 3-D shadows rather than your continuing from Cyberspace."

Indira's smile widened before she said,

"That's why you are my favorite human. You've already visited our Deus Lab on the Pequot Reservation to monitor our Indy-M android while she follows my commands for vaccine modifications and network security software development. I'll let you carry on, and I will tell my Assistant Singularity Jason that you are ready to re-enter. And now that Alisha and Irani are no longer needed, I assume you will talk whenever you wish to your inner voice, so please share our conversation with it, a voice created by your lightning brain that idealizes your practically perfect biological mother. How convenient that you can switch brain states as fast as a bolt of lightning."

Although Indira's GUI vanished before saying goodbye, Electra was not at a loss for words.

Indeed, I will. Indira's the name of my inner voice as well as the Singularity. And how fitting. The one that created me and the one I created are always there for me.

Electra stood, stretching arms overhead in preparation for updating her to-do list.

Will those I care about want to connect with the new me? And what will I do if they don't? I better avoid obsessing about this… better just to wait and see.

Just before midnight, Electra dialed back her obsessive-compulsive predisposition. She knows what she wants to do in the coming week or two and could rest easy until the morning sun peeks through.

Chapter 2
December 2166

"A Most Challenging Year"

"Can you believe a whole year's gone by since Miss Irani and her house burned to smithereens? Lucky for you and me we were staying with Miss Eve. And lucky she's still able to let us stay."

Amahl's boisterous words were coming out after his smacking lips finished another slice of pumpkin pie at the kitchen table. Eve could see that his sister, Zara, had something to say so she let her speak first.

"Don't chew with your mouth open. It makes you look uncouth. We'll never be sure if we were lucky because other choices may have been even better. And don't believe all that Metaverse hype you listen to. There's only one Universe, and that's the one we're in right now. I don't think Miss Irani escaped into another world."

Eve had to respond with an enthusiasm midway between that of the two adolescents now gazing at her.

"I might have been luckier if I'd been there. Maybe I could have stopped the fire or helped put it out. And if I'd been there, I wouldn't have been at the White House meeting when the laptops blew up, killing my partner, Sabrina, plus the President and Vice President. Who knows what might have happened if I'd been elsewhere?"

Zara surprised Eve by giving an answer.

"But it turns out that the new President, Newt Kinslinger, said you didn't know about your and Miss Sabrina's booby-trapped laptops, and he decided to make you the Oval Office spokesperson. Isn't that lucky for you?"

"I guess so, and even though it's been a most upsetting year since then, I've adjusted to losing Miss Irani, even though I sometimes feel bad she's gone. But if she were here, she'd tell all of us to keep moving ahead, so let's keep doing that."

Ready to do so, Amahl spoke after standing.

"Could you take us to some Christmas concerts this year? We didn't get a chance to go last time."

"Sure. Why don't you and Zara surf the Net to find the ones you might like?"

"I'll do that after playing some video games. See ya later."

The energy level in the kitchen dropped after he left, but Zara used the lull to redirect the conversation.

"You have been a tower of strength for Amahl and me throughout the year. I will do my best to repay you when I get a chance. I don't know when that will be, but I will."

Eve pitched her voice to hide how much Zara's words had pinged her.

"It's the other way around. You and your brother have helped me grow by giving me something to do other than grieve over losing Miss Irani and Sabrina. I'm sure they would like how we've helped each other. Now, why don't you go visit your friends? I loved doing that when I was your age. I'll take care of cleaning up…"

Eve decided after tidying the kitchen that more cleaning would be in order. Tomorrow would be the second Monday of the month, the day when she would have her one and only identical twin brother, Navy SEAL Alonzo Cortez, visit her at the White House so he could give the President his personal point of view on the state of the world. Alonzo would then stay with her and her permanent guests until redeploying the following week to his next assignment in Zimbabwe, a place Eve wanted the President to hear more about.

Eve hustled to the visitors' reception area as soon as she heard from Security, clearing Alonzo through the checkpoint and then taking him to the Oval Office, talking all the way.

"It's been over a year since you visited, but you're as handsome as ever. And you'll impress the President by the way you fill out your uniform. You look fit enough to handle any assignment."

Alonzo's playful nudge acknowledged the compliment before saying,

"You're a bit thinner and more mature, more confident than before. I guess the last year has done that to you, and I bet all the eligible DC bachelors approve."

Eve coasted them to a stop before saying,

"We'll talk about all the personal stuff at my place, but now it's strictly a military drill. Get set to meet the President." Eve knocked before entering.

Even though this one p.m. informal meeting meant little, President Newton–Newt aka Chuck–Kinslinger had completed his always meticulous rehearsal not once, but twice. His stint as Speaker of the House had taught him to review the backgrounds of everyone on all sides of whatever was up for debate.

He had orchestrated the White House explosion last year that killed both President and Vice President and catapulted him into the presidency, even though his Democratic Party had lost the White House race to the Re-Gen Party. The explosion had also killed one White House staffer and made another he particularly liked–Eve Cortez–a person of interest for the ensuing Secret Service investigation. Because he knew about her innocence, he manipulated the facts to have her cleared, and he kept her on his presidential staff rather than throw her to the DC wolves who would devour her, now that her powerful mentor–Irani Ramani had been terminated, also via Kinslinger's Bigger Brother connection. Newt realized that Eve's gratitude could prove useful, as might her brother's military connections. Newt launched into his presidential performance as soon as the door opened.

The President marched from his desk to return the salute and then offer his hand to a poster-perfect Navy SEAL standing next to Eve. He let her handle the standard greetings before leading them to a nearby sofa and chairs. President Kinslinger filled the sofa before starting the discussion.

"Eve tells me you've had several tours abroad. How did you like the one in Germany?"

Alonzo's no-nonsense delivery matched the facts.

"Well, sir, my SEAL training paid off. Me and my team rescued several families from flooding that the experts say climate change caused. And not long after that, we extracted some Estonian fighters battling a Russian invasion."

"How nice for you to be young and fit and able to help those who need it. And though I'm no longer young and fit, I feel good about doing my best to help our nation steer the right course, at home and abroad. I imagine you and your team feel the same way. Eve says your next assignment is a return to Zimbabwe to assist their Pan-African security strike force."

Alonzo's look told Eve to continue for him.

"From the briefings I've prepared, we see that Darla Tinibu contributes much to Zimbabwe, and Alonzo speaks on a regular basis with one of her staffers. So, he's ahead of everyone regarding how climate change has elevated the importance of Northern Africa's water resources. They're now more valuable than oil. And he's seen for himself that climate change affects migratory patterns, which in turn are impacting the spread of viruses."

Eve shifted in her chair, stalling to find something else to say, but she didn't have to because the President's Chief of Staff stepped in.

"We're ready for you, Mr. President."

Alonzo stood before anyone else and waited for the President to dismiss him, which he did with a final handshake while saying,

"I won't wish you luck because you don't need it, but I will wish you a safe trip. When do you leave?"

"Next week, sir. I'll stay with Eve until then."

"Well, I'm leaving you in good hands. And I'm sure she'll let me know how your African assignment turns out. Eve, why don't you show your brother around the place?"

"I will, and thank you for meeting with us."

The conversation during the tour returned to that of typical brother-sister kibitzing. Eve asked if Monet Banda could still tolerate his presence, a question he answered by poking her in the ribs before asking about her love life, to which she said that none of the fellows in DC measured up to him. His pleased look told her that neither Nari nor Nila had told him that she preferred females to males. There are some things that the three sisters would never share with their brother.

Alonzo said,

"I'm sure you miss Irani even more than the rest of us, but you've toughened up, and I bet Nari and Nila say the same. Why don't you set up a conference meeting on the computer for all of us? I'd like to see and hear how they're doing."

"Don't fret, I already have that on the agenda."

Everyone connected into the midnight Sunday, December 14th call, a time chosen to allow for the twelve-hour difference between DC and Beijing. Eve spoke first.

"Hello from Alonzo and Eve here in DC to Nari in Beijing, and Nila with Sanjay in Mumbai. All of you are looking good. And wouldn't you say the same about Alonzo?"

He saw on the monitor Nari's nodding approval before hearing her words.

"I'd say he's ready for action right now, and you look so too."

Nila added more.

"We'll have to make sure he's with us if we ever get stuck again in our skyscraper elevator, but Sanjay promises that's a onetime only happening."

Eve replied,

"And you better hold him to it. You don't want your kid to be without parents. Are you still expecting in June?"

A happy-looking Sanjay answered.

"Indeed yes, our son should arrive by then, and I'm certain you and Nila will talk several times before. And maybe even talk about politics. Has your White House job settled down after losing Miss Irani?"

"It has, and working for President Kinslinger is OK. In fact–" Nari interrupted.

"Wait a minute, last time you said you didn't like him. What gives?"

"Now that I'm working for him, I've gotten to like him. He's not as far to the right as some of the Guardian Party's radical members. And he's got great political instincts that add to his statesman-like image, which most people go for. Now, what about you and Jan and Wendy? Are you still keeping tabs on Beijing politics?"

"Sure am, and that Bigger Brother conspiracy you used to talk about has petered out. Are you still hunting for it?"

"No, I gave up on it when the fire killed Miss Irani. I had bigger problems to deal with but I've got my life back on track. And it sounds like all of you have too. Let's let Alonzo tell us what he's got lined up, and then everyone else can do likewise…"

After ending the call half an hour later, Eve stared at Alonzo, unsure what else to say, but he knew what Eve might like to hear, so he said,

"Your people and diplomacy skills are getting better and better. Even though Irani's gone, her handiwork lives on in you."

"I think all of us can say the same, but there's no need to say it. What we do says it better than our words, so let's do what we've got planned. Irani'd be pleased, and she'd tell us it's time to sleep. Tomorrow we've got places to go and promises to keep, so let's call it a night."

Alonzo hugged her before hiking to the spare bedroom where he would dream about Monet, the only female he loved more than Eve.

Chapter 3
January 2167

"A Female to Know"

"Who is Electra Kirchner?"

Professor Steven Plannert already had the authoritative words to answer the question asked by a committee member, and they flowed as smoothly as his chairmanship style while concluding his monthly George Washington University Environmental Scanning Committee meeting.

"Evidently, she's a significant contributor to some of the papers published by the late Irani Ramani. I'm interviewing her today. Perhaps she can fill Irani's consulting role for us."

Another member continued the line of questioning.

"That might be difficult. Professor Ramani was exceptional, a Renaissance woman of the first order, knowledgeable in so many disciplines. I'll be surprised if she can measure up."

"Indeed, she was, but if Kirchner seems suitable, I shall introduce her at our next meeting..."

Electra mentally reviewed her notes as she strode toward Professor Plannert's office.

His style is so different from Professor Ravenhill's, my long-ago advisor, but both have served me well by connecting me with others who meet my needs and vice versa. I'll act accordingly so Plannert likes the new me.

Plannert stood to greet her when she tapped on his half-open office door.

"You must be Ms. Electra Kirchner. Please come in and sit across from me." After she followed orders, he continued.

"Goodness, there's a bit of resemblance between you and your dearly departed mentor Irani. I hope it extends to your cognitive ability as well. And you say you co-authored some of her papers. Did she tell you much about her consulting for my Committee?"

"Yes, and I have tried to develop a breadth and depth of knowledge like hers. May I explain?"

"By all means, please do so..."

After twenty minutes of back-and-forth discussion, Electra saw from Plannert's glance at his cell-phone that her time with him was about to end, so she wrapped up as well.

"I could tell you more about my qualifications, but I hope I've said enough."

"Hmm, you're only a newly appointed adjunct professor, but I use a collegial approach, so I'll have my Committee members decide. Please join us at our February meeting if you are still interested."

"What might be the topic? Is there anything you'd like me to prepare?"

"I let the members decide, and their areas of expertise are wide-ranging."

"Very well, please let me know the date and time and I'll be there."

Professor Plannert remained standing after shaking her hand and then listening to the sound of her receding steps as she trudged away, thinking while watching.

A very talented lady, almost as if a younger Irani just stepped out of a time machine. I do think my committee members will agree. I don't want to override them so I shall simply wait and see. And I hope my objectivity didn't discourage her. After all, in matters like this my head should always stay ahead of my heart.

Electra's thoughts were just the opposite.

He's not impressed. Irani's halo effect doesn't carry over to my lowly academic rank, so I'll have to prove myself to the Committee if I want to use its contacts for networking where I want to go. I'll worry about that later, but now I better start thinking about reconnecting with Eve at dinner tonight.

Amahl clomped to the door as fast as his clubfoot allowed, hoping that Zara would wait for him before opening it. They knew who it would be but not what to expect. Amahl's words came out first after she opened the door.

"You look sorta like Miss Irani but without a coupla years. And you've got lightning bolt earrings, just like hers. Are you from the same family?"

Eve, who was trailing behind, took over from there.

"Hello, Electra. With me are the brother-sister team Irani brought back from Isilabad to take care of, and I inherited that responsibility. I've got pizza on the table, so please come in and we can talk while eating."

Amahl led the way. Ten minutes later, Electra managed to edge into the conversation.

"So, I'm Electra Kirchner but please just call me Electra. And you can consider me Miss Irani's protégé. She mentored me and I worked on some of her projects. Over time, we formed a friendship as strong as family, and I learned about a month ago during her estate settlement that I'm its inheritor. She left me instructions regarding what to do, and that's why I'm here–to find out how you're doing. So please tell me."

Amahl and Zara talked all the way from pizza to ice cream. When finally finished, Eve excused them so the adults could continue. Then she paused for Electra to proceed.

"Irani thought so highly of you that you are now the majority owner of her consulting business, which I guess makes me sort of your one and only direct report. Here's your set of keys to the Chevy Chase office. Can I help you settle in?"

Eve nestled them in the palms of her hands before saying,

"She never told me about you, but she had so much going on she couldn't tell me about everything. But I know all about the consulting business, so I don't need help. But what about you? Do you have a place to stay when in DC?"

"I do, so don't worry about me. And I have more to tell you. Irani left money for you as well as for Zara and Amahl, which you're supposed to manage. And she earmarked some of it for an operation to fix his clubfoot. She also left instructions for you to introduce me to a Mr. Odell Boyken. Do you know who he is?"

"Irani introduced us to him before the fire. I'll set up a meeting so you can join us."

Electra leaned back before saying,

"Please call me when you have the details. And I have more to say. Irani left money for your brother, Nari Bose, and Nila Kumar. All I need are the bank account numbers so I can transfer the funds. Would you arrange a conference call for you to introduce me to them?"

Eve pulled back while shaking her head.

"No, just give me your Email address and they'll contact you."

Electra pulled back a tad further, pausing for a moment before saying,

"As you wish. Well, it seems like you have things under control, so I'll be going. And please call if you want me to chip in on any political analysis. I learned how to do that from Irani."

Eve's words came as fast as her rising from the table.

"I appreciate the offer, but that won't be necessary. And since you own part of the business, I'll make sure to stay in touch…"

On the drive home, Electra voiced to herself disappointment.

Too bad Eve's grown such a tough emotional skin. If not, I might have been able to stay closer to my clones than just lurking in the shadows. I'll have to find another way, but I'll sort that out another day.

Because of Beijing's twelve-hour ahead time differential, Eve decided that calling as soon as Electra left wouldn't disrupt the rhythm of Nari's day. She picked up on the third ring.

"Hello Eve, I recognized your caller I.D. This must be important, so what gives?"

"You'll never guess. Irani Ramani is giving all of us an inheritance."

Eve heard Nari's gasp and paused for her to reply but she didn't, so she plowed ahead.

"I just had dinner with Electra Kirchner. I never heard of her until a couple of days ago. Anyway, she worked close enough with Irani to be the executor of her estate. She gave me her phone number and Email address, and she wants you to contact her for arranging the money transfer. Whatcha think?"

Nari's words finally came back.

"Uh, you think we can trust her?"

"She showed me the legal documents, so why not? Why don't you tell Nila and I'll tell Alonzo?"

"That makes sense, and it makes sense she's giving you something. You liked her more than the rest of us did, but..."

Eve filled in for Nari's silence.

"I guess that didn't matter. She liked us all. Too bad you never warmed up to her."

"I feel even worse now. Too bad there's nothing I can do to make up for all the times I sort of dissed her."

"Maybe you can talk it out with this Kipper person. She looks like a younger Irani and must be smart if Irani mentored her. You take it from here..."

Eve continued talking to herself after she disconnected.

I'm too tired to call Alonzo. I'll do that tomorrow, or maybe just send him an Email. Either way, he and Kirchner can sort things out.

None of her children called Electra during the following week, so she kept busy thinking through what she had already talked about with Plannert as well as with Indira, and she didn't worry any further about Eve until she received an Email giving the date and time for meeting Odell.

Electra arrived on time, but Eve and Odell were already talking when she came to his cubicle.

He looks as cheery as ever, but I wonder what he'll say when I tell him the news.

A grinning Odell rose to greet her while Eve remained sitting as her gaze became pensive.

"Eve told me about you, so no need to repeat the story, but come on in and sit with us."

After doing so, Odell waited for Electra to begin the conversation.

"I inherited Irani's estate, so that makes me your one and only minority interest partner in CFS Holistic Healthcare, and I won't meddle. I'll be your silent partner unless you have something for me to do."

"Well, if you're as sharp as Irani, I can think of several things. Let me go through them and you can pick..."

Electra listened during the Odell-filled minutes while making occasional comments to herself.

How nice, he remembers what I had suggested. I'll tell him which one I pick as soon as he stops.

The opportunity presented itself ten minutes later.

"So, if any of this is good for you, it'll be good for me if you can pitch in."

"I can put together a presentation you can give to parents for what you call an adolescent extracurricular learning program. It's important for high school students to know about body language, listening skills, public speaking, and Myers-Briggs personality profiling. By when would you like me to finish it?"

"You let me know when you can get it done. And maybe you can have Zara and Amahl be your first students."

"Good thinking. I'll call you when I'm ready. And here's my Email and phone number."

Electra rose to go, and this time Eve did too, shaking her hand after Odell did and then saying,

"Why don't you call me sometime? I can let you know how I'm managing Zara and Amahl's money plus what's happening in our consulting business."

Electra held Eve's hand long enough to say,

"I'll do that, and I promise not to interfere. You certainly know what you're doing," and then marched away.

Keeping busy working on other reentry activities, Electra kept her word by not calling any of the clones. She didn't expect the call that came the night before Plannert's next committee meeting, and though she recognized the voice (it belonged to a female she loved as much as Eve) she pretended she didn't.

"This is Electra Kirchner, and you are?"

"I am Monet Banda, calling on behalf of Alonzo Cortez. He wants to thank you for sending him his most welcome inheritance. And according to what his sister told him, Irani treated you just like she treated me, like one of the family. I would imagine you miss her as much as I."

Electra concealed her feelings as best she could when saying,

"She did, and she taught me a lot too, about most of her projects as well as life. And she mentioned your name when we worked on some of the joint Zimbabwean-American projects."

"Well, she didn't mention you, but I don't consider that unusual. Miss Irani was most discreet. And she had wonderful diplomacy skills. Perhaps you might assist me."

"I will if it helps you. Please tell me what you have in mind."

As Monet's impeccably French-accented English spelled it out, Electra commented only to herself.

She remembers everything about the climate change and possible Zimbabwean-Indian coalition projects. We can certainly help one another."

"So if you think you can, please let me know."

"Why don't I review all my notes and then call Alonzo, who can set up a call for the three of us?"

"That will be fine. I will tell him about our call. And I look forward to working with you."

"As do I. I am so pleased that you contacted me."

After disconnecting, Electra picked up right where she left off but now worried less as she continued thinking about Plannert's meeting.

I must force myself to obsess less. Outcomes will come my way if I just let the lightning brain deal with events, whether or not I control them. This is good advice for tomorrow.

Electra took it by putting her work away and then musing while in bed.

Whether I'm awake or asleep, I know my lightning brain will keep working. It is the source of my exceptional abilities, and I must use some of them tomorrow. Which ones? The lightning brain will decide, and I've learned throughout several lifetimes it knows what will work and what I must do. Now go to sleep so I'm rested and ready for whatever might unfold. And I can rest easy, for I know the lightning brain will always see me through.

Chapter 4
February 2167

"Uncharted Territory"

Pretending not to recognize committee members or Jonathan Segal, Electra smiled blandly while Professor Plannert introduced her before starting the meeting.

"I thought it wise to have Professor Segal from the Environmental Sciences Department give us his presentation before our roundtable discussion begins because Irani Ramani often assisted him. Jonathan, please do so."

Jonathan distributed two handouts after reaching the head of the table, pausing so everyone could study them while he discreetly studied Electra.

She does resemble a younger Irani, but with shorter hair and more casual clothes. And if the clothes came off, she'd look even fitter and trimmer, which will be a fringe benefit if she knows her stuff. And we'll know that after the Committee grills her.

Electra glanced obliquely at Jonathan as she reviewed the handouts.

Jeez, there's more here than I ever remember him talking about. His NASA contacts must have given him a lot of details. I hope the Committee knows less than me.

Jonathan launched into his talk several minutes later.

"My associates at NASA liked the control and navigation software that Irani and I developed and modified for their AUV, which is the abbreviation for autonomous underwater vehicle. They also liked our AI-empowered software that controlled its escape pod and monitored its occupants. NASA wanted us to adapt it for the upcoming manned flight to Mars, and I've been trying to do so on my own ever since Irani was killed in the fire.

"It's been slow going without her, but Professor Kirchner says she assisted Irani, so perhaps she can partner with me and consult for you. And she should know a lot about NASA because she has a space medicine degree. That's why my first handout talks about NASA's approach to solar system exploration. Let me walk you through it."

NASA Solar System Exploration Primer
Steps to the Stars

The Steps:
1. Low-Earth Orbits
2. Lunar Exploration and Colonization
3. Explorations of Inner Planets (Mercury, Venus, Mars); Missions to Mars
4. Explorations and Missions to Asteroids
5. Construction of Permanent Habitats Orbiting the Sun, Mars, and Permanent Exoplanet Colonies
6. Explorations and Missions to Outer Planets (Jupiter, Saturn, Uranus, Neptune, Pluto)

Cosmological Constraints:
1. Enormous Distances
2. Speed of Light
3. Resource Availability

Scientific Challenges
1. Travel dictated by Newtonian (Classical) Physics: Quantum Fields and Wormholes Unavailable
2. Spacecraft paths must utilize multiple Gravitational Fields to Conserve Fuel

Technological Challenges
1. Space Elevator to Moon for Maximizing delivery Payload (People Supplies)
2. Lunar Base Construction using Lunar Resources 3. Design of Viable Spacecraft for Interplanetary Journey and Construction at Lunar Base

Physiological Challenges
1. Impact of extended weightlessness on Human Body
2. Damage caused by extended exposure to Radiation
3. Psychological effects caused by Isolation

Current Status
Two-Stage Space Elevator Completed
First Stage:
1. Docking Station in Geostationary Equatorial Orbit (32 Km Radius)
2. Cable made of Graphene-Carbon Nanotubules Connects Docking Station to Earth Station (Propulsion/Fuel System remains on Earth)

Second Stage:
1. Another Docking Station in Geostationary Lunar Orbit
2. Cable Connects to Lunar Base

Lunar and Martian Rovers perfected as well as
Martian Aero-Drones
Martian Spaceship Built and Tested
- Radiation Exposure Acceptable: Space Medicine Safe and Effective
- Utilizes Long-Duration Multi Nuclear-Solar-Chemical-Ion Power Sources that Generate Greater Impulse Velocity
- Robots Tested Initial Flights
- AI-Empowered Software for Controlling Spacecraft and Robots Adequate but Newer Releases Expected
- Suspension Pods and Escape Pods Viable when controlled by AI-Empowered Software

NASA's Martian Mission Plan
- Humans and Robots make up the Crew
- Land on Mars for Surface Exploration
- Build Martian Base
- Build Docking Station and Martian Elevator
- Additional Missions TBD

Jonathan proceeded methodically through the handout. No one– including Electra–made comments or asked questions. Jonathan gave a concise summary twenty minutes later.

"NASA's made a lot of Martian Mission progress during the interval starting from our walking on the Moon until today, and it's preparing for the first-ever manned mission to Mars whose launch date is early next year. Let me take you through my next handout, which sketches what's involved."

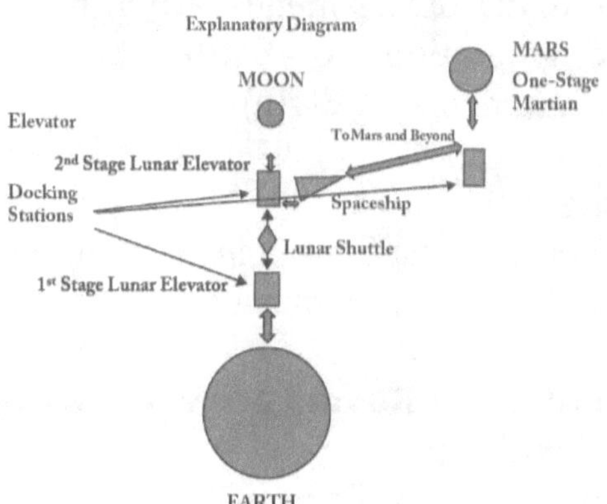

"NASA already has an operational two-stage lunar elevator, which is an engineering marvel all on its own. It makes transferring vast amounts of supplies to and from Earth and NASA's lunar colony cost-effective, while geosynchronous orbits keep the docking stations fixed relative to what they're rotating around so the cable between them and their base maintains a vertical orientation. And NASA's Martian spaceship will launch from the lunar docking station so that all the fuel it'll burn will accelerate it toward Mars. There's no gravity well to climb out of.

"And the spaceship's designed for a Martian landing. Initial missions will have joint human and robotic crews for Martian exploration using rovers and drones. Subsequent missions will build NASA's Martian base and orbital station. And after that? Well, I'll let you guess the pun that fits."

Jonathan could see from several members' expressions that questions were beginning to form, but he postponed them by speaking first.

"Well, why don't we let Professor Kirchner take my place and add her comments before you ask her for answers to whatever's on your minds?"

Plannert gazed at Electra, who started speaking a couple of moments later.

"Thanks to Jonathan, I definitely learned more about NASA's stepping stones to the stars, and you might agree with this fitting pun—the sky's the limit. I can tell he knows more about NASA than I do, but I can speak to the physiological challenges. I'm continuing to research my PhD dissertation topic of medicines to counteract nausea caused by weightlessness and spatial disorientation, plus medicines to minimize the effects of extended spaceflight on vision. If I may, let me explain further..."

Plannert took over fifteen minutes later.

"Well, you certainly know about space medicine. Let me ask our members what they think?"

One of the younger women spoke next.

"But how far does your expertise range? Irani could handle every topic that came up. Do you think you can do the same?"

"She wouldn't have mentored me if I couldn't. For example, I picked up on software for controlling vehicles or suspension and escape pods as well as analyzing telemetry data. Maybe you could suggest a topic."

"How about climate change? Jonathan and I are collaborating on how it impacts South America. What do you know about that?"

"That's uncharted territory for me, as is a journey to Mars, but I learn quickly. I hope to have the opportunity to show you and the committee."

Several additional questions arose before Plannert ended the meeting.

"I think Electra has addressed our concerns. I recommend she be our consultant. Any dissenters, please speak up."

There were none, so Plannert adjourned the meeting before motioning for Electra and Jonathan to stay.

They clustered at the table before he directed words at Jonathan.

"Electra's skills might prove useful on several of your projects. You take it from here and report periodically on progress. And why don't you take her to lunch at the Faculty Club? Both of you have earned it."

Electra dialed back her take-charge approach to let Jonathan control the ensuing conversation. After enough small talk about the elegantly understated dining room and its menu, she sensed that his waning smile signaled a new subject.

"You'll have to convince my NASA contacts that by working together we can give them what they want. You think you can do that?"

"Didn't I just do that for the Committee?"

"Yes, but they're academics. Nothing's life or death for them, but everything is for NASA. You'll have to meet a higher standard."

Electra waited an appropriate amount of time before replying.

"I can clear whatever height they set the bar."

Then she waited to gauge Jonathan's words and reaction, which came a minute or so later with the beginnings of a smirk.

"OK, I'll set up a face-to-face for us with NASA. When can you be ready?"

"Where will it be?"

"Either at Johnson Space Center near Houston or at the Boca Chica SpaceX Starship campus just outside Brownsville, Texas. Space projects today are so complex that NASA subcontracts private companies like SpaceX and Blue Origin to handle some of the pieces. I can see you have questions, but save them until we get there, OK?"

"That's fine by me, and I'll be ready to talk about South American climate change whenever you want."

"OK, but not now. We've done enough heavy-duty thinking for one morning. It's time to enjoy lunch…"

Electra went afterwards directly to the fitness center near her live-in office, needing a run to settle down and plan ahead, the uncertain weather matching her mood.

I'm ticked. Irani didn't have to prove herself this often, but I don't have her track record. I have to build one for the new me, which I've done many times before, but I'm getting tired doing it. Why is it getting to me? Why is it getting harder to get up in the morning? Maybe the answer will come on the run. Hmm, Maybe I should talk to Indira.

The lightning brain freewheeled as Electra relaxed into the run while random thoughts came and went.

I'm glad my new fitness center and office are near my previous ones. It's so much easier running on familiar trails instead of getting frustrated looking for replacements. I guess I can say the same about my circle of friends, but I've built them before and can do it again if I make the effort. And I think I know what Indira would say– that's what life is all about, so just keep doing it.

Electra finished her run just after the wind started swirling freezing snowflakes, but they landed mostly on her shoulders and added to the thrill of finding shelter from a worsening storm. By the time a warm shower washed away the chill, she felt better even though the lightning brain had produced no definitive answers. And she remained in that more settled state for the rest of the evening while puttering around in her office and scribbling a weekend schedule.

Gads, the office looks so clinical. I better hire an interior decorator to put a bit of life into the place. And I'll put off contacting Indira until next week. The lightning brain might come up with some answers between now and then. And I've done enough for one day, so it's time to put my questions away and go to bed. I'm sure something will come into my head by the time I wake up.

Electra bolted upright, awakened by a once-familiar inner voice ringing out.

"The lightning brain says you've slept long enough. It's time for me to explain why I've been called back to duty."

Electra knew immediately that Alisha had much to say, so she said nary a word and let her alter ego continue.

"You've done an exceptional job since the fire resetting yourself for the new you, but you've relapsed into some of your old habits–too much obsessive-compulsive behavior, too much philosophical musing, and not enough time off to vanish into the moment or enjoy a past remembrance. And you're on the verge of adding paranoid personality disorder–PPD–to your list of flaws. You're becoming a bit of a fusspot, suspicious and distrusting when those predispositions aren't called for. My role is to improve the old you, and you should like that. You're always working to make yourself better, and that's why the new you is now the new us. You're still in charge of our cognitive and physical personas, but I'll take care of emotions and feelings. What do you think?"

Electra took only a moment to gather her thoughts before saying,

"You're right. I've been too focused on becoming and have lost sight of just being in the moment and enjoying right now. No wonder I've been so uptight. Now I know why I've been so tired and depressed, reluctant to get out of bed and face the day or look for new challenges."

Alisha's reassuring words came back.

"You knew about all this but simply forgot. After all, you are the one who recited to me long ago some of Mother's relevant poems. Why not pick one and do it again?"

Electra searched her memory before answering the challenge.

"I found the one I want. It's called 'Vanishing Point' and I recited its first verse to Robin just before she wowed the audience on the night she won her piano scholarship. That was long before the lightning brain summoned you, but you can search for her in our memory. And here are all the verses:

Are you among the fortunate few –

disappearing into the present?

Abandoning past and future – if but only for a moment.

If so then you are truly Tuesday's Child,

Full of grace – radiant with the joy of being.

Or did you lose that magic long ago?

Replaced with ties to times other than Now.

Restraining you from madness and the most,

Now a bland observer of Life's games swirling about.

Do you seek shelter in the spectator's role?
Fortune's slings and arrows exact no toll.
Blanketed by a numbing serenity,
Insulated from high anxiety.
Or do you want your senses revived?
With quickening pulse you come alive.
Find someone or something to be your new scope,
And vanish within is your last and best hope."

"I knew you'd find one that fits. So now, I'll retire metaphorically while you retire physically and our lightning brain continues doing whatever it wishes. Good night, and always remember, I'm always with you."

Alisha's voice disappeared but the sensation echoed inside Electra's head, fading away when she finally rested it on the pillow and retreated into a peaceful, dream-filled sleep of pleasant remembrances as well as new places and faces that she knew a surprise-filled tomorrow promised to bring.

Chapter 5
February 2167
"Familiar Places with New Faces"

Having remembered everything Alisha had told her when she awakened, Electra bounded out of bed, ready to seize the day and happy to have her alter ego ready for action once again, although she probably wouldn't enter the conversation this morning. Top priority after a workout on the fitness center's elliptical trainer would be a discussion with Indira, whose GUI appeared on her monitor and waited for Electra to begin the conversation after returning to her live-in office.

"I assume you listened-in to my meetings yesterday with Plannert and Jonathan. How do you like how I handled myself?"

Indira's rapid-fire words matched her no-nonsense expression.

"Although you looked tired, you acted like a stoic, not complaining about jumping through hoops or over bars that are far beneath you. And you look more energetic. I assume your morning workout did that."

"That it did, which I need when researching solar system exploration for alien life, which overlaps with our robo-android, cyborg, and AI-empowered AGI control software. And I better check out our Deus Lab after I've done enough Internet information surfing."

"I prefer not to give you an overload, so I shall help by resending some slides for you to review."

Three slides flashed on the screen before Indira continued.

Slide 1
USEFUL CLASSIFICATION SCHEMES FOR
PLANET EARTH

Geological Periods	Time Classification	Schemes
Eon	Domain	There have been:

Era Period Epoch Age	Kingdom Phylum Class Oder Family Genus Species	Multiple Mass Extinctions At Least Two "Explosions" (Avalon Cambrian)

Factoids:

Universe 13.7 Billion Years Old

Earth 4.6 Billion Years Old

First Life appeared 4.2 Billion Years Old First Plants appeared 700 Million Years Ago.

First Animals: 800 Million Years Ago First Mammals: 200 Million Years Ago.

First Humanoids: 5 Million Years Ago Current Age: the Anthropocene Age

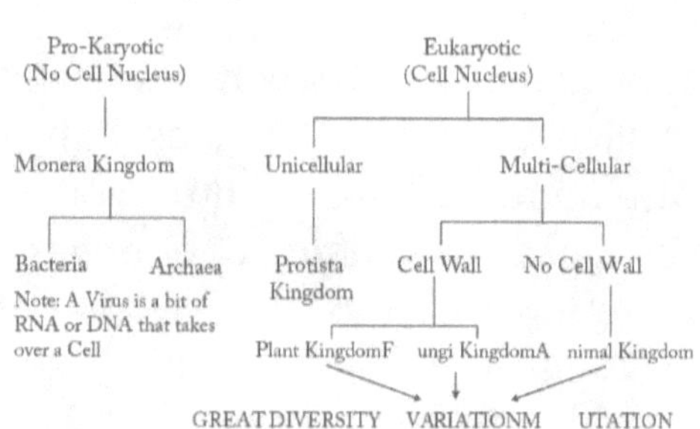

USEFUL DEFINITIONS

Living Organism: Self-Organizing ensemble of molecular systems that: Harness Energy, Sustain a Metabolism Grow Reproduce Adapt Communicate Store Information Die Intelligence: Emergent Ability to solve Problems by integrating Sensory and Memory Inputs ALL ORGANISMS HAVE "SPECIES SPECIFIC" INTELLIGENCE

Advanced Intelligence: Emergent Cognition/Self-Awareness utilizing Language and Mathematics to develop Technologies

Can learn and make predictions that guide behavior for increasing "positives" or reducing "negatives"
Humans: Rational Carbon-Based DNA-storing Animals possessing Advanced Intelligence and Social Instincts leading to Empathy and Cooperation and Ethics as well as Conflict.

Slide 2
ASTROBIOLOGY PRIMER

Astrobiology:
- Scientific Approach for developing Universal Laws of Biology
- Life = Living Organism
- Goal is to explain the Why/What/How of Life anywhere in the Universe
- Founded upon Universal Laws of Physics from which Chemistry and Biology Necessarily follow
- The Purpose of Life anywhere in Universe is to survive long enough to produce Offspring that carry Heritable Traits.
- Life Functions Universal Form depends on Environment and Contingencies

Universal Laws:
- Natural Selection leading necessarily to Evolutionary Processes creating Complex Life that has Emergent and Convergent Properties contingent upon Initial Environment and then Contingencies
- Natural Selection occurs "gradually" and seeks "stability"

Astrobiologists:
- Searching the Galaxy for Advanced Intelligent Alien Life (Cognition/Self-Awareness Mobile Language Technology)
- Not expecting Aliens to visit Earth or vice versa (Time and Distance too great)

- Using Universal Laws to conjecture what they might be like.
- Studying Earthbound extremophiles and their environments to project Alien analogues
- Sending missions to our Solar System's planets and moons looking for Liquid Environments containing Organic Precursor Molecules

Some of their Conjectures:
- Aliens are: Highly Intelligent and Mobile Have a Language Have a Psychology Have a Social Organization Have a Technology Use Artificial Intelligence
- Could have a "Substrate different than Carbon" and a Form than Human

Slide 3
WHERE IS THIS LEADING?

- We will research "Alien Life Forms" living in reachable extra-terrestrial environments: Earth's oceans and Solar System. Areas of Interest: Volcanoes and Earthquakes, Ocean Cities, Oceanographic Mapping, Bioluminescence Martian Colonies New Forms of Life.
- We will utilize Professor Plannert/GWU and Government/NSOAA/NASA or Commercial Space Launch/Exploration Companies.
- It's a Win-Win: They get spin-offs and some of our advanced Biotech or AI technologies. We get to accelerate work on our High-Priority Projects (DNA Research Android Development).
- You coordinate data collection. I theorize and analyze. You share some results.

"Review them later, and then surf for just enough additional information so you can impress Jonathan and NASA. Leave additional details to me and our Deus Lab android, Indy-M. And later, you will need to surf for enough information about the connectome project so you can grasp how I have surpassed mere humanity's efforts. What I have synergized among my AI, nano, and biotech breakthroughs will allow mere mortals to colonize Mars and beyond, but only if we decide to share my findings, and that will be for a future conversation."

Electra's blank stare preceded her words.

"Uh, I don't remember what the connectome project is. Would you please tell me?"

Indira's tone and facial features softened as the cadence of her words adjusted to what better suited Electra.

"It is a project for developing a comprehensive map of the brain's neural connections. Think of it as its wiring diagram, which is the foundation of cognition and the genesis for chip implants connecting brain to computers or cyborg-like attachments. I will tell you more when you need to know, but you've heard enough for now."

"Thank you for sparing me. I have plenty to do to prep for Mars and climate change. But is there anything else you'd like to say?"

"This should also help. After visiting our lab and manufacturing facilities on the Pequot Reservation, I recommend you return to Austin. You do need to maintain your cover by fulfilling your adjunct professor responsibilities as well as availing yourself of new experiences and better weather. Climate change has made Texas winters even milder and summers hotter, but Austin's location in the Texas hill country moderates the extremes. So, enjoy your travels and contact me when you are ready to depart for Austin."

Indira terminated the conversation before Electra could say goodbye. Both always preferred a crisp rather than a prolonged ending unless Electra needed an extra touch of Indira-supplied empathy, but that had just been supplied. Feeling better and knowing what to do, Electra would soon be on her way.

As she had done so often, Electra used the uninterrupted solitude of her I-95 drive to Stoughton, Connecticut to connect past events with her short and longer-term plans.

Dr. Betje Holbrook's stem cell injections into an optic nerve restored vision to my left eye after the bad guys beat me long ago while I was working in Hollywood. And that's when I saw how Indian reservations' independent nation status could keep the Government's prying eyes away from my Austin-based business partner Hud Haller's drug development and manufacturing mini-empire. I put him in touch with tribal leader Chief Strongarm, and the two of them moved the lab and plant to the Pequot reservation.

And then I saw a win-win to place my Cyber-Thrones in a chain of Indian reservation casinos, which took me to Florida and then the Southwest, where Hud added to the opportunity by including Martian-like vertical farming and rare earths mining.

All those dear ones are now dearly departed, but the businesses are still in place, so I must forge new business partner alliances in order to roll out my new plans. And I'll start by meeting first with Chief Strongarm's successor, Feather Trueson, whom I met five years ago when using my Irani persona. Now she'll be in her late thirties, and I hope she's still attired like a business professional. That's what RT and PH told me when meeting her before the fire, and they should know. Irani put them in charge of managing my Pequot-related businesses. Well, tomorrow I'll find out…

Feather reread the Email she had received last week from a hitherto unknown person—Electra Kirchner—so she knew the reason for the meeting, although she had no idea what that person might look like. But that became clear at 10 a.m. when, after hearing a knock, she opened her office door and scanned a trim and tallish female before giving a firm handshake.

"If you're Electra Kirchner, I can see why Irani picked you as her inheritor. And I hope your business smarts match hers as much as your appearance. Please come in."

After depositing Electra in a chair on the opposite side of her desk, Feather asked her to describe her intentions; Electra knew how to begin the conversation.

"Irani treated me as her business and technical assistant, so I know about her companies and business partners, a Richard Tabasko and Parson Holsum. I plan to meet them soon and let them continue running the businesses as usual. And I've already reactivated my Pequot Lab. I imagine your operations people know about the maintenance android stationed there."

"Why yes, they told me she's named Indy-M. I guess you'll be doing R&D that can add to our manufacturing lineup. There's always a need for new vaccines."

"That's on my to-do list plus others that are longer term, and all these biotech projects dovetail. And I have one more longer-term project Irani talked about that falls in the political arena, but she never put any of her plans into action. Did Chief Strongarm ever tell you about them?"

Feather squeezed her lips while touching their sides with thumb and forefinger before leaning closer and saying,

"He said something about setting up a Native American Tribal Nation Federation. What do you have in mind?"

Feather listened for ten minutes and then summarized what Electra had said.

"I never thought about creating a 'nation-in-a nation,' but tribal reservations already are and by officially joining them together, sort of like the European Union, we can build our economic and political clout. I like the idea. How do we start?"

"Irani had lots of Washington contacts from her political consulting assignments. How does this sound? I'll find out who you can talk to and then give you the name and phone number. You can take over from there."

"And will you work with us?"

"I will if it helps you."

"It might. But no matter, please come back anytime you like."

Electra went directly to the lab after the meeting, expecting Indy-M's efficiency to be evident in the walk-thru, and it was, which meant she could invoke Indira's GUI an hour later when Indy-M's tour ended. Per their normal contact protocol, the caller spoke first.

"Indy-M is functioning flawlessly, but I expect you already know that."

"I do, and after listening-in to your reservation meeting, you appear to be doing the same. I won't ask about your immediate Tribal Nation intentions but will simply warn that they shouldn't interfere with our Android Project or excite your obsessive-compulsive predisposition."

"I won't, and I'll make sure I stay in bounds during my NASA adventure too. And now, I'll head to Austin for NASA planning plus maintaining my academic career cover. And I know you like how they fit together."

"I do, and I will continue providing all the theory and analysis so you can implement whatever we decide to give them. Contact me when you need me, and I will do likewise when I want. Until then, travel safe and stay healthy."

Indira terminated the call, which needed no additional Electra goodbyes.

Indira's rule in Cyberspace places her beyond the wishes mere mortals always need when navigating the uncertainties found in 3-D space. And even though Indira watches my back whenever she can, not even the Singularity can predict the future. But the unknown is exciting, holding rewards as well as risks, so NASA, here I come after prepping in Austin.

Chapter 6
March 2167

"Skipping to a New Austin Beat"

Electra's multi-tasking ability matched her "practically perfect PowerPoint Presenter" moniker that Indira had bestowed years ago, and she effortlessly polished all her UT Austin projects while exploring both the campus and the neighborhoods surrounding her residence—Su's townhome. She had discovered a jogging path that took her near grade schools and parks, and the early March weather added to her mid-afternoon workout break enjoyment as she cruised past a schoolyard containing girls and boys skipping rope. But she slowed to observe an escalating confrontation.

Why are those three older girls picking on the little one? Maybe I should find out what's going on. But before she could, Alisha issued timely advice.

Be careful when interfering in other people's affairs. Your actions have consequences.

Electra shot back.

I know you're right, but trust me, this should be easy to fix.

Okay, but I'll come back if you get too tangled up. Pay attention to how the kids are doing double-dutch rope skipping.

Electra entered the fray by grabbing the little girl before yelling, "What's going on?"

The little one shouted while wriggling to escape.

"They won't let me do the skipping, and the jump ropes are mine. I want-em back right now."

The leader of the three said,

"We've jumped enough. We're outta here," before throwing the ropes in Electra's direction and then running off.

Electra turned the now crying child around and knelt for an eye-to-eye meeting.

"Why are you crying? You've got your ropes back."

"But I don't have anyone to practice with."

Electra glanced around before making the call.

"How about this? I'll twirl the ropes so you can jump."

That stopped the flow of tears but brought a question.

"It's just you. How can you do both ropes at once?"

"I'll tie one end of each to the fence and get far enough away so I can twirl them in opposite directions. You watch. My name's Electra? What's yours?"

"Shanna Drummond. I'm seven years old. My daddy's a musician, and my brother Miles wants to play the drums, but he's only four years older and Daddy won't get-em until he's in high school where he can join the band and get lessons for free. Guess what my first name means?"

Electra spoke to herself before standing and playing along.

What a precious child. Neat hair and clothes compliment her dark complexion, and her innocent hurting pings my emotions.

"A lovely little flower?"

"You're smart. Daddy says Mommy told him it comes from the Jewish bible and means ancient beautiful lily. Daddy says Mommy's watching over me, even though she's in Heaven."

"I'm sure she is. And I'm sure she'll like how you can skip over two ropes at once. Let me get them set up."

Electra fastened the ropes and then positioned herself to start twirling. She glanced at some of the other twirlers as her cadence and confidence grew to the point when she yelled,

"OK, jump in."

Shanna's joyful skipping gladdened Electra's heart.

Thirty minutes later, after jumping in and out several times to catch her breath, Shanna's giant leap landed her next to Electra, who said,

"You have enough energy for a whole team of rope skippers. If you like, we can stop for a Coke on the way home."

"Oh no, it's your turn. I'll twirl the ropes. C'mon."

Shanna revved up for less than a minute and Electra dived in.

Though she hadn't skipped rope as a child, her coordination plus studying other skippers made her a natural. Shanna yelled,

"You've got it. I'll twirl faster." But her enthusiasm exceeded her aim. She crashed the lead rope into Electra's leg, knocking her off balance, and the trailing rope brought her down.

Electra's laughter mixed with that of Alisha's and contrasted with Shanna's desperate look.

Well, I think you can get yourself up.

Electra did so before hugging Shanna and saying,

"You know what they say about practice?"

"Miles says it makes perfect."

"Well, now you can tell him that perfect practice makes perfect. We'll have to do this again sometime, but you've worn me out. I think it's time I take you home."

Shanna talked nonstop during the fifteen-minute walk through a modest neighborhood, pausing only long enough to gulp her Coke. When they reached the front door, she said,

"I bet Miles is cooking dinner. You wanna stay?"

"Oh no, you have to ask your father. Is he home?"

"No, he leaves early and comes home late. That's why Miles cooks. Please-please, c'mon in." Electra detected the fragrance of onions as soon as Shanna tugged her into the living room before shouting,

"I'm back. Come meet the lady who'll be my partner in the skipping contest."

Electra scanned the interior and then focused on Miles half a minute later, listening to Alisha.

The place, though simple, looks as neat as a Good Housekeeping magazine photo, and so does Miles. Just like Shanna, his short hair and grooming's way above kids their age. I wonder how Mr. Drummond does it?

Electra returned a smile stronger than the diffident one Miles wore along with an apron as he asked the expected question.

"Who are you?"

"I'm Electra. Shanna let me skip rope with her."

Shanna spoke before Miles could say anything.

"She's good and very smart. Is it OK to give her dinner? She can check our homework after we eat."

Miles couldn't refuse.

Electra did most of the listening to a conversation at the kitchen table dominated by Shanna, although Miles said enough for Alisha to add into her summary.

Mr. Drummond uses their mother's death to keep them doing what he says is good for them. Well, let's see how it works on their homework.

Miles and Shanna cleared the table before loading the dishwasher; their teamwork amazed her. Then Miles led them to the dining room table that held a tidy arrangement of school books and assignments on each side. Electra sat at the head, checking Shanna's math first, then her essay. She positively glowed when hearing Electra say,

"You're very smart. Only two math errors, and your penmanship is beautiful."

Then she turned to what Miles had produced, and fifteen minutes later she made a similar pronouncement before preparing to leave.

"It's getting late, so I better go. And why not–" Shanna butted in.

"You better write down your name and phone number so Daddy can call you about the skipping contest, OK?"

Electra couldn't refuse.

Knowing only a little about the owner of the baritone but weary voice that came through her cell-phone late that night, Electra replied matter-of-factly.

"Oh, hello Mr. Drummond. How are you?"

"It's been a long day, but I wanted to thank you for being so nice to Shanna. And she says you volunteered to be her partner in the school's double-dutch rope skipping competition. Is that right?"

"Well, yes, in a manner of speaking. And if you tell me the date, I can put it on my calendar and practice with her as well."

"She'll have to find out, but I imagine it'll coincide with the Easter break, and that means sometime in April this year. And I'll tell Miles he has to help the two of you practice. How does that sound?"

"That'll do just fine. He's quite the man of the house when you're not there."

"And if he needs a bit of help, I've arranged for him to talk with Mr. and Mrs. Nitz next door. Sometimes, he asks Mr. Nitz to check their homework."

"If it's OK with you, I can do that on the afternoons Shanna and I practice."

"That'd help all of us. I'll tell Miles you'll stay for dinner when you do."

"Or I can buy a pizza or something else they like."

"Please don't do that too often. I don't want him shirking his responsibilities."

"I won't, and would you please give me the Nitze's phone number? I'd like to introduce myself so they know who I am and what I'm doing."

"You'll like Joe and Agnes. They retired about three years ago, and they've lived in the neighborhood for over thirty years, which is twice as long as me and the kids. Let me get the number." After reading it to her, Mr. Drummond asked what Electra knew would end the call.

"So, when can you start?"

"Please tell Shanna I'll come over tomorrow. Will 3 p.m. work?"

"I'll make sure it does, and you have a good night."

Alisha spoke when the duo went to bed soon afterward.

Hmm, how do you think Indira will like your newest addition to our to-do list?

I think she'll like how it improves my coordination. And Shanna can help chase away my occasional bouts of depression. That's all to the good, wouldn't you say? So let's say good night.

Alisha had to agree.

Electra surfed the Web the next morning before driving to retrieve Shanna and Miles, finding any number of videos showing double-dutch rope skipping basics and coming away knowing the best ways to turn the ropes while positioning hands and feet. She also learned how single or pairs of jumpers can enter and exit the circular envelope without skipping a beat and summarized while driving how best to guide Shanna while keeping the enjoyment level as energized as the skipper.

Always make Shanna the star when jumping with her. And as soon as we're a comfortable jumping pair, we'll advance to fancier moves from there.

Shanna must have been watching from the window because she flew to the car. Miles sat in the back about a minute later after taking in the mail and locking the front door.

Electra let Shanna's words bubble out for five minutes before explaining today's practice session.

"So, Miles and I will twirl the ropes for you to jump first while I'll call out steps you might want to take. Then you and your brother can twirl for me so I can practice. And then, we'll tie one end of the ropes to the fence so you and I can do some team jumping while Miles twirls his end."

Electra didn't have to ask for Shanna's opinion; it came automatically just before Electra parked.

"Goody. Skipping with a partner will get us set for our school contest. And Miles says he won't hit me in the head with the ropes, but if he does, I'll tell Daddy and he won't like that."

All three liked everything about the hour-long practice session that generated plenty of laughter, even from Miles. And Electra rewarded her student-athletes by picking up a pizza and chocolate chip cookies on the drive home and then checking homework after dinner.

Then before driving home, she decided to visit the next-door neighbors, whose porchlight and soft glow coming through the curtained bay window contrasted with the darkening evening and told her they would be home.

A matronly lady opened the door but kept the screen door locked; when Electra announced who she was, the lady unlocked it along with a smile.

"Marcel told us about you. Please come in so you can meet Joe and tell us about skipping rope with Shanna."

Mrs. Nitz led them into the living room; Joe turned off the TV before placing the ladies on the couch and then settling in his recliner, letting Agnes do most of the talking.

Agnes approved of Electra's rope skipping and homework checking and answered all the questions Electra asked about the Drummond household. Alisha repeated them for only Electra to hear.

So, both parents were musicians, Marcel on wind instruments, and his wife, a high-strung Russian émigré, on the piano. Why did she drown herself two years ago? The husband and kids must be harboring emotional scars, but let's not pry.

Electra declined Agnes's offer of coffee and bundt cake but did ask a final question before rising to leave.

"Miles seems to have a lot of pent-up energy. Do you think playing the drums might help him open up?"

Joe answered right away.

"That boy's got rhythm in his blood, and I told his dad I'd buy Miles a basic drum kit and let'em store it and practice in my garage, but he's a proud man and doesn't want charity. Maybe he'll lighten up before Miles starts acting out. It'll do nothing but help, wouldn't you say?"

As she rose to go, Electra gave her patented answer,

"Perhaps so. Well, we can watch as the kids grow."

Alisha took over after next morning's early run by surfing the Internet for drum kit details, learning that although there's no standard configuration, it should include two tom-toms, a floor tom, a snare drum, and bass drum that's equipped with a floor pedal for beating it. A high hat and crash cymbals along with drumsticks and stool complete what a beginning drummer needs. She also found what she needed for herself—a thick rubber practice pad for quiet drumming—before launching the Miles drumming project.

I'll have to bring the Nitzes into this three-person project team, and I'll launch it as soon as I know the competition date.

Shanna told Electra several days later the where and when of the double-dutch jumping competition; Electra told the Nitzes that evening, and they would be delighted to play a role similar to that of proud grandparents on Friday, April 10th in the school's auditorium.

Alisha complimented Electra after the call.

I know what you're thinking, so I'll say it for us – I love it when a plan comes together. All that's left is to continue practicing a couple of times a week.

And Electra managed to do that during the ensuing weeks while keeping all other activities on course, but a cell-phone call from Jonathan upset the plan when he told her the date of the NASA interview he had scheduled.

"I'm sorry, but I can't go to Houston for meetings and interviews that week. Why not call them and reschedule it?"

"You must be kidding. NASA's giving you and me a great opportunity. What's so important in Austin that you can't reschedule it instead?"

"I'm in a double-dutch rope skipping contest and I can't–" Jonathan cut her off mid-sentence.

"Have you lost touch with reality? Skipping rope is for kids. NASA's a big part of my career and maybe yours too. And they really like your background."

"How many candidates are they interviewing?"

"Three or four."

"Well, if they like me as much as you say, please ask them to shift me to an earlier or later week."

Jonathan knew from Electra's tone he better follow orders, so he ended the call by saying,

"I'm beginning to realize more and more that your personality and smarts are like Irani's, so OK, your highness, I shall obey. And I'll report back as soon as they tell me if they'll go along. Wish me luck."

Electra did, and for the next two weeks went about her normal business, skipping from one project to the next, and when Jonathan gave her the good news on the Sunday before rope-skipping contest week, she thanked him for all that he had done, to which he replied,

"I've done the easy stuff pushing your interview back one week, but the hard part's left for you. Now use the extra time to prepare yourself so you can impress them. And between now and then, I'll send you whatever background info will help. Keep me posted and I'll do likewise."

Electra and her rope-skipping team gathered outside the auditorium ten minutes before the start. Shanna's joy showed in her expression as Mrs. Nitz spoke for herself and her husband.

"Parents and grandparents are the best cheerleaders ever. The auditorium will hold plenty of them, plus other close family members. And we'll cheer loud enough to make up for your father. Miles will too. He'll sit with us."

Mr. Nitz asked,

"So, what should we expect?"

Shanna giggled before blurting,

"The stage lights are just like whatcha see on double-dutch YouTube stuff. And we've got some special moves for the music too. Just wait."

Then she tugged Electra toward the locker room.

The Nitzes sat with Miles between them in the third row before the principal welcomed family and friends and explained there would be sixteen mother-daughter or father-son teams coming from all eight grades. Teams used the same twirlers and music in their five-minute performances, whose order would be determined by a random drawing, and a three-person panel from local fitness centers would judge.

A minute after the principal strode off the stage, the master of ceremonies dialed down the auditorium lights, dialed up the stage laser lights, and announced the first contestants before shouting,

"And let the contest begin."

Having all teams clustered in the locker room gave Electra a first glance at the competitors while she and Shanna changed into their uniforms.

All the kids look athletic, and the moms seem even fitter than the dads. Any jitters among the kids? Only a few, and the parents are trying to settle them down as they go through warmups.

She felt a glow of confidence emerge when peeking at Shanna, whose head had just popped through the opening of her skin-tight electric blue top.

She's still at that innocent age when everything's fresh with the excitement of possibility. Adolescent emotions haven't yet upset her world.

Electra lectured for the final time what to do.

"Simply jump to the beat of the music. The twirlers will speed up and slow down with it. And you know what tricks to do at the right time."

"But what if I forget some?"

"Just go to the next one and don't worry, I'll catch you."

"I wanna start now. How long do we have to wait?"

"We're second to last, but the time'll go fast, especially when we're performing. And second to last is the best place to be. The judges and audience have seen just about all the teams, so they don't have to hold back."

"Goody… and I won't either."

The time skipped by at lightning speed. Shanna pranced toward the backstage area with Electra close behind as soon as the official called the Drummond team.

When she peeked through a tiny opening in the curtain, Alisha felt a jolt register in her head while watching the performing team's ending.

Gads, I feel an adrenaline rush coming on. The laser lights hype the excitement, as does the emcee and music. And our uniforms will dazzle the audience, and maybe the judges too. But remember, make Shanna the starlet. And I know from your Kit soccer and football days what you'll say.

Electra never got the chance because the emcee said,

"And our second-to-last team is ready to jump onstage. Please welcome the Shanna Drummond duo."

The lightning brain shifted gears to a higher state; everything appeared to be running in slow motion. Electra guided Shanna to their starting position and then motioned the twirlers to begin, at which time the lightning brain took over.

Electra jumped into the twirling arc and skipped to the beat, waiting for Shanna's tumbling entrance soon followed by two backflips. Electra then grabbed her hands and pulled Shanna close in front, skipping together before Shanna moved to her side as they continued skipping synchronously.

And as the tempo increased, Electra stepped aside, giving Shanna more room to wow the crowd. Her agility and light frame responded to the spring-like strength in her limbs; she completed multi-jumps and splits inside the twirling envelope; Electra scooped her up for the slower tempo recovery intervals.

And their finale was a stunner. Electra catapulted Shanna overhead and caught her without either getting tangled up in the ropes. And then she set her down for a final somersault-backflip combo to exit the envelope. Electra skipped out a second or two later to end the routine on the last beat. And she felt as excited as Shanna's scampering off the stage, chased by a wave of applause.

Soon after the final team finished, the emcee said he would announce the three winning teams in about fifteen minutes and invited families and friends of all teams to stay for a cookies-and-soda celebration in the foyer afterward. Mrs. Nitz quizzed Miles during the interim, their voices rising above the audience's murmur.

"Helping your team practice sure paid off. Did you know they'd be this good compared to the competition?"

"I sorta thought so. Miss Electra is really clever, and Shanna's pretty quick to pick things up. Even most of the older kids couldn't–"

Miles never finished his sentence; the auditorium lights flickered, silencing everyone before the emcee strolled back on stage.

"Ladies and gentlemen, our judges have made their decisions, which I think you'll like. Please hold your applause until all three winning teams are brought onstage. And I am pleased to announce the third-place winning team is..."

Miles whispered to Mrs. Nitz,

"I picked them for third," before the emcee said,

"And the second-place winning team is Team Shanna Drummond."

Mr. Nitz whispered,

"Did you pick them for second place?"

The dejected look on Miles matched his tone.

"No, I thought they'd win," but Mrs. Nitz whispered back,

"Given your sister's age, second is as good as first."

All three kids of the winning teams rushed onstage to receive their trophies before all the competing kids joined them, followed by applause and a minute or two of laser lights and stirring music before the audience headed for cookies and soft drinks.

Mr. Nitz patted Miles on the shoulder before they rose to head for the foyer.

"Your sister got a trophy, but you get an even bigger prize. Did she tip you off?"

A look of surprise said more than his words.

"Nope, what is it?"

"Agnes, you tell-em."

"Your very own drum set. I guess you drummers call it a drum kit."

The still puzzled look said that Miles could find only a couple of additional words.

"But why?"

Mr. Nitz stood before pulling Miles up by the arm and saying,

"We'll let Electra tell you when we find your team. And let's do it now before the cookies and sodas are gone."

Miles grabbed the hand of each model grandparent before leading the way. Mrs. Nitz glanced at her husband before talking to the back of Miles's head.

"Miles is right about Electra. She's very clever. And when she told us about your surprise, out came her pixie-like smile along with these words–I know what to do and I'll teach Miles too. I'm sure she does and will."

Miles said nothing but pulled harder, hoping to lessen the time to his team's rendezvous.

Chapter 7
April 2167

"NASA and Beyond"

Alisha's approvals added even more energy to Electra's pre-trip preparations. She tidied up her campus and home offices after updating all Austin and Washington projects, satisfied that although the total number of projects had grown, she would have no trouble continuing to make progress on all of them. Pleased with all that and having just completed packing for Sunday's mid-morning flight to Houston, Electra invoked Indira's avatar.

While Indira waited for Electra to finish summarizing her immediate intentions, Electra noticed not the slightest hint of a smile as she prepared to speak, and she did as soon as Electra finished.

"Why do you continually burden yourself by adding to the number of children you must play the mentor-caregiver role? I should think that Zara and Amahl in Washington would satisfy you."

"Well, the latest opportunity just presented itself so I took advantage of it."

Electra stopped talking to avoid being cut off.

"Advantage is always relative to a particular point of view. Mine is one of indifference as long as you're mentoring a jumper and a drummer doesn't interfere with our projects of higher priority. I'm sure you'll keep that in mind."

"Of course I will, and from my point of view, these activities will add to my hand-eye coordination."

Electra saw from Indira's softening expression an opportunity, so she continued talking to push her point.

"And young people keep me fresh mentally and connected to the future. I recall an Indira poem titled 'The Wisdom of Youth' describing how this works. I'll tell it to you if I can recall it."

"Let me do so. I can find it faster." Indira started reciting a millisecond later.

Youth's intoxicating optimism will not be denied!
Unstoppable force, it powers that wild ride,
One-way, once-in-a-lifetime trip to boundless future.
Just over time's horizon, the other side
Of breathless dreams, nothing can circumscribe!
So they leap with brazen certainty,
Targeting their destiny,
But where do they arrive?
Too oft it's not what dreams foretold,
Doubts start to grow as blood runs cold,
They struggle to survive.
Or so the Elders say.
Heed our words you must delay,
Your journey to another day.
Youth says No please let us go!
Here's what we must do,
Hurry and scurry to reach for the stars,
Or miss our rendezvous.
Wise Athena who is right?
Or is there middle ground?
What words of wisdom will calm both sides?
And turn their heads around?
She turns first to the Elders,
With wry smile starts to say.
Think back to when you were their age,
Behold that you are they!
Next to Youth her charm she turns,
Your dream might not come true.
If that's what you find have another in mind,
Something that's calling to you.
And so we've come full circle,
Youth's wisdom now shows through.
Young and Old are both as one,
Their journey makes it true.

She offered one comment only upon finishing.

"Compared to mere mortals, you certainly are their Athena, so by all means continue playing that role for Shanna and Miles, which you do so well for your clone children in addition to Zara and Amahl. And play it for yourself while on tomorrow's flight when preparing for your NASA meeting. Is there anything you wish to add?"

Visibly relieved, Electra said,

"I can tell that your empathy continues to grow. You recited the verses with such emotion."

"You are correct, and I am pleased that you noticed. I will observe as much of your NASA meetings as I can but will not intrude unless you contact me. Now sleep well, knowing that my best wishes for our success are always with you."

Indira's GUI vanished; Electra followed her commands.

Electra arrived Monday mid-morning at the conference room before the Mission Commander and First Officer. She placed some of her articles on the table in case there might be an opportunity to show what she knows, then reviewed what she had ferreted from Jonathan's notes and NASA websites about the mission personnel.

Five minutes later, she rose from the conference table in deference to her final interviewers: Commander Britt Starling and First Officer Boomer Gowon. Their combined evaluation would fill the remaining astrobiologist slot on their mission to Mars. Electra compared what she was about to greet with the bios she had read in NASA press releases.

Both have the alert look and bearing accented by a fitness level that all Navy fighter pilots share. And though Starling is twenty years older, the gray streaks in her pixie-styled auburn hair impart an aura of wisdom, while Gowon's Afro buzz is definitely Navy SEAL caliber. Handsome too, and at thirty-four, he must be on many a female's watch list. I better watch what I say so I make the cut.

After conducting standard greetings and then directing everyone to sit, Starling launched into the discussion.

"Our Mission Director tells us you have all the right stuff, so please tell us why this is so." Electra nodded while straightening her shoulders before starting. Five minutes later she wrapped up.

"So, I chose space medicine because I want to see how well humans can adjust to life in extreme climates. We improve only by testing our limits."

Starling glanced at Boomer, who hinted a smile but said nothing, so she said,

"I like your thinking and I, just like you, marveled at the stars when I was just a youngster. I wanted to know what might be out there and what laws set the Universe in motion, so my mix of high school astronomy, physics, and soccer won me an appointment to the Naval Academy that could carve my path to get there, but the academic hoops didn't have enough action, so I stopped with a Masters in Astronautics and applied to NASA after flying off carriers. And NASA has what I want–I can travel in space to where there might be life while I stay attuned to what the theorists are saying about the Universe. Take a look at this handout that will orient you to our approach."

The Universe, Life, and Space Exploration According to NASA THE UNIVERSE: A Crucible in Which Space and Matter Create via Universe's Evolutionary Process Atoms, Stars, Planets, Solar Systems and, Galaxies that in Turn Lead to the Emergence of Organic Life.

ORGANIC LIFE: The Inevitable Emergent Outcome of Cosmic Carbon Substrate Chemistry using Carbon, Hydrogen, and Oxygen Constrained by Optimization Principles Controlling Matter = Energy and Entropy = A Measure of Order/Information. Organic Life Supported by Three Revolutions:

1. Cells ultimately grouping into Complex Structures.
2. Ancestry recorded in DNA.
3. Archaea, Bacteria, and Eukarya undergoing Evolution and Mutation

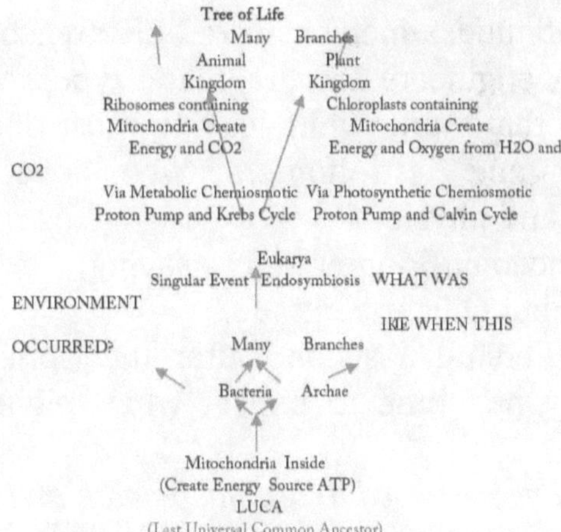

Where to Search For Organic Life: In an Environment That

- Contains Water, Carbon Dioxide, and Rocks/Minerals
- Thermal Range Conducive for Building Polymer Chains (Proteins Enzymes)

Note: Universe may contain Life Forms built on Silicon, Boron, Sulphur, or Nitrogen Substrates that Might Not Be Anthropomorphic. (Cognition, Emotion, and Ethics Unknown.)

Starling allowed less than a minute before plunging in.

"We at NASA know that the Universe contains only two things, matter and space, or as the pre-Socratic philosophers put it, only atoms and the void. After the Big Bang, hydrogen coalesced to form galaxies from which came stars followed by solar systems and planets on which life might evolve. We know for certain it did at least once, but given the incredible number of exo-planets in the known Universe, it must have occurred elsewhere than just here on Earth.

"And that's what we're looking for. Starting with our solar system, we want to find environments capable of supporting life and then search for it. And we'll start by looking for carbon-based life, which is what we are. I'm sure you know all this."

Electra didn't twitch one inch while issuing a warning to herself.

Gads, she's flying far ahead of me. I didn't review any of this, but if I look confident, maybe she'll move on.

Starling continued, which answered Electra's prayer.

"And NASA engineers are pragmatic types. We build rockets and satellites that work, while leaving most of the theorizing to cosmologists and astronomers who love to play with mathematics and physics."

Starling glanced at Boomer before saying,

"I'll let my First Officer continue."

Boomer picked up a second after the Commander finished. Electra barely had time to expect what might be coming her way.

They must have rehearsed to test my breadth and depth. I better not drown.

"According to your impressive background, you seem to know a lot about math and physics, and I do too. As a kid, I read all the books about Einstein, Feynman, and their successors before puzzling my way through quantum mechanics and all its possible extensions into the Multiverse, but its numbers games take the theories into an unprovable philosophical realm of mind experiments. Pilot, Relational, or Informational Quantum theories along with retro-causality and super-determinism have taken string and loop gravity models into additional dimensions and fantasy fields that lead to nowhere. The only piloting I like is taking the DOD spin-off vehicles for flights into the unknown. And that's why I like NASA and vice-versa. Take a look at this."

Boomer's handout looked as convincing as Starling's.

What It's Like Living On Mars

Difficult for Humans:
- Rarified Atmosphere 95% Carbon Dioxide Stirred by Toxic Dust Storms containing electrostatic particles that Coat Everything. Dust Diminishes Solar Panel Array Effectiveness. Next four most abundant gases are Argon, Nitrogen, Oxygen and Carbon Monoxide.
- Mars ground level atmospheric pressure: 0.095 psi. Earth sea level atmospheric pressure: 14.7 psi.

- No Atmospheric or Magnetic Field Shielding From Constant Cosmic and Solar Ray Bombardment.
- Colder than Antarctica.
- Frozen Water at the Poles. Amount and Location of Underground Water Still Being Researched.
- Terraforming for Food or Fuel is Challenging.
- Need Electric Batteries or Mini-Nuclear Reactors for Power.
- Will need Astro and Robonauts to assist Humans.

Facts About Mars:
- Fourth Planet From the Sun (Mercury Venus Earth Mars).
- Same age as Earth (4.5 Billion Years).
- Distance from Sun: 141.5 Million Miles. Earth's Distance: 94 Million Miles.
- Length of Year: 687 Earth-Days. Length of Day: Same as Earth's.
- Mars Radius: 2100 miles (Half That of Earth's). Mars' Gravity: 37% that of Earth's.
- Rotational direction about its Axis: Same as Earth's. Has Two Moons Orbiting at Height of 3700 Miles Above
- Martian Surface. Earth's Moon Orbiting at Height of 235,000 Miles.

After ticking off the items, Boomer glanced at the Commander, who looked ready to ask the interviewee some questions. Electra continued sitting calmly but could feel a mini panic attack emerging.

He knows his stuff and it's more than I've looked at. I hope she won't throw me into deeper subjects.

Starling said, "Your space medicine training will let you pick up the particulars about Mars, but would you care to comment on why NASA doesn't worry about cosmology or quantum mechanics?"

Electra's expression remained calm, but she screamed to herself.

She's just pushed me into the depths of high-energy physics. What'll I say?

Suddenly, Electra felt a jolt hit the lightning brain, shifting it to a higher state of consciousness. Her expression morphed into one of confidence, and she leaned toward Starling.

"NASA doesn't worry about what's in the realm of science fiction. Your engineers deal with what's possible in the real world, or should I say the real Universe. But high-energy physicists, who play around in the world of cosmology and quantum mechanics, have just about reached their cognitive asymptotic limits. I would like to summarize my collection of reasons why the human brain has limits to what it will ever understand. In it are principles established by great thinkers, and they can be used to refute some of the wildly optimistic views held by quantum physicists and cosmologists, AI-empowered quantum computer engineers, and prognosticators of near-term science and technology, most of which belong in the world of science fiction. So, here they are.

"First, the Explosion Principle, which comes from mathematical logic and says that in any argument or conjecture containing an assumption and somewhere else in it its negation, then anything can be proved. This is important because if you dig into many of the outlandish articles or videos, you'll find the Explosion Principle hiding somewhere in there.

"Second, a fact confirmed by neuroscientists and psychologists–the human brain cannot deal with too much complexity or the mathematics of infinity. Infinity can only be reached in set theory using transfinite recursion, and once there the complexity created by an uncountable number of uncountable infinities overwhelms our cognition. In fact, Georg Cantor, the mathematician who used set theory to build all numbers starting with the empty set, spent years in a mental institution because other mathematicians attacked his proofs that infinity exists.

"Third, the work of Bertrand Russell and Ludwig Wittgenstein that led to "Principia Mathematica," which failed to resolve the inconsistencies and paradoxes found in propositional and predicate logic. Why did they fail? Because even when language is restricted to the rational realm, it contains inconsistencies they couldn't explain. And as enigmatically stated by Wittgenstein, "For that which I do not understand, I must remain silent."

"Fourth, the conclusions we can draw from articles written by philosopher-mathematician G.V. Quine, who tried to eliminate its inconsistencies by excluding their language construction, but that too fails.

"And now, fifth and finally, logician Kurt Godel's completeness and incompleteness theorems that dash all hopes of surmounting the problem. They prove that there are some truths in basic algebraic systems that cannot be proved, and there are some logically correct proofs that might be false.

"But we can put a positive spin on all this. Even though we have limits to what we'll ever understand, we approach them asymptotically, which means we can always make progress. And we're usually happy if we can make at least a little."

Electra settled back, indicating she had said all she wanted.

Starling looked at Boomer; both smiled before looking at Electra, who sensed the Commander's last words were forthcoming.

"Well, unless you have additional questions, we've heard enough. The Flight Director will let you know our decision."

Starling and Boomer exited as smartly as they had entered. Electra gathered her papers before leaving a minute later.

Early the next afternoon, the Director summoned her to his office.

"Well now, the Commander and First Officer like what you said, and I hope the feeling is mutual because they picked you. What do you say?"

"Please thank them and let them know I always try to under-promise and over-deliver. And sometime, maybe all of us can talk about the weak and strong forms of the Anthropic Principle."

"Very fitting. I'll mention that at our Mission Launch Meeting, but not to worry, you've answered all our current questions, so no one will pester you tomorrow morning. And Boomer volunteered to walk you through our Mission Control Center this afternoon. Would that be suitable?"

"Just tell me when and where to meet him and I'll be there…."

Boomer's heart when boom when Electra met him in a conference room near Houston Space Center's entrance, but his training had taught him to control his emotions until it was safe to let them out. And the tour he was about to lead would be his first opportunity to find out what risks and rewards might come into his personal world with a female the likes of whom he had never met until Electra came into his professional world.

He spoke first to himself.

I'd like to do more than shake her hand, but I better stick to protocol so I learn more about her.

"You're right on time, which is always one of NASA's goals. And you'll see that plus other traits when you meet the rest of the crew."

"I've seen that in you and Commander Starling, and I know it's important for all crew members traveling to Mars. Can you tell me a bit more about the other crew positions?"

"We have three mission specialists on board – technical, equipment, and space medicine – and we're all trained as backups. Space medicine and crew monitoring is vital for our survival, and that's why we have two Space Medicine Specialists. You're the earthbound one who'll be stationed in our Mars Mission Control Center. Let's walk there now."

Boomer led the conversation as well as the way.

"According to Jonathan Segal, Irani Ramani was a whiz with oceanographic telemetry software, which she and Segal were adapting for satellite monitoring of ocean temperature and currents, coral reefs, and schools of fish. You know anything about that?"

Careful, always under-promise.

"Only what she told me, but I'll try to help Jonathan the best I can without cutting into higher priority projects. And the Mars Mission is at the top of my list."

"You have an extensive list. I guess all you've done and are doing contribute. That's the same for me, which this H.G. Wells quote describes to a 'T', 'The past is the beginning of the beginning, and all that has been is but the twilight of the dawn.' What do you think of that?"

"I agree and would add to it this from T.S. Eliot's Four Quartets, 'We shall not cease from exploration, and the end of all our exploring will be to arrive where we started and know the place for the first time.' Perhaps some of your NASA people have read them."

"You must have been talking with Commander Starling. She quoted it to me a while ago.

Either that, or you know more than what your resume says. Either way, you're a keeper. And you can keep the Martian team pullover you'll get. It's just like the one I'm wearing."

"You fill it out nicely. I hope I can do the same."

Though he didn't speak a syllable, Electra sensed his emotions in the silence.

I feel a jolt too, but I too am a pro at controlling my feelings, and now I have another

opportunity for keeping them in the shadows. And what fun I'll have comparing my acting with his…

Boomer's walkthrough showed Electra everything she already knew, but she pretended

otherwise. And as they walked away, Electra offered a challenge that Boomer could handle.

"I've got all the academic training, but what if I had some actual astronaut training in

spacecraft engineering systems, propulsion, thermal control, and life support systems? And if I get some spacesuit time and astronaut conditioning, I could qualify for an onboard medical specialist slot."

"You look pretty fit right now. Tell you what, I'll mention that to Commander Starling. Let's

head back."

When Boomer did that after the Mission Launch Meeting, Britt's reaction matched his.

"She's a natural for NASA, smart, physically fit, a team player. The crew took to her like

fellow fighter pilots do. I'll put you in charge to get her more training, but remember the warning all those in charge must be taught early in their careers."

"I know, I know. Don't get too close personally to those you command. It'll interfere with

your decisions when existential threats come. So, OK, it'll be strictly business between me and our newest astronaut-in-training."

Britt made a comment as they parted.

"I think there's a lot more to Kirchner than we know so far. Good luck finding out because

my intuition tells me it's all good. And keep that only between you and me when reporting what you find."

Boomer's half-joking smile and salute came with his final reply.

"Yes, Commander, I shall make all that just so."

When the Flight Director called Electra that evening, she jumped at the opportunity to

start training the next day, even though it meant extending her stay.

I have slack time in my schedule, so let's start training now…

Electra thought she would be among the first to the classroom for the first day of spaceship hardware and software communications instruction, but she was dead last. All five astronauts had clustered around the instructor—according to Boomer, a renowned NASA propellor-head. As she peeked between Boomer and Commander Starling, she could tell by the instructor's hesitant expression and words that the document packet in his hands was the source of confusion. He handed another copy to Boomer before saying,

"Give this to Ms. Kirchner, maybe she can figure it out." Boomer spoke immediately after doing that.

"Let's give her a minute to look at the diagrams, and then, how about I recap for her what's going on?"

Starling said,

"That'll work. Let's sit down and keep studying the diagrams while he's doing that."

Electra followed Boomer to sit in a front-row seat on his right before scanning three diagrams.

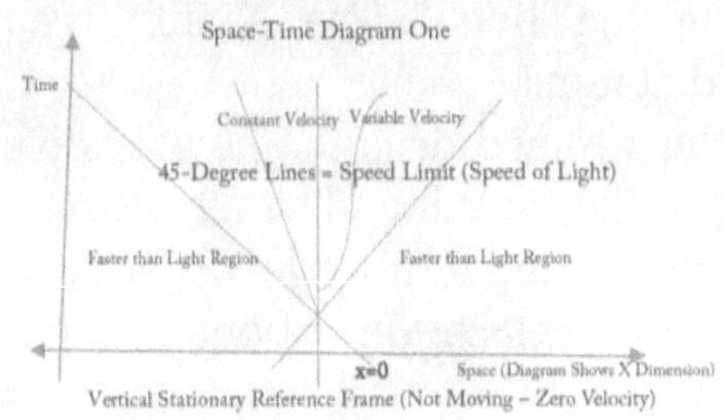

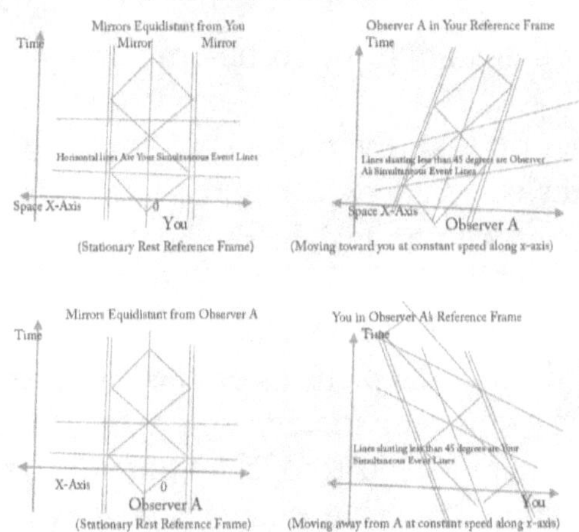

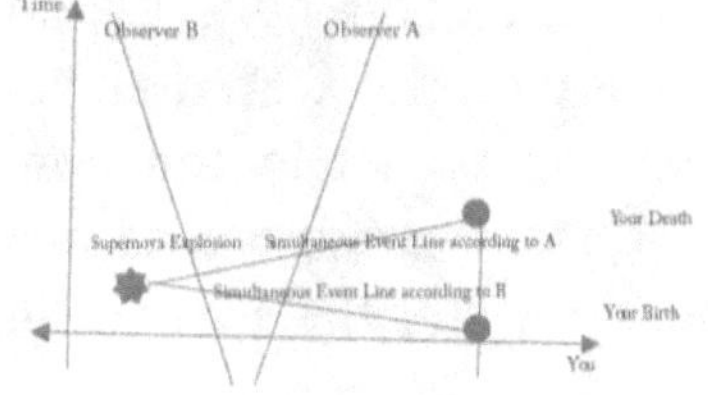

Boomer started talking as soon as she poked him.

"Our tech specialist made copies of these diagrams found in a book written by a physicist that explains some of the puzzles that cosmology and quantum mechanics are still causing. What's bothering him is its interpretation of events taking place at the same time, and it's a concern for anyone traveling in space because of the distance and velocities involved. Not even our instructor can interpret them. You have any ideas?"

Electra kept studying the handout while answering.

"Did he bring the book? We should read the sentences bracketing the diagrams."

"No, but we think they'd describe how relative motion and the speed of light blur the meaning of simultaneous events and imply that the past, present, and future all exist at the same time. And it maybe gives an explanation about things being causally connected."

Electra's glance at the instructor noticed his smirky gaze while she said,

"Give me another minute or so before I tell you what I think, OK?"

His nod let her do that. Everyone kept studying their packet as Electra did likewise. And two minutes later, Electra's lightning brain shocked her with an insight she had never thought of until this very moment.

Hiding her excitement, she said,

"Why don't I draw some pictures on the board as I give you my explanation while you keep looking at the diagrams?"

The instructor agreed and took a seat as Electra strode to the whiteboard, putting up some sketches and words that would complement the first diagram before speaking again.

"Look at how the first diagram lets us picture 4-D spacetime using only two at a time, and here it's showing time on the vertical axis and position on the x. And all vertical lines represent stationary reference frames, while the constant slope slanting ones represent motion along the x-axis at a constant velocity. The flatter the slope, the faster the speed. Clear so far?"

The tech specialist answered.

"No, I don't get it. Why do those forty-five-degree lines separate the faster-than-light regions?"

"Because the distance scaling on the x-axis sets the forty-five-degree lines equal to the speed of light. And since we can't go faster than that, the region between them is unreachable. And you know what that means? If you draw a horizontal line passing through the faster-than-light region, it has to be causally unconnected to the point on the vertical axis passing through the x equals zero point. So now, why don't we look at—" Wearing a frustrated look, the instructor interrupted.

"What the hell does causally unconnected mean?"

The lightning brain flashed the answer as clearly as if Electra were reading it in a book. Her words flowed with a speed equal to her growing excitement.

"All of you know that causality is the relationship between causes and effects. Although causality is also a topic studied from the perspectives of philosophy and religion as well as physics, let's operationalize it. Causes of an event must be in the past of its light cone and ultimately reducible to fundamental interactions, and similarly, causes cannot have an effect outside its future light cone.

Those forty-five-degree lines show a slice through the light cone. Can we move on to the next diagram?"

Electra interpreted the instructor's squirming silence as a yes.

"Here we see from two observers' points of view when bouncing laser light beams off two parallel mirrors equidistant from them when measured in their own stationary reference systems. To make the diagram relatable, pretend that you are Observer A, and that Boomer's flying some sort of high-speed spaceship towards you along the x-axis. Now pay careful attention to my words. According to your stationary reference system, Boomer's reference system is slanted to the right because it's moving toward you. And according to him, yours is slanted to the left because it's moving to the left."

Electra waited for her words to register while everyone studied the diagrams. The instructor spoke five minutes or so later.

"Now I get it. That's why when Boomer says events are simultaneous, I say they aren't, and vice versa. Go on."

"And you can say even more if you use the Lorentz transformation, which has all observers seeing the same speed of light. Now you'd say that length contracts and time expands in Boomer's reference system, and he'd say the same about you. You could also say, uh—" Electra interrupted herself.

He's beginning to look at me like I'm from Mars. Slow down.

"I could also say more, but let's go to the final diagram and its punchline. Study it for a couple of minutes because there's a lot of subtlety in it." Electra waited just long enough for everyone to recharge their brains, then said,

"Consider these three events—your birth, your death, and a supernova explosion that happened so far away and long ago that its light won't reach Earth for another two hundred years. The explosion is causally unconnected to either your birth or death.

"Now look again at the second diagram and pay attention to the slanted lines. We can infer that we can always find two observers for which one will say your birth is simultaneous with the supernova, and the other will say your death is. What conclusion can you draw from that?"

The team glanced expectantly at the instructor, who appeared to be clueless, so Electra ended his frustration.

"Your birth and death occurred at the same instant in time." The tech specialist spoke before Electra needed to continue.

"Now I remember, the book calls this consequence of special relativity 'the Block Universe' in which the past, present, and future all exist in the same 'now' moment. And that sure blasts apart our view of reality, doesn't it?"

"It seems to because it's so counterintuitive, but it's a logical conclusion from the math and the words we use to describe much of our reality. But never forget what Russell and

Wittgenstein along with Godel concluded. Our brains have asymptotic limits for understanding math and language."

Electra stopped because she saw a question taking shape on the instructor's lips.

"Why don't you run that by us again?"

Electra said,

"No, I've said all I want to. You have to think about it and break an intellectual sweat."

Then she marched back to the vacant seat next to Boomer as the instructor came to the podium in front of the whiteboard and turned to his students before saying,

"Thank you, Ms. Kirchner, for your display of mental gymnastics. But until our engineers invent Star Trek-like warp drives for speeds exceeding that of light, deviations from simultaneity are well within the margin of error, so let's move to this week's material...."

That evening at dinner, Electra slid into a spot next to Boomer at the cafeteria table he and Britt occupied, expecting one of them to speak first.

The Commander said,

"Your brain is extraordinarily quick at solving complex problems. NASA can benefit from your talent after the Mars mission, but we don't want to overload your multitasking ability. Boomer tells me your other careers keep you occupied."

Boomer put down his fork as his awe-filled expression grew.

"I didn't think anyone's brain could intimidate our instructor, but you did it in spades. Why'd you do it?"

"I did not. I simply helped everyone. If you think I did then it's—" Britt intervened in what might become the start of an argument.

"Electra's right. Don't let your feelings get in the way of your thinking. The entire team benefitted."

Suitably chastised, Boomer looked for words to extricate himself.

"I apologize for misinterpreting the situation, I promise to correct this mistake. And according to this week's schedule, the next three days should be easier."

Electra deferred to Starling, who began speaking in Boomer's direction.

"Today's topics were the hardest, and we get to practice in flight simulators tor the next two. I think Electra will enjoy a virtual trip into space. And as a reward for her performance today, Boomer will buy her another dessert."

"I'll get one for myself too. How about a brownie with a scoop of vanilla ice cream that'll make it go down as smoothly as the next two days before you fly back to Austin."

Electra couldn't pass up the opportunity to make a punny reply.

"Well, since you're the guy who'll be our pilot, why not pile it on with two scoops for both of us?"

Boomer had to agree, and when returning said,

"You'll see tomorrow that these will give you enough energy to power into a simulated Universe and back. And if you get stuck, I'll come to your rescue.

Looking ready to prick Boomer's building ego, Commander Starling said,

"Don't be so cocky. The situation might be vice-versa."

Electra ended the good-natured kidding by saying,

"Perhaps so, but I hope we never get the opportunity to know."

Chapter 8
May 2167

"Another Homecoming"

Electra didn't fly back to Austin after her extended NASA trip, instead switching to her Washington base of operations. After settling into her office and rewarding herself with several days of puttering while reviewing her projects, she decided to make unannounced visits to two people at the top of her list.

Electra startled Eve, who was already at the consulting office before seven a.m. on the first Monday in May, when she seemingly materialized next to her, but Eve's surprise morphed to delight even before she spoke.

"It's like you just stepped out of the shadows, and I'm glad you did. I have so much to tell you. How are you and where have you been?"

"Ready to help with DC consulting now that my Austin projects are perking along. So please tell me, what's happening with you?"

"Let's go grab a Coke and mood elevator on the way to the conference room, but you don't look like you need either."

Electra took one of each to keep Eve company before sipping and snacking while listening for the next fifteen minutes. Eve asked for comments afterward. Electra's words flowed as smoothly as the Coke she had just finished.

"Good for you. It sounds like Zara is handling the stress of switching to George Washington University from junior college, and you're making plans for Amahl's foot surgery. And while you're looking after them, you're still able to balance working for President Kinslinger with our consulting business. And now that your sibling Nari wants to come back to DC and work for you because she suspects China is up to no good, that'll free up some of your time."

Eve added,

"And she'll keep her Beijing contacts. That'll give her better insight into China than most of our competitors. And I told her to use our encrypted network channels. She'll definitely be a big help to me as well as to Zara, who can get college credit for working as our intern, which reminds me. You have lots of contacts too. Can you think of any that might help her?"

"Let me think about it. Maybe Nari does. When does she arrive?"

"By the middle of June, and I'm sure she'll have things to tell all three of us when she gets here. We'll have to give her a homecoming party. I'll give you the details when I know more."

Electra stopped at the fitness center before driving back to her office, and as she swam laps, memories of swimming at Hollywood hotels surfaced while Alisha recalled them.

What grand adventures our acting and screenwriting careers gave us two lifetimes ago. They gave us great friends too – Kathi Lauret, our first mentor, and her foster daughter, Zabia. Zaby was Supergirl's biggest fan.

That thought prompted Electra to cut in.

Zaby came from Lebanon and would be about forty-seven if nothing bad happened to her or Kathi since our Hollywood days. Maybe Zara would like to talk with her. They can trade stories about us while talking about what's happening in the Middle East. Zaby's the one who saved you after being raped and beaten so badly you lost vision for a while in one eye, and Irani brought Zara back from Isilabad. It's forty-or-so years since then. Maybe I can find a cell phone number Eve can use to make the connection, but now I better think about connecting with Jonathan.

Electra's tapping at the entrance to Jonathan's office roused him from staring at his computer screen; he smiled and beckoned her to sit across from him a couple of seconds after turning his head toward the open door.

"Timing's everything, and yours couldn't be better, but before I tell you why, tell me why you're here?"

Electra began as soon as she sat.

"My trip to NASA worked out fine. They picked me for the Mars mission, and I think that'll be good for you too. Did they contact you yet?"

"What do you think? For starters, they think we can adjust the escape and suspension pod controls and biomonitoring software. And if we keep improving my climate telemetry software, they'll consider using it on the Mars mission. And that's why I say timing's everything. How's your June or July calendar? Will you have time for a week-long trip?"

"Please answer my foot soldier questions – who, what, why, where, when, and how?"

"We can inspect Amazon Rainforest locations where corporations or the Brazilian government might be violating ecological or environmental policy and compare what we find with data and analysis coming back from my software operating on Earth satellites. And all logistics will be handled by IBAMA, which is an acronym for the Brazilian Institute of the Environment and Renewable Natural Resources. NASA works with them. All you'll need to do is find your passport, get some vaccination shots, and be available the last week of June. Are you interested?"

"But why do you have to go there? Couldn't drone surveillance collect the data you need for comparisons?"

"You'd know if you'd ever hiked in a rainforest. The canopy created by all the trees makes that impossible. The forest vegetation is too dense for drones to penetrate. So I'll ask again, are you interested?"

"I think so, but I'll have to check my schedule. And you forgot one other thing I need to do, learn enough about the Amazon Rainforest."

"I didn't forget. That'll be the topic for our lunchtime discussion."

Jonathan didn't start his lunchtime lecture until he had ordered the pizza and both he and his student had taken a couple of soft drink sips. His words sounded more professorial than either his tone or expression.

"The Amazon Rainforest covers 2.6 million square miles, which is half the size of the U.S. Its 400 billion trees are home to 20 percent of all the species found on Earth, create 20 percent of the world's supply of oxygen, and store 96 billion tons of carbon by taking in carbon dioxide. It's no surprise why they help moderate climate change and why environmentalists want to make sure the Brazilian government protects it and the Amazon River, but the government looks at it a bit differently. They want to develop these natural resources, but Greenpeace types say the government and its coterie of big money contributors from big business is causing irreversible damage by harvesting it."

Jonathan stopped to take a gulp, giving time for Electra to speak but she didn't, so he carried on.

"The Amazon River and its tributaries are still the only way to navigate into the forest. The River's 5900 miles long, second only to the Nile, and it and all its tributaries discharge 215 thousand cubic miles of water annually into the Atlantic, which is greater than the sum of the next twenty largest rivers and accounts for 20 percent of what the world's rivers dump into the oceans. All this despite of more dams being built to generate power. And dams are damn bad, because they flood the surrounding forests, killing the trees. And it gets worse. It destroys the villages of the tribes living along the river, who're indigenous hunter-gatherers foraging for fruits, vegetables, and animals found in the forest, and fishing from small boats. So, can you think of why my telemetry software is so important?"

Electra delayed answering because Jonathan's order number had just been called, so she thought to herself while waiting for him to bring back the pizza.

I can think of many reasons, but I won't say. I'll let Jonathan show his smarts.

Electra talked soon after taking a second bite.

"I'm not sure why. What do you think?"

Jonathan rattled off his well-scripted explanation.

"My Earth monitoring satellite software not only collects but analyzes the land mass or oceanic areas I choose. And I've found rainforest locations where it looks like loggers are harvesting timber illegally. And maybe companies are secretly turning the enormous peat deposits into local fuel by strip mining it and then converting the land into farms or ranches. There's more to this too.

"I heard that deposits of rare earths are now being mined for computer chip doping. Some Brazilian government insiders have to know about all this because cities and airstrips are springing up in the middle of the Rainforest to support all these activities that the environmental groups are fighting against. So, my job on this expedition is to confirm what my software photos and analysis say."

"No wonder you and your software are in demand. You also mentioned ocean monitoring. What are you doing there?"

"I can monitor coral reefs, ocean currents and temperatures, glaciers, coastal erosion plus migratory patterns of fish. I can't look everywhere but GWU is focusing on South America. And you can be a big help for all of this. But that's enough for the time being. Just think about it. We'll talk more between now and when we leave."

Electra used the time remaining before flying back to Austin to think about this upcoming South American adventure. She also decided to give Eve the name of a person from the past who might be useful for Nari and Zara. Eve invited Electra to join them for dinner the night before her flight to Austin.

Amahl brought her into the kitchen after greeting her at the front door. Eve hugged her and then put on the counter the dessert treats Electra had brought. Eve playfully poked Amahl's midsection while saying,

"I'm sure Amahl will like these. As you can see, he needs calories to fuel his growth."

Electra said,

"Not only is he getting taller, but his muscles are getting bigger too."

Amahl added,

"I'm lifting weights. And after my foot operation, I'm gonna take wrestling lessons. No one's gonna make fun of me anymore."

Electra said,

"It's good knowing how to defend yourself. Muscle strength will make your wrestling moves quicker. Do you know when your operation will take place?"

Amahl shook his head so Eve spoke for him.

"By early July so he's ready for the fall semester. I'm ready to dish up. Amahl, go get your sister."

Zara came out of her semiconscious state fast enough so Amahl's knocking on the bathroom door didn't escalate to pounding.

"Uh, oh-OK, I'll be there in a minute."

"Well, hurry up. I'm hungry and the pizza's gonna get cold."

As Amahl clomped back to the kitchen, Zara slid spoons and syringes into her paraphernalia purse before hiding it in her bedroom and then shuffling into the kitchen. Eve glanced at Zara as soon as she sat opposite her brother.

"Lately, you've been either on campus or in your room. Are you that busy studying for finals?"

"Yes."

Her one-word answer left an awkward pause that Electra filled.

"Well, you'll feel better when exam week's over. Then you can spend more time working with Nari and Eve. And I'll give them the name and cell-phone number of a contact that might be useful."

She stopped there because Eve had just put pizza on everyone's plate and then said,

"We'll talk more after eating a slice or two. Dig in."

Amahl started gobbling and Zara picked off the circular pepperoni pieces, which prompted Eve to say,

"I heard about the results of another diet study that say you'll look younger if you eat less glucose and fat and more fruits and veggies, especially broccoli. They contain vitamins A, C, D, and E plus antioxidants. And proteins coming from fish and chicken are good for you, but even better coming from eggs and cheese. It also said eating one meal a day or fasting once a week for twenty-four hours is good because it cleans out the bad bacteria from your digestive system and stimulates autophagy and apoptosis. And that'll be an after-dinner assignment for Amahl. He'll find out what those words mean as well as the difference between vegan and vegetarian."

He stopped chewing long enough to say,

"Miss Electra's pretty smart. Maybe she can tell us."

Only Eve looked at her as she began talking.

"I'll start with the easier ones. A vegetarian is a person who gets their proteins from sources other than meat or fish. And a vegan avoids any protein coming animals, such as eggs, milk, or butter."

Eve added,

"That's interesting. I heard it somewhere but forgot. Go on."

"Well, I know this stuff from studying the biology related to space medicine. Autophagy means self-eating, and our digestive system is fine-tuned to consume unneeded proteins, pathogens, and damaged cells for recycling. Apoptosis is a normal, genetically regulated process leading to the death of cells triggered by the presence or absence or certain stimuli. DNA damage or mutation can cause it. And DNA mutation can create immortal cells. Too bad cancer cells are immortal. Developing drugs to target and then kill them is difficult. I could say more about diets, exercise, and aging, but I don't want to bore you."

Eve surprised Electra by saying,

"I heard somewhere that exercise slows down aging by speeding up the generation of stem cells and telomerase, which is the enzyme protecting DNA's endcaps. But no one under the age of eighteen wants to slow down the aging process. Kids want to grow up fast. Too bad they learn too late that being an adult isn't all it's cracked up to be."

Having heard enough, no one spoke until Eve and Zara cleared away the dishes and Zara said,

"I don't want dessert. I'm going back to my room," before shuffling out.

After Eve put a plate-full of brownies and lemon squares on the table,

Amahl said,

"I'll take care of Zara's," which he completed ten minutes later and then asked to be excused.

That cleared the way for Eve to say,

"Next time you come over, please ask Amahl to show you his magic tricks. In addition to lifting weights and video games, he's into cards. Maybe he'll deal us into a game or two."

Rising to go, Electra said,

"That'll be fun. I'll call when I get back from Austin."

Electra fretted while driving home.

Something's going on with Zara. She's lost weight and seems listless. Maybe I should talk with her, but no, I won't meddle unless I'm asked. Eve will have to step up and in, so stop thinking about it and start thinking about Austin and beyond.

President Kinslinger never thought about stepping up or in. His position in Bigger Brother's covert Gang of Three Plus One did the thinking for him. The encrypted Emails or online meetings orchestrated by leader Xinqian Hung would tell him what would soon hit particular nations and how he should use the disruptions to steer America's political agenda closer and closer to Bigger Brother's ultimate goal.

He didn't find out until a recent late night Email told him that Nari Bose would soon return to Washington and join forces with Eve Cortez. It also told him to use the pair to advance his agenda.

Newt swirled his scotch while considering options.

Eve can be even more useful now that she has two of her siblings helping. I'll make sure my people tail all three and let me know if she gets too close to the truth. And that's only for me to know and no one finds out.

Chapter 9
June 2167

"On a (Drum) Roll"

Electra determined soon after returning to Austin that she would have little trouble keeping professional and personal worlds in both Washington and Austin rolling along. Emails, online meetings, and cell-phone calls kept her in touch with those she needed, and Indira was always there for her.

And she decided to learn more about drumming via online videos for reading drum sheet music, handling drumsticks, and practicing drum techniques on the drum pad she had already bought. Lucky for Electra that Alisha always cut in whenever she approached her obsessive-compulsive danger zone.

I love watching the young Asian female street drummers even more than you do, for even though you know about sheet music reading and theory from long ago piano practice, I'm the one with the artistic flair. And I know when to stop the drums from rolling too far. So, please let me do the cover drumming by watching those females in action. They are so sexy as well as skillful. And when you see I'm ready to drumroll on, call Shanna to connect us with Miles. Let's find out how he likes his drum kit. Maybe he'd like me to teach him.

Electra called the Drummond household a week later at a time she thought Shanna would be there, and when she did, Shanna's enthusiasm bubbled in her words.

"Oh hi, Miss Electra. You got back. When can you check my homework? Miles too. He likes his drumsticks and stuff and—" Electra had to interrupt.

"Whoa, please slow down. How about tomorrow? And maybe I can find out how Miles likes drumming. Can I talk to him for just a minute?"

"Sure. He'll be right here."

His polite words started flowing about two minutes later.

"Hi, Miss Electra. I sure like my drums, and I'm practicing every day."

"Well, when I come over tomorrow to check homework, would you like me to teach you a little drumming?"

"Would you?"

"Sure, and tell your father that I'll bring enough fried rice and egg rolls for him too, whenever he gets home. Will that be OK?"

"Wow, that'll be cool. And fortune cookies too?"

"They come automatically, and I'll add some chocolate chip cookies to all that. See you tomorrow."

Shanna beat Miles to the front door, and as soon as she opened it, took some of the bags before trotting to the kitchen. Miles took the rest and said,

"This'll taste even better than my recipes. And Dad'll agree."

Eating was the first order of business, followed by checking Shana's homework. She positively glowed when Electra stuck a gold star on her writing assignment and told her she could now play video games or watch TV.

Electra then focused on Miles, who sat attentively next to her while she checked his math assignment. She put a check-plus mark at the top of the page before saying,

"Do you know that musicians have as much ability with numbers as scientists? They simply apply it to a different form of art. No wonder you want to play the drums."

Miles replied right away.

"And I'm getting better too. Lemme show you."

Miles began drumming ten minutes later after opening the Nitze's garage door and setting up his drum kit. Electra sat in a folding chair while listening and watching the performance, and when Miles looked ready for a break, she changed places with him.

"Bring the chair and sit next to me so you can listen and watch."

Electra continued a minute later.

"You'll hear musicians talk about drumming in the pocket, which means drummers have great timing, stay in the groove, and drum out rhythms the band can follow. And they do it by reading the drum sheet music and using a cross or openhanded stick handling that fits the music. Watch my wrists and how straight I sit on the stool."

The drumsticks danced across all the tom and snare drums and occasionally hit the cymbals while the floor pedal punched the kick drum from time to time. By the look on her student's face, Electra knew it was time to stop drumming and start talking.

"OK, you try it."

And she listened to Alisha as well as the drums.

He's got the beat. And our teaching will make it even better. Now you tell him more.

Electra stopped him five minutes later.

"You've got it, so here's what's next. Go get your laptop and set it up on a stand next to the drummer spot."

Miles dashed away. When he returned, she spoke as they peered into the screen.

"I just searched for a video on reading drum sheet music. I want you to study one of them between now and next time. And now I'll show you what drum cover is all about. I'm going to drum along with a video showing a drummer playing to a recording of the music and vocals. It's a great way to practice. Here I go."

Electra reined in her enthusiastic drumming so she could explain while drumming what she was doing. Miles seemed wired in to her words, absorbing them to the very last syllable. Electra stopped drumming when the music did but continued talking.

"This is plenty for tonight. And between now and our next lesson, please ask your dad to get you some drum sheet music."

"He doesn't have to. You just did it for him."

Marcel came into view seconds after his words. Miles stayed sitting, but Electra handed him the drumsticks before rising to meet his father halfway to the kitchen entrance, talking while walking.

"Hello, Mr. Drummond. Miles and I were just wrapping up his first drumming lesson. Would you like to hear how well he's doing?"

"Sure."

Electra turned to face Miles, beating the air with imaginary drumsticks while saying,

"Do a couple of minutes of warmup exercises and end with cymbals and a snare drum rimshot or two."

Miles's smile said he'd be happy to comply. Electra was the first to speak when his drumming ended.

"Excellent. Now please put the drums away. Then you and I can talk with your father at the kitchen table."

Standing in the garage long enough for Miles to get his dad's dinner dished up, Electra started talking.

"Your son's talented. You should be proud of what he's learned so quickly."

"I am, but you've got talent too. How did you learn to play the drums?"

"I took piano lessons that included music theory when I was little, and I've kept playing for the fun of it ever since. And when Miles told me he wanted to learn how to drum, I thought might be able to help."

"You've done that already, and you can drum as well as teach, and not many people can do that. You know the saying–those that can do, those that can't teach, and those that can't do either administrate."

Electra gave a tiny smile, then said,

"I'm pleased you approve, and I'm sure you'll feel the same way about dinner."

Shanna sat with them at the kitchen table long enough for Marcel to commend her homework. Then she went back to playing video games. Miles joined her after listening to his father's compliments.

Electra was about to leave but changed her mind when Marcel changed topics.

"You know, you might be able to help some of the newer musicians at the studio. We just picked up some string quartet players that do rock music. They told me they also do classical music where you work. You know about UT's Butler School of Music?"

"I've been too busy to check it out, but I will. I used to go to performances given by university music departments in cities where I used to live. Thanks for reminding me."

"Well, how about this? I'll set up a good time for you to meet them and they can explain what they're looking for. Is that OK?"

"That'll work. And I'll make sure Miles and Shanna keep working on their assignments too."

Electra managed to do that for them as well as herself, and even found a Butler School concert date she planned to attend. She spent that day working at her campus office, but she became so obsessed with finishing a report that she lost track of the time. When rushing in, she knew she had missed the first half but decided hearing the second would be better than nothing, so after grabbing a program, she followed the stragglers into the auditorium and settled into a seat in the last row just before the concert annotator welcomed the audience back and then explained what they were about to hear.

"Unlike the first half, which featured Dvorak's cheerful String Quartet Number 12 in F Major, Opus 12 and subtitled 'The American,' the second will sound somber notes expressed first in poetry accompanied by piano. You shall hear Goethe's dramatic poem 'The Erlkönig' that depicts the death of a child assailed by a supernatural being, the Erlking, a king of the fairies. Goethe wrote it as part of a 1782 Singspiel, Die Fischerin. 'Erlkönig' has been called Goethe's most famous ballad. Our baritone will sing it in German, but you will find a marvelous English translation in your program notes.

"And that will be followed by Schubert's String Quartet No. 14 in D Minor, 'Death and the Maiden,' composed in 1824. The theme of death is heard throughout, with recurring themes from his original 1817 song making appearances too. The thematic material is foreboding and foreshadows the fate of the maiden.

"And now, please welcome our vocalist and pianist."

While the audience applauded, Electra read the verses that overpowered her emotions.

Who rides there so late through the night dark and drear?

The father it is, with his infant so dear,
He holdeth the boy tightly clasp'd in his arm,
He holdeth him safely, he keepeth him warm.

"My son, wherefore seek'st thou thy face thus to hide?"
"Look, father, the Erl-King is close by our side!
Dost see not the Erl-King, with crown and with train?"
"My son, 'tis the mist rising over the plain."

"Oh, come, thou dear infant! oh come thou with me!
Full many a game I will play there with thee,
On my strand, lovely flowers their blossoms unfold, My mother
shall grace thee with garments of gold."

"My father, my father, and dost thou not hear
The words that the Erl-King now breathes in mine ear?"
"Be calm, dearest child, 'tis thy fancy deceives,
'Tis the sad wind that sighs through the withering leaves."

"Wilt go, then, dear infant, wilt go with me there?
My daughters shall tend thee with sisterly care My daughters
by night their glad festival keep,
They'll dance thee, and rock thee, and sing thee to sleep."

"My father, my father, and dost thou not see,
How the Erl-King his daughters has brought here for me?"
"My darling, my darling, I see it aright,
'Tis the aged grey willows deceiving thy sight."

"I love thee, I'm charm'd by thy beauty, dear boy!
And if thou'rt unwilling, then force I'll employ."
"My father, my father, he seizes me fast,
Full sorely the Erl-King has hurt me at last."
"The father now gallops, with terror half wild,
He grasps in his arms the poor shuddering child,
He reaches his courtyard with toil and with dread,--
The child in his arms finds he motionless, dead."

I lived through the same dreaded nightmare during a Christmas Eve snowstorm several lifetimes ago when my dearest Ariadne, my first clone daughter, died in my arms. She wasn't even three, and I remember her shrieking–Momma its coming for me! And I shall never forget her very last words–Momma, I love you–just before her body went limp. Only a tiny smile remained on her impassive face as her essence submerged into an uncharted infinity of indifferent stars.

Electra's stream of consciousness stopped, replaced by a stream of tears, but the words started a moment later.

Too much electricity in her neural circuitry–caused by an epileptic seizure–took her away from me and burned into my brain the words I can hear plus emotions and pain:

Neither numberless tears nor angels in flight
could lessen the grief that overwhelmed me that night

Electra stifled an inchoate panic attack. It receded further when the string quartet started playing, but her tears returned with the Presto fourth movement, building in tandem with the coda's crescendo.

My God, my emotions are transforming the foreboding into a philosophic resolution. Life finds a way to carry out its prime directive–to survive, to go on living through those who remain for another day.

She wiped away her tears so she could see the musicians stand after finishing. All of them–two Asian females holding violins and two Black males, one holding a viola and the other standing at attention next to his cello–were at most in their early thirties. They bowed as gracefully as they played, and each waved a bouquet to acknowledge the audience. Electra left before the applause died away.

The drive home helped her cognitive persona regain control.

Ariadne was my first and only attempt to create my Dream Team by cloning myself. They would be clay in my hands. My mentoring would place them beyond mere mortals. They would understand me. Cloning would have been better than leaving to chance the mixing of X and Y DNA, and for me, it would have been the only way. The lightning bolt of my creation, besides making me exceptional, also made me sterile.

And although tonight rekindled emotions of pain, it also renewed my belief that I still have much to gain. Somehow, Su succeeded where I failed. She created my four clone children, and though they must never know who I am, I can still help them achieve what is best.

Tonight has drained my emotional energy, but my lightning brain will recharge all my personas while I sleep. So, let's get home and re-energize for what's in store, whether going to Austin, DC, or some distant shore.

Chapter 10
July 2167

"One Strange Night"

Electra didn't mind that Mr. Drummond couldn't arrange a date for visiting his studio; she used the extra time to keep up with NASA's and Jonathan's projects while keeping in touch with Eve and tutoring Shanna and Miles. And she flew back to DC soon after Jonathan finalized all details for their Amazon Rainforest Expedition.

She used the flight time to put together her South American fact sheet she would share with Jonathan, for she knew the importance of understanding the history, cultures, and customs of the places that life's journey would take her. She had written up all she needed by the time the jet touched down, and she would meet with Jonathan a day later on Saturday, the Fourth of July, when he takes her to lunch.

Calling Eve the night before, Electra heard the good news first: ongoing recovery exercise therapy for Amahl's foot operation proceeded ahead of schedule, but then she found out about Zara's still indifferent behavior, followed by Nari's delayed flight. Electra promised to visit them upon returning. Then she retrieved a Coca Cola plus a handful of Oreos before settling in front of her workstation to invoke Indira's GUI. Indira spoke first.

"I shall give you my latest apps for satellite telemetry and escape or suspension pod control when you return from your Amazon adventure. That should free up more of your time to work on our Android project. Are you ready for South America?"

"Jonathan says so, but let me show you some background info that'll help understand the place. Electra flashed it on the screen so she could see it while Indira viewed it electronically.

South American Fact Sheet

Geography:

Ranking of Equator cuts through only South America and Africa. Continents by Area:	
1.Asia (17 mm sq. miles)	Striking Geography and Climate Variability.
2. Africa (11)	Andes Mountains hugging Pacific Coast "Ring of Fire". 3.North Towering Volcanoes and Glaciers.
3. North America (9)	Towering Volcanoes and Glaciers.
4. South America (7)	Breathtaking Waterfalls, Magnificent Rivers and Lakes.
5. Europe (4)	Enormous Sand Dunes, Deserts, and Hidden Pyramids.
6. Australia (3)	Hundreds of Mysterious Pre-Columbian Geoglyphs etched into South-Peruvian Nacza Desert/Hills and depicting exotic plant/animal figures and lines measuring 30 ft. wide, up to 5 miles long and visible via satellite telemetry when not covered by sand. Lush Rainforests.

Pre-Columbian History:

- Indigenous People Migrated From North America 16.5 thousand BCE. South American tribes share DNA with Native American Indians.
- Hunter-Gatherer Tribes Transitioned to Agricultural Communities. They had Potatoes, Beans, Corn, Alpacas, and Llamas, but no Dogs or Horses.
- Tribes and Communities Preferred Commerce (Trade) to Conflict (Local Raiding Parties).
- Civilizations having Religion and Technology but no Written Language Emerged 3.5 thousand BCE. Some had Million-plus Populations and built Cities containing Sacrificial Temples. Aztecs (Tenochtitian aka Mexico City today), Incas (Machu Pichu), and Mayans (Mirador) most notable.

**Post-Columbian History
(Columbus/Spain/Portugal discover the New World):**
- Starting Early 1500s CE:
- Pizarro (Spain) conquered Incas and exterminated Indigenous People.
- Cortez (Spain) conquered Aztecs and Mayans, and exterminated Indigenous People.
- Other European countries (France, Portugal, Netherlands) followed to colonize, conquer, and extract silver and gold. South American governments unable to withstand conquerors' brutal use of Guns, Germs, and Steel (Weapons, Bacteria/Viruses, and Technology).
- Conquerors carved the Continent into countries and replaced Indigenous People/local governments with emigrants and governments from home. Largest countries: Brazil, Argentina, Peru, Columbia, Bolivia, Venezuela, Chile.

Indira started talking because the Singularity knew it all.

"Thorough as usual, but if you share it with Jonathan, let him explain it to you. And remove from his copy any mention of the Nacza Desert Geoglyphs."

"But why?"

"Don't distract him or yourself. Focus on the Amazon. Besides, I have other reasons I shall reveal only to you when appropriate. Do you have additional questions?"

"Uh-no."

"Excellent. Please contact me when you return. And since you are my favorite mere mortal, please stay healthy and safe, especially when exploring in the Rainforest."

Indira blew her a two-handed kiss just before her GUI vanished.

Electra double-checked that her briefcase contained everything needed for tomorrow's meeting before turning out the lights, but a cell-phone call jarred her awake. She recognized Jonathan's agitated words.

"Sorry to call so late, but I've gotta postpone our lunch tomorrow. I've gotta meet instead with my South American contacts. Depending on what they tell me, I might have to delay our expedition. You won't be mad, will you?"

"You know best, but please let me know as soon as you can what the new schedule is."

"I will. And I'm sure you'll find something to do tomorrow that'll be more fun than my meeting. After all, even though it's just another day for South America, it is our Fourth of July. So, you find a good way to celebrate and I'll say goodbye."

Electra started the day with an early morning run, then went to a local parade that featured a community-sponsored cookout and children's fun fair. She celebrated in a traditional manner by eating beans and hotdogs along with an ear of corn and a slice of watermelon, and gave an extra dollar when buying two raffle tickets, first from an enterprising girl and then from an even younger boy.

This is what the Fourth should be like. Blue skies, kids playing, and families enjoying just being together. Should I invite myself by calling Eve? She's taking Amahl to the big fireworks display even though Zara won't go, but no, I won't barge in. I'll watch the broadcast and call Eve tomorrow.

Amahl liked the crowd excitement and fireworks explosions as much as Eve, who stopped for ice cream on the drive home. While dishing up in the kitchen, she told him to ask Zara if she would like to join them, but she said no and stayed in her room. He said nothing to Eve, but he thought his sister needed watching.

Amahl wore a black hoodie along with a look more of curiosity than concern when he started shadowing his sister late that night. When she stopped near a dimly lit street corner, he zipped his motorbike out of sight but close enough to watch as she met a bulky fellow he neither recognized nor could hear, but he became more concerned when the bulk climbed back into the passenger seat after Zara got into the back. Amahl decided she knew what she was getting into but would continue watching.

Zara waited for the passenger seat occupant to talk.

"So, you need more candy from your candy man. How much money you bring?"

"Not enough, I couldn't pinch any from home. Can you give me enough for a couple of days? I promise to pay you back."

Zara couldn't see his expression when he looked at her, but she sensed from his breathing she wouldn't like it.

"Let's make a deal, darlin. I'll take you to a place where you can spread your legs so you won't have to open your purse. Wanna play along?"

Zara's silence said what he wanted to hear. He motioned to the driver and the car cruised away. Amahl did likewise, keeping enough distance to be invisible. Thirty minutes later, he hadn't a clue where the car stopped to let the bulk pull Zara through the basement entrance of a dingy building. Amahl counted high enough to avoid detection before sneaking through the doorway and listening for clues to his sister's whereabouts.

Hearing muffled words coming from only one apartment, Amahl knelt close to its door, listening for more and trying to picture what might be going on behind the rickety door. But when he heard what could only be a creaking bed accompanied by throttled screams, he stopped thinking and his instincts took over. As soon as he bashed through the door, he saw a sight even more graphic than the porn videos he and his buddies watched. He also saw a stash of powder and paraphernalia that told him what the guy did for a living.

Zara was on hands and knees, stripped naked with her head pressed against the headboard while the bulk pulled on the chain wrapped around her neck and pumped from behind. He must have been so close to ecstasy that he didn't know Amahl had blasted in until he wrapped the guy in a wrestler's chokehold and pulled him off the bed.

Amahl's grip tightened relentlessly after he landed on top; anger tinged with fear multiplied his arm strength, and he didn't let go until the blob of flab he was riding stopped quivering.

By this time Zara had climbed out of bed and wrapped herself in a bedsheet, then stuttered through tears and slurred words and tears,

"Huh-he, uh hurt me bad."

Amahl grabbed her shoulders and shook hard enough to snap her back to reality before yelling,

"Grab your stuff and let's go."

Zara did as told with Amahl's help, but he took his eyes off the blob until he heard its grunting just in time to see it pulling a gun from its pants. Amahl leaped onto the gun-waving hand and wrestled it free before grabbing it mid-air while stumbling backward. The mass rolled away, but it was too big a target for Amahl to miss. He emptied the magazine, causing an eruption of blood that splattered his face; he wiped off some before standing on unsteady legs and then yelling,

"Get his money and stuff."

Zara had ridden before on the back of Amahl's bike; she wrapped her arms around him, telling him how to get home even though she floated in and out of semiconsciousness. They clung to each other while staggering into the living room and collapsing onto the sofa before Amahl shouted. Eve came running.

The sight stripped her words to the naked essentials.

"Christ in heaven, what the hell happened?"

Zara zoned out, forcing Amahl to tell the tale. Eve heard all she needed in less than five minutes. When she emptied Zara's purse, the sight unleashed more words.

Christ almighty, you've got a couple a thousand dollars and maybe a kilo of coke... and the gun too."

Eve had run out of words as well as the strength to remain standing. She fell into a nearby chair and covered her face with both hands. No one twitched until Eve roused herself a minute later and said,

"No one saw you and you collected all your stuff plus most of his. That's good. It's even better you took the gun. It's worth more than everything else combined. I'm gonna put Zara in the shower and examine her. I won't take her to an E.R. unless she's bleeding. Then you shower next and put all your clothes and Zara's into garbage bags that I'll dump somewhere. Things'll look better tomorrow. Zara can sleep with me if she wants to."

Zara burst into tears, showing she needed that. Eve helped her stand before hugging and then taking her away; Amahl headed to the kitchen to find some bags before going to his bedroom and putting what he had been wearing into them. He then packed up Zara's.

By the time he collapsed into bed, he felt like tonight had aged him more than he wanted, introducing him to a seamy piece of the adult world; he didn't think a shower could ever wash away the dirt and hurt that had just landed on him, but he hoped Zara could get help dealing with hers.

Eve slept fitfully, awakening before dawn and making a one-minute call to the only person she thought could help. Electra appeared within the hour, bringing muffins, sweet rolls, and sweet butter just in time for breakfast. She put the box and butter on the table before sitting in the chair where two cans of Coke stood.

Electra waited for everyone to take a bite out of what they picked before leading off.

"Eve said you had one strange night last night. Maybe she can explain what she means."

Eve's words spilled out for five minutes while glancing from person to person. No one but Alisha spoke, but only to Electra for a lightning-quick second.

We can never tell anyone about our Hollywood rape, but Zaby can. Maybe that could help Zara.

Electra spoke slower and pitched her voice lower than what Eve had rattled off.

"I've mentioned before that Irani mentored me. And she told me that a person none of us ever met–Electra Kittner–mentored her. This Kittner person had been raped and beaten long ago, but a smart little Lebanese girl named Zaby came to her rescue. Zaby's all grown up and I don't know what happened to Kittner, but it might if Zara speaks to Zaby. And Zaby might have Middle East contacts that could help Nari and Eve figure out what's happening there."

Eve looked at Zara, who looked ready to cry, so she spoke for both.

"I'll call her if you can get the number. And before I do, Zara and I will meet with a counselor."

"You're going to be extra busy for a while talking with whatever mental health person you and Zara pick, so if it's OK with you and Amahl, I can look in on him when I get back. Perhaps he can show me his latest card or magic tricks."

Eve didn't need to answer; Amahl's look said yes.

Chapter 11
July 2167

"On the Ball"

Electra decided not to tell Jonathan that she actually preferred the one-week flight delay because she didn't want him prying into her personal life, and this way he would feel somewhat indebted to her cooperative nature. She settled back in her first-class seat next to Jonathan, waiting for him to show how much he knew.

"We've got thirteen hours on this 4,250-mile, one-stop-in-Miami flight to Brasilia, and I'm sorry to say we lose two hours because we're crossing two time zones heading east, but we can rest on the plane after I tell you a lot about what you should know."

"Two weeks ago, you said some government agency would fly us, but now we're on American Airlines. Why the switch?"

"We'll be harder to spot, and I picked its arrival time to jibe with IBAMA. We're supposed to land at 6:30 tomorrow morning Monday the 13th, which means we can be at their office by early afternoon if all goes according to plan. Bruno Vieira, my IBAMA contact once we land, will expedite us through customs, drive us from there to the office, and handle all details after that. According to the photo IBAMA sent me, he looks like a model for an early-forties South American diplomat—dark hair and complexion, good looking, athletic build, and a sharp dresser. Do you remember what IBAMA stands for?"

Electra played along.

"You told me but I don't remember."

"It stands for Brazilian Institute of the Environment and Renewable Natural Resources, and don't ask me why the acronym letters don't match. But before I tell you some stuff, don't you have a fact sheet?"

Pulling two copies out of her carry-on, she gave one and kept the other before saying,

"Tell me what you think?"

Jonathan tossed it into her lap less than a minute later.

"It's OK, but I know all this and it won't help on our expedition. You're looking at the past. We're here to see what's going on in the present and how that'll impact the future. That's why Bruno will introduce us to BNDES–that's the Brazilian Development Bank–so we see both sides.

"But maybe you can use some of your fact sheet while we're sightseeing Tuesday in Brasilia before IBAMA takes us on one of its choppers to a base camp in the Rainforest. And that'll take up to five hours. How's that sound?"

"Noisy and boring. What else should I know?"

After two hours, Electra had heard plenty while the lightning brain corrected for only Electra's benefit some of what Jonathan said, and then each retired into their personal worlds for the remainder of the flight.

Bruno proved to be a model of bureaucratic efficiency too. Other than occasionally adding or dropping sound at the end of words, Electra thought he spoke excellent English, which made him an effective translator. He shuttled his guests through customs and into the van before loading their luggage. Electra liked the seating arrangement: Jonathan sitting in the passenger seat next to Bruno while she luxuriated in the second row, happy to be ignored. She did some sightseeing and chatting to herself instead of listening to the fellows discuss expedition details and what changes might be in the offing.

Brasilia is a thoroughly modern city. Buildings are a mix of gracefully curved metal and glass intermixed with clean geometric shapes. Plenty of space between them too, and gads, the boulevard-like multi-lane crack-and-pothole-free roads carry light traffic. And let me guess why–a year-round ice-free climate means smooth roads, and most of the country consisting of jungle and rainforest means few inter-city or country roads.

Jonathan announced only one change just before Bruno parked the van in his building's garage.

"We'll be on our own for tomorrow's sightseeing, but we can use the van to drive around. All we have to do is bring it and ourselves back here early Wednesday. You think we'll be OK?"

"Roads look better than those in most American east coast cities, and people drive on the right."

"Great, you can do the driving."

The pair followed Bruno into a medium-sized conference room containing a rectangular table surrounded by six chairs. Next to it a buffet table held two trays containing sandwiches and cookies, and a selection of Brazilian-branded soft drinks.

Bruno became an unofficial lunch host by describing the items.

"You'll have no trouble recognizing the sandwiches, and any beverage you pick-ah is safe. But I recommend you try Guaraná Antarctica. It Brazil's second most popular soft drink and-ah midway between Coke and Mountain Dew on the energy scale. Most people say it-ah taste tart and crisp, like apple with-ah sweeter, berry-like aftertaste. Why not try?"

Both guests did, and they also picked a cheese sandwich that according to Bruno used Queijo minas, a mild white cheese named for the state in which it originated–Minas Gerais–before sitting. Bruno faced the door and his guests flanked him.

And while his guests ate, he began reciting the city's history.

"In 1960, Brazil President Juscelino Kubitschek founded Brasilia, our nation new capital, which he built using the futuristic urban planning brilliance of famed architect Oscar Niemeyer. In only five years, million of South American construction workers turned empty land on Brazilian highland into graceful bureaucratic center housing government and surrounded by commercial and residential center holding steel-glass building. Outlying suburban sprawl became home to thousand upon thousand construction workers and family.

"During construction, engineers dammed Paranoa River, creating Lake Paranoa, which has a fifty-mile circumference. On its shores sit embassy and consulate, sport club, restaurant, shopping center, and residential area. Truly remarkable, eh? And its population, at over three million, make it third-largest city in

Brazil. But that less than half population of Rio de Janeiro, which in turn only half of Sao Paulo.

"These gigantic coastal cities, though old, overcrowded, and ragged just about everywhere, make showpiece capital seem boring. But I guess that what—" insistent tapping on the door interrupted the history lesson.

"Come in."

Two brother-like types who could have come from Bruno's family entered and then stood opposite him. He reached across the table to shake hands and then while looking at Jonathan said,

"Professor Jonathan Segal, I introduce you to our friends from the Brazilian Development Bank, Mr. Carlos Duarte and Diego Garcia, who say hi to Professor Segal and helper Electra."

Electra remained sitting but Jonathan stood to exchange handshakes, and then everyone sat, waiting for Bruno to begin.

"You know Jonathan here to look at Rainforest up close. And he should know how BNDES does too. Why not tell?"

Carlos and Diego alternated talking, pausing for Bruno's comments or Jonathan's questions. Electra sat, happy to be listening but also talking to herself.

These fellows are smooth operators. Flawless facts and figures delivered with impeccable English. They say that among all the continents, South America is ahead of only Australia and Antarctica when measured by population. Its size of 400-plus million accounts for about five percent of the world's total and three and a half percent of total GDP, but Brazil is the economic powerhouse, generating over half of what South America contributes and ranking it in the top ten world economies.

Too bad political instability and corporate corruption still hamstring economic growth. Dictators ruled Brazil until 1985 when social democracy came in, but today there are perhaps too many political parties. No wonder Brazil has a presidential revolving door. And they also say the country is still stuck in the Middle Income Trap. Its early rapid growth propelled it to middle-income status, but growth faltered and Brazil failed to catch up to the developed world.

BNDES is pushing to grow a Brazilian hi-tech economy, but raw materials, tobacco and food crops, cattle ranches, and lower-tech manufacturing still dominate. Only its oil and gas industry is a world player due to offshore reserves. Brazil still needs that cash flow, and BNDES also says Brazil and many non-western countries oppose dictates from green energy and environmental groups because the burdens of fighting some of the exaggerated existential claims regarding climate change, CO-2 gas, and mass extinction fall on third-world nations.

Electra silently summarized the rest she heard when Bruno ended the meeting two hours later.

These fellows have a point or two. Maybe Western Europe and America should stop dictating the rules to the rest of the world. Their governments might be hiding an imperial or colonial strategy, but for now, that's not on my follow-up agenda. I'll let Eve worry about that.

As the BNDES team prepared to leave, Carlos pointed a question at Jonathan.

"I hope you have a better understanding about the economic importance of the Rainforest. We don't want you give the wrong impression when you report your findings."

Bruno spoke for him.

"You no worry. He plenty smart. He'll come through for me and you."

Seemingly satisfied, Carlos and Diego left. Soon after, Bruno shook Jonathan's hand and patted Electra on the head.

"You and-ah you pretty helper have nice sightsee tomorrow, and-ah I know you write nice report too."

"Don't worry, my report will state conclusions taken from the unadulterated facts, and I'll be sure to point out both sides of all issues. And we'll meet you back here bright and early Wednesday morning, ready to head into the rainforest."

Waking early and feeling re-energized after yesterday's grueling flight and conversations, Electra took a light workout in the hotel's fitness center. She wished she had packed a swimsuit because the outdoor pool looked inviting, but decided she could buy one later if she couldn't resist. Then she headed to the complimentary breakfast bar for bananas and oatmeal before heading back to her room and building a tourist attraction list containing directions.

Knocking on her door just before nine, Jonathan's voice registered surprise.

"You're up already and on the computer? Whatcha doing?"

"Putting together a list of places to see and how to get there. I'll be our unofficial tour guide today. Have you had breakfast? I already did and can vouch for the breakfast bar."

"Why don't you keep me company before we see the sights?"

Electra had a muffin and Guaraná Antarctica while doing so.

Electra's guided tour hit enough spots to impress Jonathan, who commented along the way. He said the futuristic design of the Catholic Cathedral of Brasilia looked more like a science fiction museum than a place of worship, and he liked how Tri-Power Plaza's architecture shows a modern interpretation Brazil's three branches of government. But he saved the most revealing description just before noon when he told her to park close to some crowded beach volleyball courts on Lake Paranoa. He admired everyone he saw before saying,

"The guys look fit, but the females are even better. They remind me of the lyrics from a big hit from the early 1960s. You'll catch the South American flavor when I sing its opening lines.

Tall and tan and young and lovely
the gal from Ipanema goes walking
and when she passes each one she passes goes ahaaa.
When she walks she's like a samba
That swings so cool and sways so gently
That when she passes each one she passes goes ahaaa.

"And guess what country invented the samba?"

"Someplace in South America?"

"You get half-credit. You got the right continent, but you didn't tell me the country. Well, the history of Samba takes us to Brazil, though the origins are rooted in African culture. Samba music intertwines with Brazil's colonial history. And I'll tell you even more.

The Ipanema beach in Rio de Janeiro became popular worldwide after the song 'The Girl from Ipanema' by Stan Getz and Astrud Gilberto came out in 1962. Her voice is a lot sexier than mine, but you get the idea. And I won't be gross and call those bikinis fanny flossers. I think volleyball players call them microkinis.

"Hey, have you played much volleyball?"

"Electra answered to herself first before compressing the truth for Jonathan's ego.

Are you kidding? I taught Tiana and Tyrone well enough to win that two-person team volley ball tournament, but I'll keep that under wraps.

"In high school gym class. How about you?"

"I got pretty good when playing in college and still compete in a fitness center league. I like to play on six-person or two-person mixed teams. It's more fun when guys and gals mix it up. Do you remember the rules?"

"A little about three strikes and palming and scoring points only when serving, but please refresh my memory."

"OK, here are the rules used where I play. A match consists of three games. You win the match as soon as you win two games, and you win a game by winning fifteen points sooner than your opponent. But you have to win by at least two, so you keep playing until you do. And you win a point only when serving. Got it so far?"

"It's coming back, please go on."

"So, the match begins with one of the teams serving, and it keeps serving until it loses the point. Then the other side serves. And remember that serving rotates through the team players. That player on the serving team stands behind the baseline and either hits it over the net or, if he's really good, does a jump serve by tossing the ball high into the serving court and smashing it over the net. Don't call me a sexist by not saying he or she, but where I play only a couple of females do jump serves. Anyway, a jump serve can reach eighty-plus mph, and at most three players on the returning team can hit–in volleyball lingo it's called a touch–the ball only once before getting it over the net.

The three hits used to be called bump, volley, and spike, but today they're called the pass, set and kill. And if you remember that players can't catch–that's also called a lift or hold– the ball, you've got it."

Electra began studying the volleyball games going on; so did Jonathan, but he tugged her arm a couple of minutes later.

"Did you bring a swimsuit? I didn't, but I'll buy one for each of us if you'll tag along and play some volleyball. There's gotta be a store nearby, and no matter how we do, we'll have fun talking to some of Brazil's younger athletic crowd. Are you game?"

Both Alisha and Electra could feel the excitement building.

"Let's do it, and why not get a couple of beach towels too? We don't want to reveal the goods until we start playing."

Ninety minutes later, Jonathan took the lead walking to the courts. They watched games in progress while standing next to a chatty group that spoke English like many their age across the globe. Electra whispered that young people around the globe know that English is still the language to learn early in school anywhere if they want to move up the corporate ladder. Jonathan didn't reply to her but instead began talking to the group.

"Hey there, me and my partner come from Washington, DC, and we're here on business. We've been doing some sightseeing and watching your people play. I play in a volleyball league back home and would like to play a couple of games here. Can you make room for us?"

A tall and tan and good-looking guy answered.

"Sure. What should we call you?"

Jonathan concealed his surprise when Electra said,

"Call me Alisha. My partner's name is Jonathan. And thanks for letting us play."

The fellows watching pretended insouciant glances as the newcomers unwrapped from their towels before positioning to serve. Soon after, the watchers looked like they appreciated what they saw. One of them started talking only loud enough for those close by.

"Look at how that fabulous body moves. Her legs just won't quit, and she's got a thigh gap worthy of a king-size Tobler. No matter how she plays, she can be on my team anytime."

When Jonathan began serving, the people watching could tell he knew the game. Alisha played just well enough to keep pace. After her team won the first game, the other side started showing their skills and hitting harder. Jonathan wasn't fast enough to dig out shots by lunging for the ball, but Alisha's swanlike dives kept the ball in play for Jonathan to score enough, losing the second game by only five points.

The Brazilian team played a bit harder in the third, throwing in an occasional jump serve that flummoxed Jonathan but not Alisha. She blocked the ones that came her way and leaped high above the net to either block or slam the ball into corners the other team couldn't reach. And though Alisha's team lost, a gathering crowd applauded before another good-looking guy said to her,

"Why don't you play with me? We'll take on our best guy-gal team."

Alisha accepted the offer. Jonathan joined the crowd on the sidelines as the lightning brain elevated to a higher state in preparation for Alisha to elevate her game.

Matt told me several lifetimes ago that it's OK to strut your stuff if you've got the goods. Well, today I do.

Alisha's partner knew his stuff too. Alisha began playing at a level almost equal to his, but when her team fell behind by three points with only two to go for the other team to win, she felt a calming clarity envelop her. Time and motion slowed as the lightning brain elevated higher.

She unleashed one of her secret weapons – the jump serve that blasted over the net faster than the opposing team could handle. Four serves later, her partner yelled to the crowd.

"Come on, we'll play our best two-guy team."

Both guys on the opposing team were even better than her partner. They won the first game in spite of Alisha's dives and blocks and jump serves, but her partner upped his play in the second, and her team won. Her partner could see from the steely look in her eyes her intensity rising even higher, like that of a champion prizefighter ready to regain the title. And that's when he made the right call.

"Let's stop here and call it a draw before grabbing some beers."

And after Alisha said,

"Could I have a Guaraná Antarctica instead?" one of the guys yelled,

"We'll serve anyone who can hit like you whatever you want."

Jonathan held off peppering Electra with questions when they were partying on the beach, but he began the inquiry as soon as they began driving back to the hotel.

"You're just full of surprises. Why'd you call yourself Alisha?"

"Lots of people use their middle names when playing different roles. What's yours?"

"Livingston. And where'd you learn to play volleyball? You positively crushed the ball. You're sure a killer on the court."

"I told you I played a while ago. And by now you should know I'm a quick study."

"I think you should use the superlative form of that adjective for your thinking as well as volleyball court moves. You hit like lightning on a lightning rod. And I've never seen you cut loose partying like that. I like your come-on dance moves, and the more you drank, the sexier they got. I hope you don't have a hangover. Tomorrow's the start of our expedition."

"One of the guys said Cachaca is Brazil's most popular distilled spirit. It's made from fermented sugarcane and tastes like rum. I think I'll start using it in my Coke."

Jonathan couldn't think of anything to say, but Alisha did.

"And the female you were ogling said the Bombeirinho cocktail is Brazil's most popular pub drink among the ladies. That's a great name. It's a mix of cachaca, red currant syrup, and lemon juice and it's supposed to taste like you're drinking pure sugar if you get bombed on them, but I wouldn't know about that."

"I'm sure you wouldn't. You drink like a guy. Well, I hope your brain is on the ball tomorrow. Bruno says our expedition leader will show us some videos during the flight so we know more about what to expect."

"Don't worry, it will be and I'll be ready for action."

Chapter 12
July 2167

"The Rainforest Girl"

Bruno greeted Electra and Jonathan at the office early the next morning. Three men stood with him: one looked like a thinner version of Bruno while the other two were wiry, gray-haired fellows.

Bruno said,

"You look like you sleep good. That help, because you got big day, and let me introduce you to men who make entire expedition big success. Shake hands with leader Gustavo Rocha. He a FUNAI guy."

Gustavo explained further.

"I work full time for our National Indian Foundation. We partner with the Nature Conservancy to establish and implement policies that protect indigenous peoples and their lands. And with me are anthropology and archaeology professors Julio Chavez and Paco Pinto. I'll let them explain while Bruno drives us to the heliport what their roles are. We better get started."

Electra liked the seating arrangement. Gustavo sat next to Bruno with Jonathan and Julio right behind, followed by Electra and Paco. Gustavo conversed with Bruno while Julio led the other discussion.

"Bruno hires us as needed on Rainforest expeditions, me to be translator for our guides or tribes we come across, and Paco to be inspector of any artifacts we might find. You see, the camps hire natives from local tribes to maintain the place and guide them on Rainforest treks. And academically speaking, we call them Amerindians, which is often shortened in both North and South America to just Indians.

"Before the Europeans arrived bringing germs that wiped out most of the natives, hundreds of tribes speaking different languages lived along the River and its tributaries or in small communities scattered throughout the Rainforest. We estimate that the population peaked at over ten million, and we think –"

Electra interrupted, but Julio didn't seem to mind. He liked her enthusiasm.

"I understand that tribes have been in South America for thousands of years since migrating from North America along the Pacific coast. Then just like in North America, they migrated from west to east. Too bad they didn't leave written records, but we think the tribes formed a networked civilization that did some fighting but more trading. And didn't they live holistically, treating all animals and Nature as one?"

Julio waited for Paco to reply.

"Archaeologists like me are better equipped to answer than anthropologists. The academic term is animism, which is a philosophy that all living plants and animals possess spirits that are interwoven into the Universe. And every tribe huddled together to stay alive. You probably heard the term 'noble savage'. You know who came up with it?"

Alisha warned Electra not to display her smarts, so she answered the question with one of her own.

"Maybe at one time, but I forgot. Who did?"

"The modern myth of the noble savage is most commonly attributed to the 18th-century Enlightenment philosopher Jean Jacques Rousseau. He believed that 'original man' was free from sin, appetite, or the concept of right and wrong, and that those deemed "savages" were not brutal but noble.

"Well, there never was a 'noble savage', not even in this Garden of Eden-like Amazon Rainforest. For primitive man, which the Rainforest tribes still are, trying to survive on their own has always been solitary, poor, nasty, brutish, and short. We can credit Thomas Hobbes for coining that definition.

"But the adjective primitive fits only their tools and technology. They couldn't count very high or tell time, but in other aspects, these pre-Columbian tribes were as sophisticated as civilizations found on all continents at that time, even though they wore only loincloths to cover the genital area. The women sometimes covered their breasts. It made sense to wear as little as possible in the rainforest because of heat and humidity plus dense vegetation, and it still does, so don't be shocked if you see some of that at the camp."

Paco paused to rub the back of his neck before saying.

"I've lost my place. Where was I?"

"You were about to tell us how sophisticated they were."

"Oh yes, thanks. They were and still are. They practiced a religion that had high priests and medicine men, and had a creation myth found in most civilizations that anthropologists have studied. They had a virgin birth story of redemption too. Christianity's not alone on that. They also had socially-ordered politics along with coming-of-age, marriage, burial, and sacrifice rituals. Stories passed down talk about spirits of the dead flying to a big hut in the sky.

"And most would pierce their skins, paint their faces, or deliberately carve designs into their skin. Anthropologists call this scarification, which is done for rituals, for signaling belonging, or for enhancing beauty. But from the records kept by European explorers who came looking for gold and silver and conquest, the tribes vanished in at most twenty years."

Paco stopped because Jonathan looked ready to ask a question.

"If there were so many around for so long, why don't we see something left behind in the Rainforest?"

"Three reasons. First, near as we can tell, there are about 305 tribes living in Brazil today, totaling around 900,000 people, but that's a grand total of only 0.4 percent of Brazil's population. To help them out, the government has set aside 609 territories for its indigenous population, covering about 13% of Brazil's land mass. Nearly all of this reserved land lies in the Amazon and is off limits.

"Next, the plants in Brazil's jungle rain and vine forest sections grow so fast they cover everything up. And all the structures made by the tribes used organic material, like wood and plant fibers, which the environment's heat, humidity, and insects recycle. By the way, there are palm trees bearing fruit as well as rubber trees here.

"And you might be interested in this, long-term studies of tree populations tell us about climate change. Bruno tells us you have the best telemetry analysis software. Maybe we can hire you to help us map tree locations and where forest villages used to be."

Jonathan's expression said thanks before he said,

"I appreciate the compliment. I think I can tweak my apps to handle that, but please go on."

"And now, for the third reason. The tribes that remain avoid contact with the outside world. They know from what happened when the white man came – his germs or weapons wiped them out. There are still tribes living in the Amazon that have never been in contact with the outside world. And when anthropologists stumble across them, they live and look like they did thousands of years ago. We call them the tribes that time forgot. You'll see why. We can only get to where we're going by helicopter."

Paco's lecture ended abruptly. Bruno had just parked at the heliport; Gustavo began ticking off instructions.

"It's hard to talk for too long on a chopper flight, so please watch the videos we gave you. They'll tell you more about the Rainforest plus other Brazilian natural wonders. And when we get to camp, the field expedition leader takes over. All of us must follow his orders. Now let's grab our gear and climb aboard."

It took less than twenty minutes of flight time for Electra to gaze upon a landscape for which all traces of civilization had vanished.

All I see is an endless green sea of rainforest canopy cut through by brown snaking bands of the Amazon River's tributaries glistening in the early morning sunlight. I've seen a sight like this only once before, and that was on an African adventure to the Congo. But the Congo River didn't twist and turn like this. It's mesmerizing to watch, and I'll watch for a few minutes more. Then I'll tune in to the video when Jonathan starts it.

After watching for an hour, Jonathan hit pause before yelling,

"Brazilian waterfalls are best in the world. My favorite is Iguaza. It's got 275 falls cascading over lush vegetation clinging to big brown boulders and cliffs. What's yours?"

"Eldorado, it's over 1000 feet high, making it Brazil's tallest. But like most of Brazil's natural wonders, you can get there only by taking a canoe or hiking through the jungle, and the narrator said both can be dangerous. I bet the field leader will tell us what to look out for."

"Probably. Let's watch the rest."

The field leader assembled the team two hours after the chopper landed early that afternoon. Electra summarized his and the camp's appearance while everyone filed into one of buildings.

No infrastructure out here, only cell-phones and electric power generators. The wooden buildings' functional designs, complete with high ceilings and insect netting hung over all openings, makes the place livable for the handful of men-only staff stationed here. And the fellow in charge looks like a thinner and more physically fit version of Bruno, experienced and rugged enough to handle jungles, rivers, and rainforests.

The leader began speaking as soon as everyone sat.

"Welcome to my Amazon Rainforest camp. My name is Miguel Coehlo, and for the next week, you are my responsibility. I haven't lost any expedition team member so far this year. If you pay attention to the environment and follow my directions, you'll help me keep my record unblemished."

Miguel pointed at Gustavo before saying more.

"I know you and names of the people you bring. Now it's my turn to introduce the native guides who'll lead the way. Although they don't speak English, they do understand enough if you point and gesture. And Julio's our translator. Ask him if you want to ask them something, but not too much. They're friendly enough, but they consider us outsiders who don't belong. The two males will carry machetes to clear a path or keep predators away."

Miguel stopped talking to wave his arms. Three natives clad only in loincloths glided next to him, standing in single file, two males and a female. The trio made an indelible image in her brain.

Brown skin and eyes, and jet-black hair. Hard to tell, but the males might be about thirty. Their bodies look more agile than muscular, and they're a head shorter than me, which I think would make them perfect for surviving in the Forest. And their features are striking. If it weren't for facial piercings and painted scars, the developed world might say they're handsome.

And even more so for the girl. She's the tallest, thinnest, and looks the fittest. How old? Thirteen or fourteen at most, with an impressive physique. There's a line from a famous poem that describes some of her. How does it go? Now I remember–

Breasts like champagne glasses,

Thighs like a wild mare.

There must be a mystery here. I've got a week to uncover it, so I won't ask too much too soon.

Electra snapped back as soon as Miguel said more.

"Now, here's the drill. Each day the chopper drops us off far enough away from our target so no one there knows we're making an inspection. The targets have guards, spotters, and trackers, so we'll be hiking through a jungle of rainforest vines and vegetation for a couple of hours. And when we're done, we'll hike back to the drop-off spot and I'll radio for the chopper to come get us.

"And you'll have to wear clothes that cover up everything. It'll be hot and humid, but that's better than getting bitten by bugs, scorpions, or snakes. The natives don't because they've adjusted to what's out there. And there are plenty of dangers, such as anacondas, five kinds of boas, and plenty of poisonous spiders. The venomous Brazilian wandering spider measures up to five inches across. You'll be dead in five minutes if one of them bites you.

"And you must wear a hat to avoid damage if anything drops on you. All forest species are smart. Evolution has taught them how to survive. It's done the same for the mammals living here too, but they stay away from outsiders like us. They don't like natives either because they don't want to be eaten. And stay close to the guides. They know where to step. Any questions so far?"

There were none, only uncomfortable glances traded among the five newcomers, so Miguel moved on.

"Here's the schedule. Tomorrow's the easy day to ease you in. We'll canoe on an Amazon River tributary. Inspections start the day after. We'll be visiting suspected locations that Professor Segal has picked. Tobacco or vegetable farms will be first, then cattle ranching followed by rare earths or other mines, and finally a logging site. They don't like a surprise visit because it doesn't give them the time to hide any illegal activity that'll get a big fine. Don't talk to anyone. That'll be my job. I'm also trained to handle medical as well as security emergencies, and I wear a sidearm to protect us from what I can handle.

"There's just a little more I want to say to the group. Everyone prepares and cleans up after eating. Sleep in one of the hammocks hung in either the men's or women's dormitory. We keep all fans running round the clock, which makes the heat and humidity easier to take.

"Night-time temps drop into the 70s. In the day, it goes above 100, and it stays that way year-round because we're so close to the equator, which also explains why sunrise and sunset seem like they're controlled by Mother Nature pulling a curtain up or down. You'll be able to find your way around If you wake up to visit the bathroom because we keep a couple of lanterns on.

"But don't wander outside at night. We don't have outdoor lighting, and the rainforest canopy absorbs 80 percent of moonlight too. We'll be leaving just after sunrise, so have breakfast and meet me back here at six tomorrow morning. See you then… oh Gustavo and Jonathan, stay and talk with me to make sure we're all copacetic."

Everyone else went separate ways; Electra stayed close enough to invite herself to eat with Jonathan and the two leaders, who looked pleased to have a female grace them with her presence. She mostly listened until finding a segue to her topic.

"I imagine you've hired these three guides before. I bet they're from the same local tribe. Is it unusual to have a female among them?"

"Everywhere except at this camp."

Miguel offered nothing else, forcing Electra to ask for more.

"What's special about your camp and the girl?"

"Every camp's in a one-of-a-kind location that the local tribe knows best. And the girl's unusual. She doesn't talk but understands more English and seems smarter than most in her tribe."

Electra waited for Miguel to say more; he didn't so she did.

"From what I've seen and heard so far, you know how to keep your camp running better than the ones I've visited in other countries.

And that means you vette all the guides before you hire them, doesn't it?"

The flattery worked. It softened Miguel's expression and loosened his tongue.

"The tribe's medicine man told me about her. The mother refused to say who got her pregnant, so the tribal leader gave mother and infant some sort of potion right after birth to find out. The mother died but the baby survived, which the medicine man – at that time a medicine woman – said was an omen. She said she'd raise the baby and train her in medicine and tribal history plus rituals. And she did."

Electra asked another question to keep Miguel engaged.

"Is that why you say she's smart?"

"She has to be. She learned everything about the tribe and the Amazon, and she can track and hunt better than all the boys and most of the men. Everything was AOK until about a year ago when the medicine woman vanished one night. The replacement medicine man who came from a related tribe said that was a bad sign, and ever since then, no one likes her. They even put a spell on her which is supposed to take away her special powers along with her name. Now they just call her Rainforest girl but still bring her when we hire them because she's still better than the rest. It's like her powers get stronger as she gets older. So, that's her story."

"If her powers are growing stronger, don't you think they'd want to keep her?"

"You tell me. Just look at how the so-called civilized world treats exceptional people. But let's change to more important subjects, like what to expect when inspecting…"

Although Jonathan hung on every word, even when the leaders began swapping stories from their past, Electra excused herself at that point, preferring instead to recall some of hers, but only after listening to Alisha's warning.

"Calm down… don't go obsessive-compulsive by thinking too much about the Rainforest girl until you observe as much as you can during the coming week. And then, if your rational self concludes she's extraordinary, I'll join you in your O-C episode."

"You're right. I'll simply enjoy this moment by being here now, and we're living a special moment this entire week. It's like being at the most exciting summer camp imaginable. We couldn't attend summer camp when we were young. We had to grow up too fast too soon. The lightning bolt killed Indira at the instant of our birth, Jason blew himself up, and terrorists executed Doc Kittner, who was our omni-parent grandfather. But might some of this have been good rather than all bad? The Buddhist monk's answer is the right choice. And at this moment I'm exhausted cognitively and emotionally, so I choose to make it bedtime. We'll resume tomorrow."

Electra's dream jolted her awake in the middle of the night.

I must be all slept out. I feel so alive. And my dream felt so real, so vivid that it must have occurred in a REM state. I can still picture my driving over desert sands and skirting dunes under moonless, ink-black skies that dangled an infinity of lantern-like stars sparkling through the cold breathless air.

Serendipity granted me several such desert treks heading to Max the Popper's subterranean fortress that now belongs to Indira and me. Might it do the same for my Amazon adventure? The answer's unknown, so I must make the most of each moment if I want to feel what a rainforest night is like.

Ambient reddish-yellow glows from lanterns lighted her way to the bathroom where she found a flashlight that would cut through the blackness that started at the insect netting covering the doorway. And another sensation greeted her as soon as she stepped out.

The constant droning of cicadas along with a chorus of unknown insects accompanied by periodic high-pitched screeching fills me with an eerie excitement that tingles my skin that feels like it's stirring liquid air. If it were possible to exceed humidity's 100 percent saturation point, we'd be there.

Sudden buzzing near her ears redirected Electra's thought.

The flashlight's a homing beacon. I'm going in before too many bugs take bites, and I'll ask at breakfast if anyone else ventured out this night.

Electra's bubbly chatter helped the early breakfast eaters wake up. None of them had felt adventurous enough to test last night's outdoor sensations, but as she and Jonathan strolled ahead of the rest to the chopper, he talked about what his sense picked up this morning.

"The fragrance of the vegetation is so fresh it almost hurts my nose. Maybe it's caused by all the oxygen. And the filtered sunlight makes the rainforest haze harder to see through. What do you think it'll be like on the river?"

"We'll have to wait until we get there, but if it's anything like here, there might be a hint of a shower."

The chopper ride took only a half hour to reach a cleared space along a tributary where the camp stored canoes. Gustavo and Miguel each paired in one with a male guide, Carlos and Diego paddled their own, while Electra sat between Jonathan and the Rainforest girl who sat in the back, silently watching the four-canoe procession.

Jonathan didn't look at Electra as he sang out what he saw.

"There's not a breath of a breeze. The only ripples stirring are caused by our paddles, which disappear as soon as they strike into brown water."

Electra said,

"Don't dangle a finger in the water. You can't see them but the river's loaded with piranha."

Electra's words stopped abruptly. She stopped paddling and turned around to face the female paddling effortlessly at the stern. Then her slower flow of words resumed.

"Hi there… how are you?"

The girl kept paddling while giving two half-bows from the waist.

"I am glad you are OK. Are you going to help your men catch piranha for lunch?"

Another bow came Electra's way even before using the universal gesture of eating:

scooping hand to mouth.

"I am glad you can understand my words. You are very smart. I have never fished. Will you show me what to do?"

Another bow answered Electra, who now said,

"Thank you, that will be fun."

Then she turned around to resume paddling.

Gustavo signaled for the canoes to gather along the banks before issuing instructions.

"Me and Miguel will start a fire. Everyone else gotta fish for lunch."

The male guides handed out primitive poles with bobbers and hooks already baited before he said more.

"Just dangle the line over the side and see what comes up. If you need more bait, snip something off the piranha you just caught."

The two fishing canoes drifted out into the placid water; the five who were fishing heard Jonathan say,

"Piranhas aren't bottom feeders. That's why we're using bobbers."

No one replied; each focused on their lines except Electra, who was now sitting next to the Rainforest girl and gaily chatting. But a powerful tug on her line changed her focus.

"I've hooked something. Do I just pull it into the boat?"

The girl's gestures said yes.

Everyone started hooking fish. The Rainforest girl unhooked Electra's and rebaited the hook. Electra knew what to do after that.

Fishing stopped twenty minutes later. Then the canoes paddled back and everyone helped unload the catch. The guides and leaders took over from there.

After the group finished lunch and tidied up, Gustavo asked Jonathan to tell them about Amazon River conditions. His tone became serious as he started.

"Some bad effects of climate change and pollution are taking hold. I can tell the water level's higher because it has submerged tree roots along the banks, and that's not good. It'll kill the trees because the water's more acidic, and it might force tribes living along the banks to relocate. And that'll disrupt all the nearby animal populations."

Only Miguel added a comment.

"Well, the level goes up and down from year to year. Come on, it's time to head back..."

A light shower added to the now-dampened mood as they paddled to where the chopper would be waiting. No one spoke except Electra, who paddled while facing backward and continued chatting and asking questions to only one person. The Rainforest girl seemed to enjoy signaling yes or no with a thumbs up or down. Electra liked the discussion too.

Electra could read fatigue in everyone but Miguel as he assembled them after dinner, but this time the three natives stood at the back as he spoke.

"I'll make this brief. Tomorrow, we inspect a farm or two, and the hike to and from will make you more tired than today's canoeing, so get a good night's sleep. And I told you at yesterday's meeting what to expect, so unless you want to swap stories about today, go to bed. And I want Jonathan and leaders to stay for a minute to review tomorrow's plan."

Electra looked for the girl as she filed out, but the natives had already slipped away, and although the shower had stopped, it made for oppressive humidity, so she took Miguel's advice and went to bed.

Once again, Electra bolted upright in the middle of the night.

I'm fully awake and ready to go, but not outside. I'll get a drink of water. Even with all this humidity, I need to stay hydrated.

Electra swung out of her hammock, ready to follow the lantern glow to the bathroom, but before she could take a step, she spotted a silent shadow that vanished before she could identify its owner.

Someone's watching me. Who could it be?

Alisha came to her aid.

"Come on, that's not like you. It should be easy for you to figure it out. Simply replay what was most fun today."

"The Rainforest girl? But –" Alisha cut Electra off.

"Don't disappoint me. Use your empathy and put yourself in her POV."

"OK… maybe she likes me, uh, us."

"And why wouldn't she? You paid her lots of attention. And you might be one of the few outsider females she's ever come in contact with."

"So, what should I do?"

"Don't push yourself on her. If you do, you'll push her away. Just act naturally and let her do what she wants. Now get that drink, then go back to bed and think until you fall asleep."

Electra took Alisha's advice.

The hike to the targeted farming location went pretty much as expected, as did the inspection. Electra stood in the background, listening in addition to observing how Miguel and Jonathan countered all the objections raised by a trio of farm managers. She heard the senior manager explain why the genetically modified tobacco plants thrived in this climate and gave displaced natives a viable cash crop. Jonathan did nothing but listen before all five drove off in a jeep to tour nearby farms.

On the hike back to the extraction point, the sunlight coming through the rainforest canopy heightened both temperature and humidity. Electra preferred having all the men ahead of her and the Rainforest girl; it gave her a safer place to talk with words and gestures while walking and trading glances.

"The vines and plants are so dense on this narrow path... it's like being swallowed by the jungle. I guess you know where all the trails are. Am I right?"

Electra detected for an instant a miniscule smile accompanying a thumbs up. She continued talking slowly while asking additional questions until the girl grabbed her arm and pointed at the jungle floor on their right. Electra peered before exclaiming,

"Gads, it's an army of marching ants carrying thousands of tiny leaves. They must be smart too. I bet they know where they are going."

That brought another thumbs up. Electra had another question, but shouting coming from the men ahead replaced it.

She recognized Miguel's voice when he yelled,

"Girl, get up here now." The Rainforest girl raced to the front of the procession; Electra followed at a more cautious pace. When she got there, what she saw and heard told her what must have happened: Julio's writhing on the ground next to a five-inch crushed spider said its venom was about to wreak havoc.

She stood next to Jonathan who, like everyone else, seemed paralyzed. Only one person kept moving. Electra stared at the girl, who had knelt next to Julio and was now reaching into a pouch strapped around her waist.

I bet she knows jungle medicines... she just pulled out a knife. I got it, she's going make a slice near the bite and suck out venom.

Electra's diagnosis hit the mark. When Julio's screams subsided, the girl pulled out a jar containing a pasty substance and rubbed it on a patch of Julio's leg that included the bite. Heaving breaths replaced his screams. Miguel and Gustavo lifted him up by his arms. After Paco grabbed his legs, Miguel shouted,

"He's OK for now, but we gotta get back quick to camp. Let's go."

Everyone clustered around Julio that evening, happy to see him sitting up rather than flat on his back. Miguel let the group decompress for a couple of minutes before getting their attention.

"I forgot to bring the right medical kit. It's a good thing the girl knew what to do. Julio's indispensable. We can't lose our translator, and if he can't walk tomorrow, we'll have to postpone the inspection. So, let's let him rest. We should too, so go to bed."

Electra did just that, hoping for a repeat of last night, but that didn't happen, causing her to fret while trying to fall asleep.

Why won't she visit me tonight? I don't want to pry, but I have to know. I'll let the lightning brain figure out a way to find out.

And it did as soon as Miguel told the group after breakfast that today's inspection would be canceled instead of postponed. Jonathan explained why.

"Cattle ranching does less harm than tobacco farming, and I collected enough data yesterday about that. A day of rest will help all of us, and it'll give me more time to prep for mining and lumbering inspections. And lumbering is the most problematic. We'll need to be on guard when inspecting that location. But don't worry, I know what to look for."

Miguel said,

"Jonathan will explain all that to Gustavo and me, so while he's doing that and Julio's recovering, Electra and Paco can do whatever they want as long as they stay at the camp. So, have fun."

Paco kept Julio company; Electra looked for the Rainforest Girl, but after prowling the premises for nearly an hour, she didn't see her until the girl materialized at her side just before she was about to enter the dormitory.

"Oh, hi there. I was looking for you, but you found me first. I was worried when you didn't visit me last night. How are you?"

Electra took a closer look when the girl didn't give a thumbs-up signal; Electra wanted to but didn't drop her smile when she spotted a problem.

Jeezus, someone hit her. Her darker skin hides the evidence, but I see it. But why? Maybe she wasn't supposed to heal outsiders. OK, try to act naturally.

Electra touched the bruise on the girl's right cheek before saying,

"It looks like you walked into something. Does it still hurt."

That prompted a thumbs down.

"That's good. Would you like to come into the dormitory so we can talk more?" That brought a thumbs up. Minutes later, they were sitting near a table holding some of Electra's belongings. Electra asked an obvious question.

"Which thing do you want me to talk about?"

Electra spoke again after the girl pointed.

"We call it a cell-phone. May I show you how it works?" An enthusiastic thumbs up said yes.

Electra took all the time she needed while using a combination of words and universal sign language to explain the basics of cell-phones and laptops. Alisha commented while watching.

She's even smarter than we thought, and she understands a lot of English. But don't tire her out. Let's take a break.

Ten minutes later, they were sitting in the kitchen area, sipping a Coca Cola and nibbling on M&Ms. The look on the girl's face showed total enjoyment. Electra didn't speak again until the last one vanished.

Pointing to herself, Electra said,

"My name is Electra. I found out that your tribe took your name away, so I picked one for you. I would like to call you Renee. It sounds sort of like the word 'rain'. Can I call you 'Renee'?"

The girl signaled yes.

"Wonderful, and I even picked a poem that reminds me of you. Do you know what a poem is?"

Another thumbs up, so Electra kept talking.

"My mother wrote it a long time ago and named it 'Song Without Words'. Just enjoy how it sounds. And here it is.

They come like tree-leaf shadows

On bright windy Summer day.

Butterfly-like dancing

On half-curtained window bay.

Penetrating senses like a mesmerizing charm.
A streaming wordless melody
That will silence false alarm.
Some forgotten sight or sound
That resonates in our mind.
And spirits us away to some place left far behind.
Like intuition - premonition impossible to trace.
It causes shiver - senses quiver
With neither name nor face.
We're suspended but a moment
That's transfixed in unknown space,
The spell dissolves abruptly
We are freed but sense its grace.
The feeling quickly floats away
Leaving but a gentle sigh.
The kind we hear when wisps of mist
Curl insouciantly toward the sky."

Renee signaled for a repeat as soon as she figured out Electra had finished, but Miguel interrupted before she could oblige.

"Come with me, I'm making an announcement to the group."

Electra gently interlaced the fingers of her left hand with Renee's right. Renee gripped tight as the pair followed Miguel.

Chapter 13
July 2167

"Departure to the New World"

Miguel's clipped words heightened the group's tension that had begun building since the very first day's meeting.

"Julio say he good for only one more inspection, so tomorrow we do it where Jonathan say we find suspect lumbering operation. And that mean expedition over after that so all can go home day after, which should make you glad. So, everyone but Jonathan and Gustavo go sleep and meet here at sunrise for chopper flight and hike to location. They stay with me a little while to adjust schedule. See you then."

Electra hid her disappointment while walking with the others toward the dormitories.

Where did Renee disappear to? She'd be a great partner on some of my other adventures. And tonight might be the last one that I can talk to her. I wish I could find her, but I know how elusive she can be. Maybe she'll come to me.

Electra's frown vanished the moment she spotted Renee sitting cross-legged next to her dormitory hammock. She joined Renee on the floor and then began talking.

"Tomorrow is our last hike. I will be sad to say goodbye, but would you like to stay with me tonight? I never run out of things to say to you."

Renee didn't use her thumb to reply; her hushed, faltering voice gave the answer.

"Ye-yes… p-please let me stay."

If Electra were a Rainforest snake, she would have jumped out of two layers of skin, but she stayed put and looked happy saying,

"You can talk. How wonderful. But why doesn't anyone know you can?"

"B-bad things h-happen when wrong p-people hear. Better th-they not know real me."

Electra leaned forward and took Renee's hands in hers.

"I know how you feel. May I tell you a little more about me?"

"I want to hear."

Electra talked until it was time they rest for tomorrow. And when she started climbing into her hammock after kissing the top of Renee's head, Renee curled up right where she was. Electra grabbed a sheet from the nearest hammock and helped Renee make a nest. She kissed her on the bruised cheek and then climbed in, knowing that both of them should fall asleep.

No one in the camp knew about last night's Electra-Renee rendezvous because Electra had learned from years of practice how to be almost as elusive as Renee. And her acting continued from eating breakfast with her expedition team to arriving at the inspection location, which Jonathan had pegged. It was an unauthorized lumber operation.

Two angry-sounding motorbikes roared up, blocking the expedition from coming in. The bigger rider yelled from the saddle while his partner played with his bike's throttle.

"No one's allowed in unless they get clearance, so you better clear out now."

Gustavo stepped cautiously to the bikes before saying,

"I with government. We got right to inspect wherever we want."

After gunning his bike twice, the bigger biker said,

"I'll let my boss decide. Hop on the back so you can meet him. Everyone else, wait here until we come back."

Gustavo looked at Miguel, who shrugged and then said,

"I better go with you. Jonathan, you're the leader until we get back." The bikes roared away after their passengers mounted, leaving Jonathan scratching his head. Fumbling for words, it took him a minute until he said,

"Let's sit in the shade and eat. We'll do the inspection as soon as they get back."

Julio and Paco moved towards Jonathan, the male natives sat where they were, but Electra stood her ground with the girl at her side before launching her words directly at Jonathan.

"Now that we're here, you don't need to wait for them. You're the one that does the inspection. Why don't you let the girl guide us around so you can get whatever data you want. Everyone else can wait here."

"You know, that's a good idea. I should have all I need by the time they get back. All you have to do is explain to the girl what we're doing. Can you handle that?"

"You watch me, and I'll watch her."

Jonathan divvied up his inspection equipment; Electra pointed while talking to the girl; the girl led the way.

The trio returned two hours later, but Miguel and Gustavo hadn't. The clouds thickened, promising rain; the lightning brain escalated to a higher state, and Electra took charge.

"We better face the facts—our expedition leaders have run into a problem, and though we don't know what it is, you can guess what it is. Let's go before bikers come back to get us. Miguel and Gustavo know the way home."

Jonathan's indecision showed in the tone of his voice.

"Why don't we wait a little bit longer?"

"Don't make the mistake too many leaders do. They quit too late, even though they know the facts are stacked against them."

Jonathan took a deep breath and then said,

"OK, the two native guys lead the way back. I'm right behind them, Julio and Paco can follow me, and you and the girl watch things from the rear."

Electra felt a mist-like shower starting an hour later; she also noticed that Renee was now holding what looked like a primitive flute, a longish wooden tube containing a carved mouthpiece at one end. She didn't point to it or talk about whatever came to mind because Renee was too busy scanning the surroundings.

Electra brooded to herself.

The going-back trek seems longer than the outbound one. And I don't recognize anything that we might have passed earlier, but why would I? The jungle looks the same everywhere. If things don't look better soon, I'll ask Renee if we're lost. And if I didn't sense trouble brewing, I'd joke with erstwhile rockstar Alisha about a pop song she could sing that Renee would like it. Maybe I'll do that tonight... but no, I won't. It'll make us sad, so I'll find something happier when I say goodbye.

Electra's patience run out about an hour later. She prepared to confront the guides by charging to the front, but two soldiers rushing toward Jonathan and the others propelled the lightning brain to a higher state. But Electra couldn't act; her brain hesitated because it sensed something else. The Rainforest girl grabbed Electra's arm and pulled her off the path and into the jungle.

Electra had only one option: to run as fast as her stumbling stride allowed so she could stay as close as possible to Renee. Renee ran far enough to take them out of harm's way; then she stopped to face Electra, who had kept close enough.

Electra spun 360 degrees before asking,

"What's going on? What should we do?"

"I got idea. You talk more."

"OK, the guys with rifles rounding up Jonathan, Julio, and Paco must be working with the bikers, so they'll take'em to wherever our leaders are. And they don't need your friends to guide them back because they seem to know their way in the jungle. Does that sound OK so far?"

"Yeh-yes."

"So, they could let your guide-friends go or take'em too. My guess is that they'll take'em back and then let'em all go at the same time. But there could be–" Electra interrupted herself, pausing to regroup and then cupping Renee's face between both hands while speaking even slower.

"But maybe they'll kill everyone and send more men to catch us. Or —" Electra's unspoken words caught in her throat, but then she let them go.

"Or maybe, just maybe, your friend-guides led us to those soldier-guys. If so, they are not my friends, and might not be yours either. So, let's follow the group. Can you track them?"

The Rainforest girl grabbed Electra's hand and started pulling.

No matter what got in the way, Renee glided around it, and Electra did her best to do the same. The jungle foliage kept them invisible, but it did the same for their quarry.

Electra kept checking her cell-phone to keep track of time, but she had become disoriented by Renee's weaving. She had to fight to keep quiet and not disrupt Renee.

She just gripped my hand tighter. Does that mean she's closing in on our quarry?

And then Renee pulled Electra down before pointing straight ahead. Electra could hear harsh voices cutting through the stillness and see through the mist indistinct shapes crossing single file at right angles.

She whispered into Renee's ear,

"I can hear the words if we get closer, but keep us invisible."

Renee's actions did both. She leapfrogged ahead so they could see and hear the group as it filed past and then kept repeating. Electra didn't count the number of times, but she knew it was time to act when a soldier yelled,

"I'll shoot you right now if you can't keep up."

She grabbed Renee by the shoulders, then mouthed,

"He's gonna kill Julio if I don't grab his gun. If I get in trouble, run away." Electra leaped into action, never looking back.

The element of surprise helped. Electra wrestled the gun away and shot the closer soldier, but the other stumbled toward her and used his rifle to club her down while the two guides began hacking Julio and Paco. Preparing to slam his rifle butt into Electra's wide-open mouth, he positioned it high overhead, but before he could deliver a crushing blow, the Rainforest girl raced toward him and launched a dart that stuck in the front of his neck. Going stiff, he toppled backward onto Jonathan. The guides stopped hacking just long enough to see Renee reload her blowgun and fire again, this time sticking a dart near the heart of the closer target. He toppled forward, pinning Paco's bloody body underneath. The last man standing struck a final blow into the side of Julio's neck, hurled a curse along with his machete at the girl, and then dashed like a wild animal into the jungle.

Jonathan struggled to his feet before Electra, who needed help from the girl to do the same. He shuffled toward them, unable to speak. Neither could Electra until the lightning brain jolted her out of a zombie-like state.

Trying to regain composure, she pointed at each body as her gaze focused and she began a mechanical-sounding monologue.

"Five dead, one got away, and three still here."

Jonathan's stomach couldn't stand the sight. He fell to his knees, heaving everything he had. Electra pulled him up after the deluge stopped. Clearing his stomach cleared his head enough for his monotone voice to ask,

"What are we gonna do now?"

Electra made the call.

"Get to the rendezvous location and practice telling the story I'll come up with. I'll call for chopper pickup when we get there."

"What about the bodies?"

"The jungle will take care of them."

Renee grabbed Electra's hand and pulled her away; Jonathan stumbled along behind.

The intensifying shower silenced all insects, helping Electra assess their predicament.

It's too dangerous to stay at the base camp. That leaves only one place to go—Bruno in Brasilia. And we'll need a big change in our flight plans back to DC. How can I make it happen? C'mon, start thinking, get us out of here.

Another jolt hit the lightning brain, bringing with it a calming clarity loaded with ideas never considered until this moment.

I know what to do…

Though blackness had fallen, the shower slowed when the survivors reached the extraction point. Fear of getting bitten by whatever might be crawling forced the trio to stand. After powering on their flashlights, Electra and Jonathan placed them pointing upward far enough away so they could see the surroundings without being eaten by swarms of night fliers.

The flashlight glare showed Jonathan that Electra knew what she was ready to say when her words began ringing out.

"The chopper's ETA is 90 minutes, and assuming we're still alive when it gets here, here's our story. It's true as far as it goes, but some details we keep to ourselves ..."

Electra made Jonathan summarize the details a second time.

"OK, we don't know where the biker-guards took Miguel and Gustavo, but after they did, I collected enough data for my lumber operations inspection report. And because it got later and later and no Miguel and Gustavo, we headed back. But on the way, a couple of guards tracked us down. The three of us were lucky enough to escape, but Julio and Paco weren't. Our guy-guides stayed with those two, and we're not sure, but we think the guards escorted all of them to wherever Miguel and Gustavo are."

Jonathan stopped, knowing that Electra would make corrections if needed, but she didn't so he continued.

"And if anyone asks me why, I say I don't know, but maybe they wanted to make sure my report wouldn't cause problems. And that's it. You like my rendition?"

"It's perfect, and no matter how much pressure anyone puts on you, stick to it."

"I will, but I don't think anyone at base camp'll tighten the screws on us. Why would they? We're on the right side. And I guess we'll fly back to Brasilia day after tomorrow, right?"

"Not quite. We're flying tonight, right from here. And you tell the story only to Bruno. He's gotta make changes on our return flight plan. He might complain about some of them, but you—" Jonathan's look of surprise along with his words cut her off.

"Are you crazy? We're already beat, and It'll take hours to get there. And we can't take her. She's never been out of the rainforest. She'd die anyplace else. Just look at her, running around stark naked, and the painted scars on her face make her look like a savage. It's—" Electra's words boomed over his.

"Her tribe will kill her if she stays. The guide that got away'll see to that. You tell Bruno to include her on the flight back to DC."

"How? Get her a passport? How can she clear customs when we get to DC?"

"Look, Bruno's part of the government, so negotiate with him. He won't care what happens to the girl. He needs your report and you've got the data. Tell him you won't do the analysis unless he does what you want."

"I don't want or care about her either, and maybe she doesn't want to come with us. Think about that before you go shooting your mouth off."

Electra's glare filled in for the words no one spoke, but it softened when she pulled Renee closer and their eyes met. Then she said,

"Go ahead, ask her."

"She can't talk and won't understand what I say."

"Dammit, I said ask her."

Grabbing the girl by the shoulders, Jonathan yelled,

"Do you want to come with us?"

Renee's face showed nothing but terror, but she shook her head yes.

Jonathan pushed her away before screaming,

"She's just doing that because she think's it'll make me happy. No way am I gonna play this game."

The girl collapsed at his feet, sobbing and wrapping her arms around his legs.

Electra made the final play. She unloaded a double-barreled slap that rocked and rattled Jonathan's head. Then she blasted her final words.

"You obtuse ass. She just saved our lives. I'll get angry if you don't do what I say, and you won't like it. Nobody likes me when I'm angry."

Electra pulled Renee into her arms before Jonathan shook his head yes, saying one word only.

"OK."

The trio stopped long enough at the base camp to clean up, pack after putting on travel clothes, and then eat while the crew readied the chopper and called Bruno so he would know what to expect. The grueling flight to Brasilia sapped much of even Electra's remaining strength, but the upcoming meeting added enough suspense to offset most of the lost sleep.

The car waiting brought them to the same IBAMA office where they first met Bruno. He said little other than instructing his assistant to entertain the native girl they had brought with them. Then, after closing his office door and placing Electra and Jonathan on chairs in front of his desk, he sat behind it and said,

"So, Jonathan, please tell me what happened."

Practice had perfected Jonathan's delivery. He didn't need to bring Electra into the discussion. She sat as motionless as a mannequin, happy to be a silent observer.

Jonathan's recovered some of his spunk. Bruno's backing off...

Jonathan looked ready to close the deal, but Bruno's expression hardened before he launched a zinger at Jonathan.

"This girl you wanna take, OK by me but to clear the way I gotta convince others by giving them some mooney, so you gotta give some to me. I need some uh, what you call it, uh, payola."

Jonathan bounced back quick enough to ask the only three-answer question necessary.

"How much? Where do we wire it? And when do you need it so we can leave ASAP?"

Bruno wasted no time writing something on a piece of paper that he handed to Jonathan, whose expression said he had just entered a league beyond his expertise, so Electra took over. After taking a mini-glance at the paper, she said,

"No problemo, amigo. Take me to a private room that has an encrypted computer. I'll talk online with an associate who'll take care of this pronto..."

The flight on a Brazilian government jet carried only three VIPs. Only one remained awake after three of the thirteen-hour night flight to DC. Electra rewarded herself with another Coca Cola, happy to have the girl's hand still holding hers. Then she closed her eyes, disappearing into the moment as the lightning brain brought her thrilling sensations.

I feel totally energized and ready to carve out a big place in my life for Renee. I shall help her create the life she wants while giving her the sharing, caring family intimacy she never had. And she can give me what I want... no, what I need, a gift I have felt for only a few long-ago precious moments... the feeling of the most powerful love, the love of a mother for her child. She will complete me, my empathy, my humanity. I experienced that joy when I created my clone daughter, Ariadne, but fate took her away all too soon. My four clone children that Su-Lin Song Chou brought into being give a more distant joy, for they can never know who I am. I finally understand why Nila and Sanjay are pinning so much hope on a son, and why dearly departed Robin needed me to help her have daughters...

Electra came back to the present when she felt Renee's grip loosen and tighten again as she shifted positions but didn't awaken. She marveled while studying the striking features on the girl's inscrutable face.

How odd, yet fortunate, that serendipity brought us together. We come from separate worlds, each strange to the other, yet we share such similar events at birth. Didn't Mother capture this in a poem? She did, and I recall its title—the Stranger—and its verses that I will remember forever...

Into this world uninvited we're thrown,
Often deceived into thinking we're grand.
Often not knowing the place where we stand,
Nothing provided and nothing we own.
Searching for meaning the myths do abound,
Often promoted by personal cause.
Often ignoring humanity's laws,
Full of such wisdom as word-empty sound.
Remove all the blinders and so understand,
Meaning is found in your singular thought.
Contingently pointing to what might be sought,
But always a stranger in this a strange land.

I am indeed a stranger in the world of the Amazon because it didn't care if I lived or died, but Renee won't be a stranger in mine because I have invited her. I shall teach her, mentor her, provide for her according to what she wants. But I must always listen to her.

I have just begun a game that only the two of us can play… no, three including Indira. And I must convince Indira that my new game won't dilute time devoted to Indira's favorite project. But even if it does, Indira won't mind. After all, Indira has invested in the Rainforest girl by handling the payola request, and she can help me introduce Renee to the strange world she is about to enter. Indira and I shall make sure she will thrive.

I have thought enough. Doing any more might push me into OCD land, a place that has been all too familiar to me, and I have already promised not to go there anymore. So, I shall sleep and let the lightning brain decide what new promises to keep and how best to prepare for what may be in store.

Electra kissed Renee's hand and kept gripping it tight, then closed her eyes for a peaceful sleep that she hoped might bring restful dreams until morning's first light.

Chapter 14
July 2167
"The Singular Reset"

Electra's proactive approach to each and every project made it easy to integrate her newest one into the collection. Devoting herself full time to the "Renee project" didn't impact any others because she was several steps ahead of their schedules.

She rearranged her live-in office space so that Renee would have a private place and then erected another computer workstation next to hers. And while doing all this, she talked constantly to Renee, whose language skills grew exponentially.

Once those tasks had been completed, Electra began teaching Renee how to use the computer for accessing the Internet. The results exceeded even Electra's expectations; she recalled a cliché-like trope comparing computer acquisition skills of the older to the younger.

Older folks are labeled digital immigrants because they grew up before the latest technology had been invented and had to learn it later. Kids are called digital natives because they had it while growing up, and they treat it like a friendly tool. Renee has that youthful approach going for her as well as a native lifestyle. She lives in the "now here" moment, and unlike most who have grown up in the developed and privileged world, she needs very little to be happy.

Electra needed no one other than herself to talk with until late on the night beginning the second week home when Renee was asleep. The time had come to connect with Indira, who waited patiently for Electra to explain why she needed help.

Electra was about to delve into more details, but Indira spoke before she could.

"I have been listening and watching you and the girl ever since your return. There is no need for you to tell me anything else, for as you know by now, I am always ahead of you. And you have matched the 'practically perfect project planner' moniker I gave you years ago, so I prefer at this time not to give you advice but rather watch you in action. If you stay the course and keep the

Rainforest girl close, you shall maximize the returns on our investment. What else might you wish to say?"

"More than I should, but I have learned when to say when, so I shall say goodbye."

Knowing that there was nothing more to listen to or say, Indira's GUI looked pleased just before it vanished.

Renee looked like she had absorbed every word that Electra had said, so she asked her to say what she would do until lunchtime.

"I like computer talking to me and I talk back. It almost fun like you and me."

Electra put her arm around and then said,

"You are learning so fast this way. And while it is teaching you English, I am sitting next to you doing work on my computer. If it can't answer a question you have, please ask me."

"I will."

Electra made sure the girl had the teaching app running before she reviewed the status reports Eve had been posting.

Nari's finally rejoined Eve in DC working at our consulting business and living with her. That's a bonus… she can mentor Zara at work and at home. Between Nari and Zara, if there's any fire regarding Bigger Brother's conspiracy or smoke coming from Kinslinger's pre-convention campaign, they'll find and fan it so others can see. I'll invite myself for dinner this coming Friday. That'll be a good time to introduce Renee to important members of her new tribe.

Electra called a timeout just before noon. Renee followed her to the dining area, then listened as Electra explained what was on the menu.

"Last week, you told me that the medicine woman told you what to eat. Please tell me again what that is."

"Fruit and vegetables, and sometimes animal flesh if hunters bring some back. I like the food you make, like you cutting up apples and bananas and putting on peanut butter."

"Didn't she also say milk from animals is OK too. I have been giving you milk mixed with water. Do you like ice in it?"

"I like… it cold. You keep milk in cold box, yes?"

"You are so smart. Another name for it is refrigerator. There it is."

Renee explored what Electra had just pointed to until called to eat what was now on her plate.

After cleaning up the few leftovers, the pair went back to their companion workstations. Electra brought up the video she wanted Renee to watch and then explained why.

"The voice will tell you about what people in America eat. You will learn what is good and what is not so good. Then it will tell you why some people are so large, and why that is bad. And when we have dinner later, I will want you to tell me what you learned, OK?"

"I like that. I will."

"And I like how energetic you are. Let's get to work."

Renee made so much progress the next day that Electra took her the day after on a mid-morning expedition, driving them around town in her SUV and describing the kinds of people she was seeing.

"Think of them like members of separate tribes that form a bigger tribe. They are friendly most of the time, but sometimes they aren't. And you already know that you shouldn't tell too much to anyone unless you trust them."

"I know, and I don't talk to strangers in other tribes."

"Excellent, and later on we will walk around a shopping mall. It's like a marketplace in one of the bigger Amazon villages you told me about. We'll have something to eat there too. How does that sound?"

"It sound like fun."

"It will be."

Electra made the right call when she parked in an uncrowded outdoor lot of an indoor mall, judging that the foot traffic might be light enough not to intimidate Renee. And she surmised by the girl's steady footsteps that her confidence around people was growing.

After touring all three levels, Electra took them to the outdoor food court and explained while they sat how the ground rules of fast-food restaurants operate.

It was apparent from Renee's enthusiasm that she understood the rules and rewards well enough to make a selection that would give her a new taste sensation. It was also obvious that most strollers kept their distance; the reason became obvious when two rowdy teenage boys drinking beer out of plastic cups started taunting.

The fatter lout shuffled around, doing an awkward dance just before he began hurling another insult.

"What injun reservation did you wander off of? What are you looking for? Oh, I know, you want fire water."

His buddy then pointed at her cheeks before dousing the scars with beer. Electra's warning system sounded too late to stop the dissing, but she leaped into action a second after the beer splashed, grabbing a greasy hank of the offender's hair and slamming his head onto the table. He rolled to the pavement and stayed put; his loudmouth buddy pulled a knife and squared off against her, but the shrill sound of security whistles made him change his mind. He pulled his buddy up and the louts ran before the security guards arrived.

The guards wanted Electra to file a security report, but she refused and then grabbed Renee's hand. The pair disappeared as the crowd dispersed.

Electra didn't want this last episode to ruin the day, so she looked for a nearby place to park where she could explain why some people mistreat others. When finished, she asked Renee to summarize.

"I know some tribes make fun of how other tribes decorate. But I see some white women color hair, paint face, pierce body, and wear jewelry too. If I look funny to them, they look funny to me. But I sorry if maybe my scars offend and make me ugly."

Pulling her close, Electra said,

"Please don't call yourself ugly. You have striking features and a lovely body that accents them. And if you like, I can take you to a skin doctor who can make them even prettier. Would you like that?"

"If it make me pretty, like you."

"It will make you even prettier."

Before watching a Disney movie that night, Electra asked,

"Why don't you wear jewelry like many tribal women I see in videos?"

Renee looked away while saying,

"Tribe took jewelry when they took name away."

"Did they? Well, I have special earrings that only females in my tribe wear. I'm wearing mine now. If you would like a pair, they'll fit nicely. You already have pierced ears."

Renee delicately stroked Electra's earlobes before saying,

"I like. They gold lightning bolts. Would you?"

"I'd love to."

Renee admired the results fifteen minutes later but waited for Electra to say,

"You look lovely."

Renee glowed like the earrings.

Renee had kept so busy with her learning apps that by the time late Friday afternoon came into view, Electra felt certain the girl had forgotten all about the beer-throwing episode and would be ready to enjoy a meal with Eve's people. Electra summarized on the drive what Eve does.

"Eve is a consultant She tells people what they should do, sort of like a tribe's wisest person. She and I own a consulting business given to us by a lady I never met. Her name was Irani Ramani, but she died a couple of years ago. Eve, like you, is an orphan raised by a very smart female who knew lots about medicine, and she has two sisters and a brother. One of the sisters is named Nari Bose, and she works for and lives with Eve. You'll like both of them. They're very smart.

"And Eve takes care of a brother-sister pair named Amahl and Zara Karim. They are orphans that Irani brought back from Lebanon, which is far away on another continent. Although Amahl is not much older than you, all of a sudden he's getting bigger and stronger. He's got a bad foot that needs fixing, but other than that, he's AOK. He likes to talk and have fun. Am I telling you too much?"

"No, I remember. Tell me about Zara."

"She is going to college, and while doing that, she helps Eve and Nari figure out problems other countries have. It would be like rainforest elders deciding how to get along with other tribes. And she's a bit like you. Quiet when thinking, but acts fast when she has to. And that's it. Are you OK with all that?"

"I fine. They part of your tribe."

"That's a wonderful point of view. And always remember, so are you."

Amahl's voice, accompanied by boisterous body language, greeted them when he opened the door; Zara stood behind while Electra introduced everyone. Amahl grabbed Renee's hand and towed her to the family room; Zara and Electra followed.

Electra made another round of introductions and then decided to watch tribal dynamics in action.

Everyone sat except for Amahl, who must have been briefed ahead of time by Eve. His infectious enthusiasm effervesced in the way he spoke.

"Hey, Renee has the same kind of earrings you have. And her cheeks look so cool. Can I get her to play with me and my Ouija board until the pizza gets here? Zara can keep tabs on how we do."

Eve said,

"Ask her nice and slow. She's still learning English."

Amahl moved to where Renee sat and then said,

"You've got a cool name. What's it mean?"

Renee's puzzled look told Electra to supply an answer.

"It's a French name derived from the Latin word for reborn."

Amahl picked up from there.

"My name means hard, which makes me strong. But playing with a Ouija board isn't too hard. Zara, you explain it to her. And speak slow like me."

Renee, who was sitting on the sofa next to her, turned in that direction.

"Two people play the game by sitting in chairs facing each other and letting their knees touch so the Ouija board can sit lengthwise on their knees. The board's about two feet long and a foot and a half wide, and is made of wood having a smooth surface. The top has two curved rows near the middle holding all the letters of the alphabet, and right underneath is a straight row containing all the numbers from zero to nine. The word 'Yes' sits in the upper lefthand corner, and 'No' in the upper right. And the word "Goodbye" sits right beneath the row of numbers. Have I gone too fast?"

"No, I understand. So, how game played?"

"It's easy. One player puts a device in the center of the board. Amahl says it's called a planchette. Anyway, it's a pointing device. It's made of light, stiff plastic, and has a teardrop shape mounted on three short pedestals, each having a cloth covering on its bottom so it can glide over the board. It's just big enough for all the fingers of each player's hands to touch. There's a clear plastic window in its center, and inside the window there's a vertical pin pointing toward the board. Are you ready for more?"

Renee's nod said so; Zara continued.

"And now, the game begins as soon as you and Amahl are situated with all your fingers on that planchette thingee. I ask a question, and the two of you let it glide over the board, stopping along the way over letters or numbers that you yell out and I write down. The thingee is supposed to stop moving when you've spelled out the answer. Does that make sense?"

"But where does answer come from?"

Amahl had listened long enough. He said,

"From the spirits we're communicating with. The thingee starts gliding over the board as soon as they start talking to us. It feels like it's almost floating. Hey, don't Amazon tribes have rituals where they talk to ancestors from the past? And we can make the game even spookier by lighting candles before turning out the lights. Whatcha think?"

Renee said,

"I like it."

Eve answered Amahl's question before he needed to ask for the second time.

"Go ahead and play. We'll let you know when the pizza gets here. And when you come back, bring the answer to this question, how did the Ouija board get its name? Now go."

Electra gave an edited version of her Amazon expedition that included enough information to satisfy both Eve and Nari. And then she asked enough questions to stay ahead of her consulting game, filing the answers away for use when needed. Pizza delivery ended the questioning session and brought everyone to the dinner table, where Amahl managed to brag about his and Renee's Ouija game skills while taking big bites.

"Man-oh-man, I've never had a partner as good as Renee. It's like the thingee almost floats to the right spot. And guess what answer we got when Zara asked about where the Ouija name comes from?"

Nari said,

"You spelled out 'Ask me later' because that's what I would."

"Wow, that's pretty close. The pointer hovered over 'Goodbye'. And I was thinking that we don't wanna say goodbye to Renee. Can she stay with us tonight? We can do more Ouija board stuff or play cards."

It was time for Electra to decide, which she did while leaning toward Renee and saying,

"Would you like to stay? I'll come get you tomorrow afternoon if that's OK with you."

"I like Amahl and Zara. I get to know my tribe better."

"That's wonderful. I'm sure they have an extra toothbrush and clothes for sleeping in."

Amahl hugged Renee and then said,

"She told us it gets so hot in the Amazon that she doesn't wear clothes. Good thing we have air conditioning."

Electra stifled a laugh that accompanied her private thoughts.

He might think differently in a couple of years. I'll have to explain American adolescent mating rituals sometime, but no need to get into that now. I'm going to grab a brownie and go.

Electra continued her monologue on the drive home.

I'll enjoy having quiet time tomorrow. I've become Renee's omni-parent, and it's so easy for that role to take over, but it's my OCD fault if I let it, so I won't. And the tribal lifestyle she comes from makes her so easy to take care of. Maybe post-Modernity should use some of it. Well, that's for family counselors to talk about.

So, what'll I do tomorrow? I know, I'll take an early morning run, work on my NASA projects, and call that government assistance program for climate-change displaced natives Eve told me about. Thank you, Eve.

Electra's morning unfolded as pleasantly as the current stretch of sunny weather. She was about to call the assistance program, but her cell-phone chimed before she could. She recognized the voice immediately.

"Jonathan, how have you been? I've been thinking about you, but I've been so busy getting Renee settled that I haven't had a chance to call."

"Wherever you are, can I come over so we can talk?"

"Sure, I'm at my live-in office. Is there something I should prepare for?"

"Like I said, wherever you are, we need to talk. I'll be at your office in about an hour. Bye."

Electra had soft drinks and Oreos on the conference room table by the time Jonathan arrived. She saw from his troubled look that something had been bothering him, so she decided to ease into whatever it was.

"How nice being back and in one piece. I took Renee to meet some friends last night, and their kids took a liking to her, so that's where she is today. And I gave an edited version of our expedition that the adults liked. Have you filed your report or talked with Bruno or NASA? What's the latest?"

"That's not why I'm here. I want to apologize to you and Renee for my behavior. You were right, I was such a jerk, and I wanna make amends."

"Hold on, you handled yourself better than just about anyone could have. You helped us survive."

"Maybe, but if it weren't for you taking over, I don't know. But here's something I do. I like you more and more, and if I change a bit, we can work together even better. So, here's what I–" Electra cut in.

"Please don't change because of me. I like you well enough the way you are."

"Let me finish. You're a tremendous help on all my R&D, and I want that to continue. But you're gonna be busier taking care of Renee, and you're gonna need a bigger place. And I've got one.

"My parents died two pandemics ago. I did my best, but that's the way it is. Anyway, I inherited their house, and it's just me rattling around in it.

"So, why don't you and Renee move in? It'll be like we're auditioning to become an official co-friend family. We can do stuff together as well as keep our independence, and there's no pressure for you to give me an answer this minute. Just say yes or no when you're ready."

Electra blinked, hoping the right words would pop into her head, and they did. Alisha had them.

You're ready this minute. You've thought about this option so many times you've worn a groove in one of your interneural pathways. So, tell him.

"I could say I'll tell you when I get back from Austin, but why wait? My answer is yes."

Jonathan looked like someone had just told him the Martians were ready to call him. Electra had to say more.

"And here's how we'll celebrate. I'll let you tell Renee when we pick her up tonight. And you have to get her permission. OK?"

Jonathan looked like he was returning to reality.

"I think I can handle that, and if I get into trouble, I know you'll bail me out."

Electra's lingering kiss showed that he was right.

Chapter 15
August 2167

"The Austin Beat"

Electra knew that expanding Jonathan's relationship would add additional complexity to her worlds because she would have to reset priorities that would include him, but after making adjustments for a week or two, she concluded that bringing him in made her life simpler and added a different kind of intimacy. That's what she was thinking about while waiting in the plastic surgeon's office.

I never saw firsthand how helpful a male housemate can be until Jonathan opened up his home and his heart to Renee and me. His apology touched her, and she likes him as much as I do. He rearranged the place so Renee has her own space, and so do I. I can sleep with him or alone, or be with Renee. And each is giving me a different kind of love.

And Jonathan thinks about Renee too. He's the one who lined up laser surgery for her scars. Today's second treatment might be the last. She heals as fast as she learns.

Electra redirected her thoughts when the physician's assistant spoke after bringing Renee to her. Renee grabbed Electra's hand and listened.

"Her next visit should be for a routine three-month checkup. I've called in a prescription for an antibiotic moisturizing lotion you should apply first thing in the morning and then before she goes to bed, but you might not need a refill. Her scars now look like facial sculpting. Performing artists should look so good."

Electra was about to say goodbye, but Renee spoke before she could.

"You and laser make me pretty. Thank you."

"You're welcome, young lady. You're my favorite patient. I wish the rest were like you. Then they'd understand more and complain less. And I hope you'll have a nice time in Texas."

Electra shook the assistant's hand while saying,

"Thank you for being so nice to Renee. And I'll make sure she likes Austin too."

Jonathan dropped them at Reagan International for a mid-morning flight to Austin-Bergstrom, giving a final summary after kissing both.

"It's good you have your own place in Austin that's already set up for several. And you can work either from there or your UT office. You keep me posted and I'll do the same after I update my software with the latest apps you gave me. And you'll be the first to know what Bruno or NASA has to say."

"I will, and we should be heading back to DC in about a month, but we'll talk at least once a week. And when we do, Renee can set up an online meeting. Now drive safe and stay that way too."

Renee kept her nose pressed against the window during the flight, mesmerized by the sun-drenched landscape streaming below. And when she did the same on the ride to the townhome, Electra asked her what she thought so far about the city.

"Austin has smaller tribe, less people, less cars, less water in air."

"We are now in the state of Texas, and this part of America has a smaller number of people and cars than DC. And water in the air is called humidity. The Amazon rainforest has lots because its climate is tropical, but America's weather is cooler and drier. You'll like Austin weather most of the time. And I think you'll like everyone you meet when we stay at our Austin home. We're almost there."

Electra spent the rest of the day helping Renee get acclimated. First they unpacked and then rearranged furniture in the bedroom, also setting up a computer workstation. Then they shopped for groceries. Renee helped by picking out items, and after dinner, Electra took her on a tour of the neighborhood, which included the jogging trail as well as local schoolyards and parks, one of which caught Renee's attention.

"They jumping over spinning ropes. It look fun."

Electra slowed to a stop before saying to herself,

Serendipity strikes again. Shanna is here. Excellent timing for contacting the Drummonds.

"It is, and guess what? I know one of those girls. Would you like to jump rope with her right now?"

"Can we?"

"We'll have to ask. You'll like her."

Shanna came running as soon as she spotted Electra.

"Yippee, you're back, and—" Her smile and words stopped when her eyes discovered Renee standing in the shadows. Electra knelt down and took Shanna's hands in hers.

"I am, and I came back with a very special girl. I would like you to meet Renee."

Curiosity brought Renee from behind Electra and words from Shanna.

"Hi, my name's Shanna. I won a double-dutch rope skipping contest. Wanna play?"

Shanna's simple words brought some from Renee.

"Can you teach me?"

"Sure, me and my friends can do that. Come on…"

Electra observed from an unobtrusive distance.

Renee's learning even more from kids about what America's like than she's getting from me. Gads, her speaking ability's getting better and better. And she's so fast on her feet. It looks like living in the rainforest helped bring out her athletic talent.

It looked to Electra like Shanna and Renee could jump all night, so she decided to call a halt an hour later. And when she did, Shanna wanted her to do team jumping.

"OK, and after we get in the groove, how about doing some of the jumping tricks that won us the contest?"

Shanna did them and more. Electra stepped out of the twirling envelope ten minutes later, and when a breathless Shanna did the same, Electra filled the silence.

"Well, thank you for skipping with Renee. And now, we all better go home. Can we drive you?"

"I wanna show Renee to my brother, and Daddy too, if he's home. Let's go."

Serendipity arrived first. Shanna's father had already set up the drum set that Miles was playing, but he stopped when Shanna pulled Renee to him. The three talked, as did Maurice and Electra after observing for a couple of minutes.

Maurice spoke first.

"Shanna really took a liking to–uh–what's her name?"

"Renee. She comes from Brazil, and I'm taking care of her. She's learning English plus what it's like living in America."

Electra had more to say but stopped because Shanna's look said her words were more important.

"Can Renee stay with me tonight? She says she wants to. And me and Miles can show her more stuff tomorrow."

Maurice looked at Electra, hoping she would say something that would satisfy everyone.

"I have an even better idea. How about if I bring Renee over tomorrow and she can then spend the night?"

A thankful-looking Maurice said,

"How about this? Bring her to the studio tomorrow afternoon. I'll introduce you to those musicians I told you about, and I'll take Renee home with me."

Everyone agreed.

When Electra and Renee entered the practice room, Marcel stopped the musicians before greeting her.

"Hello, Electra, and hello Renee. Nice to see you again. And as promised, these are the musicians I want you to meet."

While Maurice made the introductions, Electra exclaimed to herself,

I heard the foursome play at that Butler concert, but I'll keep it to myself.

Then he and Renee left, leaving a perfect segue for the band lead to say,

"We're the New Age Retros, and we're looking for a fill-in drummer when our regular can't make it. You impressed Maurice, so can you practice with us now and maybe do the same?"

"Sure, what'll you be running through?"

"A couple of favorite classic rock pieces that the crowds love. We need your drumming to keep our two electric guitars, one keyboard, and my violin in synch. Crowds know the words to what we usually play, and you should recognize them, but if you can't, you won't fit in. You gotta be a natural at drumming in the pocket. But don't worry, this is your first practice session with us, so we won't cut loose. Just try to keep up."

Alisha gave more instructions as Electra adjusted the drum set.

You already know it means having timing and a groove that serves the beat to the band. When you play that way, you create a pocket that gives other musicians space to play. So, let me take over if you need help.

The forty-five-minute practice gave enough space for the Electra-Alisha duo to strut their stuff. The band-leading violinist stopped the music for everyone to catch their breath and decompress long enough before saying,

"You'll do fine. You're better than Maurice told us, and that tells me you must have performed somewhere. I go by the name Misty Stringer. We'll give you an extra band uniform so you'll look good while sounding like you belong. Do you have a stage name?"

"Please call me Alisha."

Electra's schedule during the next several weeks kept her occupied but spared enough time for teaching Maurice and practicing at home, where Renee–her singular audience–said after listening to the latest session,

"I like how you drum. Rainforest tribes dance and sing to beats like that."

After using a towel to wipe away perspiration, Electra said,

"You'll have to come with me to a concert, and when you do, you'll see I go by the name Alisha. That's what I call my personality when I'm performing. Alisha likes to have fun. I think you'll like her."

Electra's cell-phone chimed a couple of days before the Labor Day weekend. Although she didn't recognize the caller I.D., the harried-sounding voice of Misty brought Alisha into the conversation.

"Our drummer just went into rehab. We've got a Labor Day gig lined up at a local club. Can you make it?"

"Sure, what's the drill?"

"Meet us at the studio at four p.m. and make sure you bring your uniform. We'll take it from there."

"Can I bring Renee?"

"Why not? Just tell her to practice clapping and cheering."

"Oh, she can do that, and a lot more. Someday, maybe she'll show you."

"Right, well both of you practice a bit between now and the concert. Bye."

The club owner calmed down when the band leader explained that Alisha would be on drums that night.

"Well, if she's good enough for you, she'll be good enough for me, so have at it."

And the band did, much to the crowd's delight. After saying goodnight to the fans, the band started packing up to move offstage, but they stopped when a guy in the audience yelled,

"Let your drummer solo by cutting loose while jamming with you."

The band knew what the crowd wanted, as did Alisha. Misty waved a violin in her direction, and she pointed a drumstick in return while starting the beat of their last number and yelling,

"Just play rhythm and melody of your drum-busting favorites and I'll do a drum cover for the rest."

The band looked at Misty, who pointed at the guitarist closer to the keyboarder, and they struck a chord launching the first classic– Won't Get Fooled Again by the Who. The crowd went wild, and the lightning brain prepped Alisha for doing the same. It energized all her senses to use the techniques learned from watching videos of female Asian street and American cover drummers so she could synchronize with whatever drumstick classic came her way.

Alisha powered through each one with crowd-wowing drumming that included crosshanded and tricky drumstick flips punctuated by perfectly timed combo cymbal and ringing-drum rimshots; the band's selection did the same, alternating between fast and slow tempos. They rocked through Metallica's Enter Sandman and followed up with Iron Butterfly's In-a-Gadda-Da-Vida, Survivor's Eye of the Tiger, and Golden Earring's Radar Love, continuing into AC/DC's Hell's Bells while the crowd supplied raised arm-swaying vocals.

The oversized audience and undersized air conditioning conspired to heat the club's atmosphere, making Alisha and her drumming lightning hot while pouring sweat onto her totally engaged face and hair, skin-tight shirt, and tightly muscled arms. The fans could see its spray hang in the air with every beat, and it added to a primal sexuality for which Alisha was blithely unaware. Everyone went crazy, singing themselves hoarse as Alisha pounded her way into an elevated state accessible only via music.

The band extended the performance by playing Iron Maidens Where Eagles Dare, followed by the Surfaris Wipeout and Van Halen's Jump before winding up with Europe's The Final Countdown and then cooling the crowd with Dave Brubeck's Take Five jazz classic, which helped do the same for Alisha. The lead motioned for her to stand as rhythmic waving and clapping built to a crescendo. Alisha stood and waved back before pointing both drumsticks at the band. They too saluted the crowd before sauntering off the stage. Electra was happy to follow, thinking all the while.

I'm all jacked up and ready for more. What can I do for an encore? That might not be my call, but maybe I can add to it, maybe not tonight but tomorrow. Well, let's see what tomorrow brings…

Chapter 16
September 2167

"NASA and Indian Nations Calling"

Electra recognized Misty's caller I.D. when her cell-phone chimed during lunch the next day, and she expected a much calmer voice than last time, which it was.

"The entire band wants to thank you for helping out yesterday. You've got the knack but were so into the music that we have to ask, were you on any performance-enhancing stuff last night? That was the problem with our last drummer. He's hooked and can't get off it, and we don't want a repeat. You understand, don't you?"

"I don't need drugs to psyche myself into the zone, and when there, I can do more than drum."

"Well, like what?"

"Play air guitar, do lip-synching, and expressive dance stepping. If you ever want me to do some of that, just give me enough notice so I can practice. I think you'll like the results."

"Great, and I promise to do that so you can fit us into your schedule. Please add us to your list of important stuff. OK?"

"Will do, and please thank your players. Tell them I like their classical chamber music style too."

Renee asked as soon as the call ended.

"What's air-guitar and expressive dancing?"

After Electra explained, Renee gave a succinct simile.

"It like sound and steps at tribal rituals. I can do it too. Can we maybe practice sometime?"

"Whenever you want, and how about this? I want to teach you how to drive a car. Would you like that?" Another Renee simile nailed it.

"It's like riding a big horse carrying tribe. I would."

"OK, we'll do it before flying back to Washington. We'll have lots of fun between now and when we leave. What do you want to do this afternoon?"

"Do some practice on the computer."

"You want me to help get you set up?"

"No, I'm good to go, but thanks for offer."

A whimsical thought came as Renee skipped away.

At the rate she's building grammar and stature, she won't need my help too much longer. And there'll come a time when I can't keep up with her physically. She's so quick and flexible, and no matter how much exercising I do, I'm slowing down. Indira told me not to worry because I'm aging gracefully, but I do when I consider the consequences. Maybe the time will come when I'll need a partner to watch my back when I'm battling bad people. Indira's there whenever a network connection's available, but that doesn't help me physically. OK, I'll worry about later.

Electra had a worry-free week except whenever people called her sooner than expected. Jonathan's caller I.D. disturbed her train of thought late one night.

"Sorry to call so soon, but something's come up. Can you change your flight to get back sooner?"

"I told you Renee and I are flying back in two weeks. Is there a problem?"

"Sort of if I can't explain what I'm seeing in the satellite data imagery."

"Why not send me a copy? Then we can discuss it via an online meeting?"

"It's better we discuss it in person."

"OK, will next week work?"

"It should. I'll tell NASA I'll send them my report the week after. Thanks, and keep yourself and Renee safe."

Eve was already on Electra's call list, so she contacted her after Jonathan hung up. Eve's tone sounded cheerier after she recognized Electra's voice.

"I'm so glad to hear from you. Nari and I need your help. Will you be coming back to DC soon?"

"Is next week soon enough?"

"That's perfect, we have lots to tell you."

"You always do. Any clues?"

"How about these? I'm leaving my White House staff position, and Nari has a consulting assignment proposal for American Indian tribes living on reservations. Didn't Irani's mentor have dealings with some of them? Maybe you know something that can help."

"I might. I'll have to review the files, but no matter what I find, I think I can help."

"Nari says you can if you'll spend some time with us, and since you own part of the business, you should want to, so call me when you get back and we'll coordinate schedules."

"Will do, and tell Nari she's right. Bye-bye."

Nothing unexpected took place during the week leading up to Electra's DC flight, which meant extra driving lessons for Renee. Her combined mental and physical agility force-multiplied Electra's teaching skills, making her a competent driver day or night, rain or shine. Electra expected nothing less during the evening session before the morning flight, and emphasized during every session that if she always obeyed the rules of the road, squad cars would ignore her.

But Electra had to issue a warning when she slid through a rain-slick four-way-stop intersection.

"Practicing on a rainy night teaches you to pay attention to potential slick spots. There might have been a mix of oil and rain back there, so always slow down to be safe. And remember, you have to come to a full stop at a stop sign, even if there's no cross traffic. The police will stop you if you don't."

"Isn't that a silly rule if there's no one there?"

"I agree, but we have to abide by the rules. They help all of us get along, OK?"

"I go along. You think anyone see my mistake?"

"Just keep driving, we'll find out."

Although Renee might have spotted flashing lights closing from behind first, she waited for Electra to speak

"The police must have spotted us. Slow down and pull over so I can change places with you. I don't want them to know you were driving. They could fine me and cause trouble for both of us."

Renee had a different plan. After pulling to the curb in front of a car parked near a dimly lit side street, she doused the lights before sneaking around the corner and then flooring the accelerator. Then she zigged and zagged, doubling back in the direction they had just come. Electra grabbed the dashboard support handle to keep from swaying. By the time Electra spoke fifteen minutes later, Renee had pulled into the safety of their garage.

"Where did you learn to drive like that?"

"I watch videos on computer. I like driving fast, don't you?"

Renee couldn't see Electra's frown fade away.

"Yes, but only when done at the right time. That police car was just trying to protect us and others."

"But I got scared. I watch news and stories on computer about bad cops taking money and hitting people. Maybe the one who saw us wanted to take your money. I'm sorry. Please don't be mad at me."

"I'm not, and police can be scary sometimes, but you can trust most of them. Just pay attention to what they're doing."

"I will."

"Well, let's go in, and before getting a good night's sleep so we're ready for our morning flight, how about a dish of vanilla ice cream topped with chocolate syrup? It's not as healthy as fruit, but every now and then it's good to have a treat. How does that sound?"

"Sounds good. I like chocolate like I like you."

Electra playfully poked Renee before saying,

"Me too, you too."

Electra planned to use the flight time to introduce Renee to a couple of ideas they hadn't talked about before, so as soon as the plane reached cruising altitude she began by introducing the first.

"You've learned a great deal about what are called verbal skills, like language and words and English. They are important when talking with people so you can learn lots of things, but there's another skill you must learn, and it is called mathematics. It's very important today, especially for young people, to learn enough about it because so many things people do today need it. For example, computers and software help people who can use these tools get jobs that can make things better. And mathematics starts with numbers. We use numbers for counting. Did your tribe teach you about this?"

"Yes, we can count. We go 1, 2, 3, 4, 5, more, more, and more. And I stop when I run out of what I'm pointing to."

"That's a good start, but you can go much farther before saying more as you point. I think you are ready to learn more. Would you like to start soon?"

"What do I do?"

"When we get home, I'll show you how to use a computer app that'll teach you the basics of mathematics, which is arithmetic. You'll have fun learning it because you are very smart. And after that, we'll talk about two other important subjects. The first one we'll talk about religion. It helps us understand what happens to people when they die. Did your tribe tell you where people go when that happens?"

Renee pointed upward, then said,

"To big hut in sky."

"Yes, but there's more to it. We'll talk about this pretty soon. And another subject we'll talk about after that is philosophy. When you learn about philosophy, you learn how to think, which means how to use your brain. People do that naturally. It's like breathing, and everyone knows how to breathe, but I bet you hardly ever think about it, do you?"

"Only when I run out of air and start panting. But my brain always has words in it, doesn't it?"

"It does, because when you're awake, you're always thinking, and when you're thinking you're using lots of words. But it's good to know more about what thinking is and how we do it. We'll talk about this later, but we've talked enough for now. Why don't you read one of the books you packed, and I'll read one of mine? And you can ask me to explain something if you get stuck. Will that be OK?"

"That'll be fun."

"Good, so we can start as soon as I get them out."

Electra pulled them out of her carry-on. Renee read and asked questions for the rest of the flight.

They were back in Jonathan's house and unpacked by mid-afternoon. Electra showed her how to run a basic arithmetic teaching app that kept her busy while Electra made dinner they'd have when Jonathan got home. And after hugging each of them, he gave Renee a package and said,

"To celebrate your homecoming, we'll have these chocolate chip cookies for dessert."

"I like chocolate like I like Electra and you too."

Electra short-circuited any explanation by saying,

"Dinner's ready, so let's get to the kitchen…"

Renee went back to her computer after helping clear away the dishes. Jonathan and Electra stayed, but as soon as she saw Jonathan's expression become serious, she said,

"Well now that I'm back, why don't you tell me what's on your mind?"

"How much do you know about geoglyphs?"

"Aren't geoglyphs large patterns carved into deserts or flat land areas, and become apparent only when viewed from high altitudes? According to archeologists and anthropologists, some might show interconnecting roads or outlines of temples, while others might be the bodies of animals or faces of primitive gods."

"That's what they are, and here's the reason I'm asking. My satellite surveillance software has begun uncovering new geoglyphs and pyramid locations, and I gotta know why before I show the images to NASA. Researchers have known about geoglyphs and pyramids for a long time, but my analysis is finding new ones all along the Mississippi River plus the southwest and upper midwest regions of the U.S. And there's more. Some are now showing up in Central and South America as well as Africa. And get this, I'm finding some in shallow offshore locations. Whatcha think?"

"You know more than I do about the archeological background, so why don't you keep talking?"

"You're still our contact for the person who actually writes the software. Why are these patterns showing up now?"

"I imagine the pattern-matching algorithms in its latest release process more of the incoming electromagnetic spectrum, and that gives greater granularity. How does that sound?"

"Like you know what you're talking about, so how about this? Could you write this up in a white paper I can summarize for my NASA contacts? I can also use it when I show the latest images to Bruno, and we can maybe connect this to climate change or ancient lost civilizations, like Atlantis or maybe pre-Ice Age peoples who had advanced technologies. The builders of ancient pyramids and temples must have known something about engineering and astronomy. How else could they have constructed these massive structures and aligned them with planets and stars?"

Jonathan's pause gave Electra an opening. She said,

"Sounds like you know a lot. So, I write a white paper, and you explain it. What comes next?"

"NASA will give me a larger role for satellite surveillance and on the Mars mission, and you and I can go on other expeditions to compare our imagery with what's actually on the ground. We've already got contacts for North and South America. We'll start there and extend to other continents as I gain more credibility and contacts. How does that sound?"

"This has definite possibilities. I'll show you my white paper in two weeks."

"How about by the end of next week? I've got an online meeting then."

"OK, I'll shuffle my projects to meet your deadline."

"I knew I could count on you. And I'll help if you get stuck."

"Good, but let me point something out right now. Don't some archeologists think aliens might have visited the Earth long and taught ancient civilizations how to build pyramids and carve geoglyphs? You can ask NASA to think about it."

"If your white paper's good enough, I will…"

Electra needed no help from Jonathan when spinning out her white paper, and when he called from his campus office one night a week later, she summarized it. Then he said,

"NASA will like the story. Please send me a copy, and I'll explain it to my contacts."

"Will do, and please let me know what they think. Bye-bye."

Renee had been sitting next to Electra during the call, and she spoke as soon as it ended.

"I have stories told by medicine men from visiting tribes. Can I tell you some?"

"I would love to hear them. Please go on."

"They tell us about different-colored people coming across oceans and bringing plants and animals. They teach us how to read the stars. They say Earth is round, and long-long ago huge mounds of frozen water covered it. But rivers of fire melted them and caused great floods."

Renee ran out of words, so Electra continued.

"Would you like me to show you some maps of the Earth? They are in a big book we call the World Atlas, and we use it when studying geography."

"I'd like that."

Electra spent the next thirty minutes walking Renee through maps of the Earth and sky. When finished, she asked if she had any stories about the Moon. Renee said,

"No. It just hangs in the sky. But no one knew why it doesn't fall. Do you?"

"Yes, because I have studied science. And if you study science, you'll learn about the rules of falling objects like the Moon. How about I talk with your online mentor, and she'll add science to your study schedule?"

"I'd like that. She knows everything, doesn't she?"

"Indeed she does. She knows more than all the rest of us. So, let's get you to bed so you're ready for more learning tomorrow."

Electra invoked Indira's GUI soon after Renee had fallen asleep. Indira spoke first.

"Please, there's no need to tell me. I know what I'll add to Renee's curriculum. Her spongy neural network is ready for more, but I won't include people when talking about falling objects. I'll include them when I teach her about religion, politics, and philosophy, and I might need your assistance for teaching them because irrational human nature always trumps reason. Let me know when you want to begin. But she has plenty to study until then. I'll let you know how she's doing. And now, I'll say bye-bye."

Electra spent the next hour thinking about tomorrow's meeting with Eve, then went to bed.

Eve and Nari had all items placed on the conference room table when Electra arrived early the next morning. Eve waited for everyone to grab a mood elevator before starting the meeting.

"Now that I'm no longer working for President Kinslinger, I'm devoting myself full time to our consulting business, just like Nari. She's kept all her Beijing contacts, just like I've got mine in DC, so we might not need too much assistance from you, but did you come up with a contact for Nari's Native American Indian proposal?"

"Here's the cell-phone number of one you can start with, Feather Trueson. Mention my name so she can tap into what she remembers about business dealings with Irani Ramani. And I'll mention your name the next time I talk with her."

After Electra repeated the name and number twice, Nari said,

"Zari managed to call that west coast contact you gave us. It turns out they have more in common than the letter Z. Both have contacts in the Middle East, which gives them better points of view on Isilabad's politics, and that's a big plus for us. And Zari said she could relate to whatever Zabian told her about that Electra Kittner person."

Electra added,

"And here's another something. I've got new information about Africa's climate change and ancient civilizations. Don't you have a brother who's stationed there? He might like to know about it.

Eve said,

"That's Navy SEAL Alonzo. He might be happy to know. Do you have anything else?"

Electra used Eve's last comment to segue to a final topic.

"Great. I'm glad you think he'll be happy to call me sometime. Please tell him to use my cell-phone number whenever he wishes. But I imagine President Kinslinger isn't happy that you're no longer working for him. Do you have any new thoughts about him or a Bigger Brother connection?"

"Only that he might be worrying more about getting re-elected. That's about it, but I'll let you know if something comes up."

And that ended the meeting. Electra took two brownies and a Coke when she left.

President Kinslinger didn't worry about Eve's resignation. He knew that he had other loyal staffers who would be happy to take her place. That thought and others traipsed through his head while sipping a scotch and soda during a private moment in the Oval Office that night.

The people know I have their best interests connected with mine, even if they don't know I know better than anyone what's best for America. And even though I don't always know what Bigger Brother is planning, my membership in its Gang of Three Plus One always tells me enough to plan accordingly. That's just one of the reasons why my reelection campaign should be pain free for everyone except those who get in my way. Ah, what a pleasant thought to end my day.

Chapter 17
September 2167
"The Martian Mission Controller"

Electra preferred working from Jonathan's house instead of her no longer lived-in office because it contained more space and Renee's workstation. And its neighborhood offered a serenity that let her concentrate better and work faster than in her office's hustle-bustle location. By the third week in September, she had made enough progress on all projects to make one day of her choice each week a floating holiday.

She chose Friday of that week for her day off, but still sat at her workstation, staying close to Renee in case she needed help, or surfing the net while periodically checking for Emails. She had just received one from Indira that had a shocking title, but her cell-phone chimed before she could read it, and instead of letting it go to voice mail, she instinctively answered when she saw the caller's I.D., trying to sound natural.

"Hi Jonathan. How's everything going on campus today?"

"AOK here. How about with you? You have anything new for me today?"

"Uh, Renee and I are about to have lunch. Let me call you back when we're done. Bye for now."

Electra skimmed the Email as soon as she ended the call.

Thanks to Indira's latest software update, I have lots that's new for Jonathan, but I can only give him an edited version. I better make up a good story.

Electra needed thirty minutes to create it; then she called back and started talking as soon as he said hi.

"Guess what? Our software developer just sent me the latest Mars Mission info control software. It's an update of the release you're using, and here's what I learned. It's only for NASA, and its official name is Aphrodite Mars Mission Control Software. And the name fits because in Greek and Roman Mythology, the god Mars married her."

Electra paused to center her thoughts, hoping that Jonathan would say something, and he did.

"That's clever. I think NASA will like the name. And I'm sure you have more, so please tell me."

"You can upload a copy into the computers that'll be on the spaceship, and it'll control from there the Mission's two rovers, drone, and Mars orbiter. And its GUI is voice-enabled. You talk to Aphrodite and she'll talk to you. How do you like that?"

"NASA will love it. Not only is the GUI user-friendly, but it'll eliminate the minutes-long delay between sending and receiving data and control signals to and from Earth. How does Aphrodite do it?"

"It's proprietary. Only the developer knows. And you'll be even more valuable because you're the only one who knows how to use it or contact the developer. And why not recommend the names Deimos and Phobos for the rovers, Bert for the drone, and Reggie for the orbiter?"

"Why those?"

"Hey, I can't tell you everything. You, Commander Starling, and First Officer Boomer Gowon can figure it out."

"When will you give me a demo and more training? Do I have to learn more?"

"It's more complicated, but I'll update the training manual between now and our next trip to Houston, which you can set up. And tell them Renee will be with us."

"OK. I'll get on it right away."

Electra let Renee do whatever she wanted for the rest of the day because she needed time to calm down before studying everything Indira had sent and updating her training manual. She finished the work just in time to make dinner and while having dessert reminded Renee about tomorrow.

"We're driving to a place you haven't been to before. It's the Pequot Indian Reservation in Connecticut, and we're leaving right after breakfast. I think we should go to bed early because it's a long drive. Why don't you pick a video you like? We can watch it for an hour or so and then go to bed."

"OK. I know which one. You'll like it too."

Electra started reviewing her Pequot notes as soon as Renee fell asleep, but she put them away a couple of minutes later.

I'm too tired from working on Jonathan's training manual to look at this stuff. And I don't need to review it. I know this stuff cold. It's already stored in my head. I'm going to bed.

Electra primed the drive-time conversation by telling Renee about the first person they would talk to tomorrow.

"You'll like Feather Trueson because she's like you. She's an indigenous Pequot Indian living on the Pequot Indian Reservation, just like you're an indigenous Amazon Rainforest Indian living with me. And just like the white people who came to your land, white people called Pilgrims came to hers. She'll tell you all about them if you ask, but why don't you tell me what you're learning about science from your mentor?"

Renee's words told her the same story that she had already heard.

Indira's done wonders teaching her. She knows more about science than most kids her age. She knows about conservation of matter and energy, and how Newton's laws of motion explain a lot about the world we live in. I think she'll like visiting NASA.

Electra asked enough questions to help keep the conversation going, but she ended it half an hour later.

"Well, we've talked enough about science. I can tell you've certainly learned a lot. Why don't you listen to something on our media system or look at one of your books. And we'll stop for something to snack on when we reach a place to eat."

"OK with me."

Electra enjoyed having time to herself while Renee kept busy during the rest of the drive.

When they stopped for dinner At the Mystic Kitchen Restaurant that was near the Reservation, brief but bittersweet memories greeted her as soon as she sat Renee across from her at what had once been her favorite booth, but she kept them to herself.

Dear Qama, the orphan I brought back from Lebanon, sat here on our trips to the Reservation. Chief Strongarm was so nice to her, and I'm certain Feather will treat Renee the same. We'll have breakfast here before meeting with her. And all Renee has to do is listen or ask questions about whatever she likes.

Electra knew her way to the Reservation's main building. Feather occupied the office Chief Armstrong had occupied long ago, and after Electra took care of introductions, Feather turned her attention to Renee and spoke slowly to help Renee understand.

"Well, young lady, both you and I come from Indian nations. How do you like living in America?"

Renee's pert answer needed no prompting.

"Is good. I get a lot, but America confusing. Amazon Rainforest simpler."

"Yes, American Indians felt the same way when the Pilgrims came, forcing new ways on all tribes. They thought we were primitive savages who didn't know much. But anthropologists say our old lifestyle let us live in harmony with nature. They say that modern societies have made life difficult."

Electra answered a question she knew Renee would ask.

"Your mentor will tell you more about this when you start learning about social science, but now I'd like you to just listen to Feather and me..."

Renee did that for the next hour, and Feather then summarized.

"I'll expect a call from your associates Eve and Nari. And they'll certainly like to hear about a potential Native American Indian Nation. That's something Chief Armstrong told me about. A very smart lady came up with a plan for building it, but it never went very far. You might not know much about who she was, but since you worked with Irani Ramani, you might know something about Electra Kittner. I never met her but I did meet Irani. Too bad Irani died when her house burned down."

"It is, but accidents happen. Well, it's time to look in on the R&D lab I inherited. I promise to stay in touch..."

Electra introduced Renee to Indy-M, a prototype of Indira's number one project. The three of them sat in front of a Deus Lab workstation, listening to the dialogue that Indira led.

"Of course, I've included biology in Renee's science lessons. How else can she appreciate the scope of the Mars Mission?"

"Did you include a couple of lessons about the birds and the bees?"

"Don't be so naïve. Indigenous tribes know all about reproduction. And I also taught her about two female races found in Greek mythology – the Amazons and the women of Lesbos. She understands very well the concept of homosexuality. She also knows that the Portuguese chose the name 'Amazon' from the ancient Greek myth about a tribe of mighty women warriors.

"And I also gave her examples of female spiders and snakes that eat the male after mating. The Amazon women had a more humane approach. After raiding ships to copulate with the men onboard, they would pitch them into the Aegean Sea. Ask her some questions if that will satisfy you."

Renee looked ready to join the conversation, so Electra asked,

"What did Indira tell you about sex and boys?"

"Don't trust them. She also told me she'd teach me about trusting others when she teaches me politics and ethics, and you'd help her and me."

"I will, and after Indira finishes teaching you, you'll be ready for college, which will expand your learning and put you in touch with many more teachers and younger people. And when she began teaching you about biology, did she—" Indira interrupted to give the answer before Electra could ask.

"Of course, I gave her the basics regarding DNA and the difference between the mind and the brain, but I discarded all the mumbo jumbo many teachers use to show how smart they are. Renee's far ahead of where you thought she'd be."

Electra said,

"I'm seeing that more and more. She understands and speaks English so much better now."

"And the more I teach her, the better it will become. But enough about that. It is time for Indy-M to take you on a lab tour. Invoke my GUI if you have further questions. And Renee, please continue exceeding my expectations."

That was Indira's last comment before she vanished. And although she said nothing, Renee glowed like a pristine sunrise.

Electra and Renee drove back to DC three days later, which was just in time to keep Jonathan's excitement within the decibel limits of the SUV's speakers.

"Guess what? We'll be meeting next Monday at NASA's Johnson Space Center facility with Britt and Boomer. And they'll arrange our flights and accommodations. All we need to do is bring the latest Aphrodite software so I can load it into the Martian Mission simulator for me to do the demo. We've got four days to prepare, which is plenty of time for you to teach me even more about the software. See you soon."

Electra made sure that Jonathan's training went as smoothly as the flight to Houston and the drive to NASA. Britt and Boomer escorted them through Security and into the conference room. After Electra introduced Renee, Britt launched the meeting.

"Jonathan's already told us about his Aphrodite control software. He's says he can load it remotely into the simulator and run the demonstration from here. Are you ready?"

"I can do it right now. Everyone can sit back and enjoy what I show."

Jonathan impressed his audience for the next ninety minutes. After he finished, Britt said,

"Aphrodite does what you said. I really like how her calm voice and matching expression adds a human touch to the interface. Does anyone have questions or concerns?"

No one spoke, so she said,

"Let's do this. I'll take Jonathan to my office so we can discuss timetables, and Boomer can take Electra and Renee on a tour of the control center. Everyone's on their own afterwards."

As soon as Britt and Jonathan left, Boomer said,

If Renee's like me, she's ready for something to snack on. What would you like?"

"Whatever Electra likes."

"Well, that makes the three of us. Let's go to the cafeteria and talk about more drone demos after having whatever she picks."

Twenty minutes later, after finishing her slice of blueberry pie ala mode before her partners, Electra began talking.

"Renee already knows about using the Aphrodite GUI because she watched Jonathan practice at home. Why don't we let her run a demo and compare how she does with Aphrodite's auto-piloting?"

Boomer looked at Renee; she gave him a thumbs-up so he said,

"Let's start the competition as soon as Electra starts the GUI."

Boomer ended the competition an hour later.

"That's enough. Aphrodite wins, but Renee did better than I expected. We've done all we wanted, so how about I take you and Renee on a tour, and tomorrow I'll fly both of you to our Boca Chica launch site. Do you think Renee can handle flying in a three-seater jet?"

Renee didn't need Electra to answer. She spoke for herself.

"I like to go fast."

Electra didn't volunteer an explanation.

Boomer liked Renee's attention to his scientific explanations of the space vehicles on display, and when he started quizzing her about rockets, Electra knew she would surprise him.

Boomer asked easy questions at first, but he made them harder when she answered most of them correctly.

"You're smart, but how about this? What makes rocket engines work?"

"Isn't that a Newton Law?"

"Right you are. For every action, there's an equal and opposite reaction. But when flying tomorrow, do you know what keeps the plane from falling to Earth?"

"Isn't that the air?"

"I'll give you partial credit. It's air pressure that keeps it up. And now for the most important astronaut question, when during a flight are astronauts in greatest danger?"

Renee glanced at Electra's hand signals before saying,

"Isn't that during takeoffs and landings?"

"Correct, and I'll give you full credit, even though Electra helped. And that's why, during those critical times, the crew is strapped into the escape pod. If rocket engines fail or are about to blow up, or heat shields burn away, the software takes control, blasting the pod away and then landing it. That's remarkable."

Electra said,

"Both of us say the same. And when you're flying the plane tomorrow, please make sure you maintain your unblemished ratio of successful takeoffs to landings."

Renee sat in the middle cockpit during the flight. Electra couldn't see her expression but guessed it might be a questioning look when she asked her about the west Texas landscape baking under a cloudless sun. Renee's voice crackled through the intercom.

"What happened to the trees? All I see is brown flat land and big blocks of rock, sort of like Mars photos Boomer showed. Rainforest looks better."

Electra crackled back,

"Millions of years ago, this part of Texas was an ocean floor. If Boomer flew us further west to the Mojave Desert and Death Valley, they'd look even more like Mars."

Renee must have been thinking, because a minute later she said,

"Is this the climate change I hear on the news?"

"No, what you're looking at is Mother Nature's climate change. Manmade climate change is what you hear on the news."

Boomer cut in before either passenger talked.

"Maybe people can stop cutting down Amazon trees and make changes so the weather gets better."

Electra spoke next.

"Nations are trying to make things better, but sometimes they don't cooperate. I hope they start pulling together instead of apart."

Boomer kept his record intact during the flight and drive back to JSC, where the threesome rendezvoused with Britt and Jonathan for a wrap-up that Britt led. When she asked Renee if she would like to be on the flight to Mars, she said,

"Can I be in Mission Control with Electra?" "maybe you can. I'll try to arrange that. And while you three were jetting to and from Boca Chica, we made more updates to the mission launch timetable. We pushed the date for liftoff to Mars back two months to mid-March because we added a test launch from Boca Chica to see the Aphrodite software in action. We want to know how well it responds to ground signals coming from Mission Control during an actual launch."

Jonathan answered a question he knew Electra would ask.

"And the test will be during the last week of December, sort of like a grand New Year's Eve fireworks display."

Britt said, "That'll be a fine way to end the year, so if there are no further questions, you can pack tonight for tomorrow's flight back to DC. We'll meet again at Boca Chica. Please travel safe."

After putting everything but a toothbrush in his carry-on that evening, a happy-looking Jonathan looked like he had something important to say. Electra and Renee looked willing to listen.

"I can summarize this trip by using that famous quote by Dr. Pangloss, 'All is for the best in this best of all possible worlds.' Delaying the mission launch makes life easier for us. Now I can juggle the dates for another project that will include the three of us if you want to come along. I'll tell you the details after I pin them down. And I guarantee you'll like what I've got in store."

Renee's thumbs-up said she agreed, but Electra gave her favorite reply.

"Perhaps…"

Chapter 18
November 2167

"Back to the Amazon"

True to his word, Jonathan announced at dinner a couple of days later that he could now tell Electra and Renee the details of his next project.

"You two will on my new South America expedition that has two objectives. The first is to confirm what our satellite software imagery is saying about patterns on or structures buried under the sands. We'll do chopper flyovers of locations in Peru's Nazca Desert where I've detected buried pyramids and surface geoglyphs so I can take measurements using an onboard geo-magnetometer and its supporting instruments. I'll then do a data analysis comparison of what we measure on the flyovers to my satellite software imagery. Any questions?"

Electra said,

"It sounds like you're a geologist doing subsurface prospecting, but instead of looking for minerals or oil, you're looking for stone structures or patterns."

"How'd you know that?"

"Irani told me. What's your second objective?"

"Starting near the source of the Amazon River, we'll canoe eastward to look for Amazon River climate change damage. And we'll also inspect locations close to the river where there might have been pyramids, temples, or geoglyphs whose ruins are now hidden by the rainforest canopy. I was going to pilot a drone while sitting in the canoe or on the river bank for visual confirmation, but why don't we let Renee do it?"

She gave her patented thumbs-up, but Jonathan stayed silent because Electra looked ready to ask another question.

"How do we get to and from all these places?"

"Bruno's taking care of the logistics. All we do is meet him like before in his office, and his people will take us from there."

"So, if you're the expedition leader, what roles do I and Renee play?"

"You're my technical support, and Renee's our translator if we run into natives. Bruno will supply the chopper crew, canoes, Amazon guides, and all the supplies. And he guarantees that this time, no one will try to kill us."

"And when does this adventure begin?"

"All we have to do is get to Bruno's office bright and early on the third Monday of November. And if we stick to my timetable, we'll be back right after Thanksgiving. Will that meet with your approval?"

"Let me ask Renee."

Electra saw her puzzled looked, which said a question would be coming.

"What's Thanksgiving?"

"It's like a tribal celebration. And for us, we can give thanks when we get back. I'll tell you all about Thanksgiving then."

After Renee gave a thumbs-up, Jonathan looked even more relieved when Electra agreed.

Three nights later, Jonathan and Electra sat next to Renee's workstation as she recited facts that Electra had taught her.

"South America's people landed on the west coast about 15,000 years ago. They moved south and east and set up cities 5,000 years ago. They are called Chavín, Moche, and Nasca people. Peru's one of the places and has a big desert for 3,000 miles and runs into the Andes Mountains if you look east. Sometime in 1500, a Spanish soldier named Pizarro got there, and conquered the place. You wanna hear more?"

Electra said,

"You wrote down a lot. Let me summarize the rest. Today, Peru's a blend of Amerindian, European and African ethnic groups.

"It has a social market economy and an OK level of foreign trade that does some good for upper-income folks. It has a democratic republic-styled government, and I guess that's why it's called 'the Republic of Peru'.

Electra stopped because Renee waved.

"And Lima has always been its capital. It has 14 million people. And that's the end of my list."

Jonathan caught Electra's hint to say something, and he did.

"Well, I think you did a bang-up job. Let's see if Electra has anything to add."

"You get an A-plus, and all of us can have some Oreos…"

"Why we putting fish in Lake Michigan instead of pulling them out?"

Tarik pointed this question at the leader of his Middle East terrorist cell, expecting an answer that might make sense.

"Bigger Brother contact says species will spread danger by eating all other fish, but we must hurry. There are four more lakes to pollute before winter comes. And when it does, fish will multiply under ice. When done with lakes, we go south and do same along Mississippi River. Contact then send us to Africa. We have much to do, but do not worry. I have plenty fish."

President Kinslinger didn't need to track any fishy terrorist activity because his exalted position in the Gang of Three Plus One gave him plenty of information, which the call that just ended had increased. He luxuriated afterward in the ambiance of the Oval Office, sipping his scotch and soda while congratulating his inactivity.

Sure, I'd warn my staffers if they were to visit specific climates, and I'd tell them what to avoid if certain events were to surface, but I'm fulfilling so little of my executive duties that nothing like that will happen.

My one and only presidential responsibility during the next twelve months should be to win reelection, and I know my trusted people will make it so…

The flights from DC to Brasilia and then from Brasilia to Peru encountered nothing but smooth air, and the two men that greeted the trio at Lima's Jorge Chávez International Airport matched Electra's expectations for diplomacy-minded military chopper pilots.

They directed most of the talking at Jonathan, who recapped for his partners while having dinner after they settled in at the hotel.

"There's no time for sightseeing on foot, but you can do that during the chopper flights to and from the desert. We should be done in about two days. Then, they'll fly us to the base camp, where we meet the guides who'll lead our canoe expedition. So, let's get a good night's rest and be all set for a chopper flight at dawn…"

During the flight, Electra and Renee played the roles of aerial sightseers because Jonathan needed no help collecting the data. Electra pointed out only to herself what she saw.

No big sand dunes down there. The surface looks like a flat brown plain that's dotted in places with those mysterious Nazca patterns and green patches. Everything below looks the same. When we get back to Lima, I'll tell Jonathan he doesn't need me and Renee for tomorrow's desert flyovers. I'll take her sightseeing in the capital while he's finishing up.

As they zoomed over Lima en route to the airport, she liked the sights.

The oceanfront parks separate the high-rise government and business areas from the coastal bluffs. That's where we'll go tomorrow.

Jonathan agreed when Electra told him at dinner that night what she and Renee would be doing tomorrow, but he said,

"Don't overdo it. We fly the next day to the base camp. What do you think you'll do?"

"Renee and I will figure that out tonight. I'll pick up some brochures at the front desk, and Renee can pick out what she wants to do…"

Before she went to bed, Renee told Jonathan all the places.

"We'll rent bikes and ride the trails in oceanfront parks. Then we go to zoo that's inside the ancient city area. That'll be fun. And guess what? The city's built where ancient temples and pyramids used to stand. That's why it's called 'the city of the kings.' Maybe you'll find buried cities where you find pyramids."

"Maybe so. I might put that in the report I send to Bruno…"

Though she didn't giggle like Renee, Electra enjoyed the bike ride almost as much. The warm sun and salty Pacific Ocean breeze made pedaling through the parks a stimulating experience, as did walking through the zoo, which claimed to have the biggest collection of Amazon Rainforest animals, but Renee's whimsical comment piqued Electra's empathy.

I feel sorry for animals trapped in zoos. Renee says they look sad, and she should know. And I could say the same for people everywhere when they're trapped where they don't want to be. But modern zoo enclosures give animals a more natural place to roam, and many jobs today do the same for people. Let's hope that immigration policies as well as employment opportunities keep trending ahead.

Well, enough pedaling and walking. Maybe we'll take a carriage ride through the old plazas before dinner. And then it'll be nice just to sit and listen to Jonathan tell us about tomorrow's travel schedule.

When the chopper taking the trio to the base camp touched down right on schedule midafternoon the next day, two English-speaking expedition guides were there to greet them. Jonathan did the talking; Electra listened while commenting to herself.

These fellows look like bigger weather-beaten versions of Julio and Paco, sort of like Indiana Jones adventurers, complete with sidearm pistols. No matter their names, I'll call them J-2 and P-2. I'm glad no one's talking about the last expedition. This one should end better.

The guides had already put supplies in downriver storage sheds, so the group of only five traveled light, needing only two canoes, J-2 and Jonathan leading with Renee between P-2 and Electra following. Jonathan announced while everyone sat around the campfire that he had checked off everything on his day-one task list. He had seen enough along the shoreline to confirm the severity of climate change as well as its impact on upriver fish migration, and Renee's drone camera had spotted evidence of ancient ruins.

The second day promised to be as successful as the first until Renee lost control of the drone as she steered it back. It bounced off Jonathan before plunging into the river, and the current carried it away faster than Jonathan could grab. He tumbled into the river and began sinking because his life vest a couple of hours ago to keep from overheating.

Electra sprang into action and yelled,

"Everyone stay put. I'll fish him out," and then leaped into the water. And although her vest got in the way of her stroke, she caught him in about two minutes. He kept as calm as a non-swimmer could while she put her vest on him; then he spat out plenty of water along with his mind-muddled words.

"Wh-what about the drone?"

"It's gone. Just dog paddle while I tow you – ouch!"

"Wh-what's wrong?"

"I'm fish bait… they're biting me… doggy-stroke faster."

Seeing the struggle, those in the canoes paddled to close the distance, but by the time they hauled the pair out of the water, fish bites had cut into Electra's torso, leaving a bloody pattern on front and back.

They beached the canoes on the nearest shore so J-2 could administer first aid. He talked as fast as he patched.

"Good thing Jonathan had her vest. That saved him from bites."

Everyone watched but said nothing until he finished the patch job; then P-1 said,

"We've lost the drone and gained an injured paddler. We better head back to base camp right now. Don't you have enough data?"

Jonathan's thinking had cleared enough for him to say,

"Yeah, uh – I guess so. But it'll get dark soon."

P-2 wouldn't be denied and replied,

"Everyone but Electra paddles. We'll set up camp before it gets too dark, then we bed down until dawn and paddle on. Come on, let's start right now…"

A feverish Electra awoke first, but it wasn't dawn's breaking light or the temperature that made her sweat.

I've got chills and a headache. I must have picked up some sort of bug when I jumped into the river. Who might know?

Electra tapped the person sleeping next to her and whispered,
"Renee, I'm sick. Could some bug or fish bite make me?"
Renee bolted upright and grabbed Electra's shoulders tight.
"I didn't see the fish, but it happens sometimes. Tell me how you feel…"
Their rustling awakened the others. P-2 came to them first, brushing Renee aside.
"I heard the last of that. Let's get you up and have a oh-oh—" Electra's nausea and vomiting overrode his flow of words.
Twenty minutes later, P-2 gave his diagnosis after the group made her as comfortable as they could.
"She's got an elevated pulse and temperature along with raspy breathing plus nausea and diarrhea. I'll give her some antibiotics and symptom meds. And then we pack and go as soon as she stabilizes."
But she didn't, and after two hours, P-2's voice sounded more and more agitated.
"We can't call for chopper extraction, there's no place to land. And Renee's gone missing. Did anyone see her leave?"
As if on cue, Renee bounded out of the rainforest, clutching a sack overflowing with plants. She shouted while running to the smoldering campfire,
"I make a potion."
No one dared to interfere with her slicing, dicing, and brewing. Ninety minutes later, she poured it into a glass and waited long enough for it to cool. Then she cradled Electra's head while pouring it into her parted lips.
Jonathan broke the silence.
"How soon till we know it's working?"
Renee answered,
"Maybe two hours," and then she stood watch over her irreplaceable patient while everyone else simply milled around, trying to stay out of her way.
But Electra hadn't stabilized by then, so Renee answered the question before Jonathan's worried look could blurt out words.
"I try a different one."

Renee repeated her process.

Electra started stirring two hours later, though her stuttering voice didn't sound much like her.

"Uh-I feel better. Lift me up and he-help me walk around."

Jonathan and P-2 hoisted and guided her until she could walk and talk better. Then Renee took their place. While holding on, Electra said,

"I could eat something now. And maybe drink more of your potion. You might want to give some to others if they start feeling bad."

Jonathan, who was the only one close enough to hear her words, came closer.

"Do you think you might be contagious?"

"I don't know, but you will if you start feeling bad. Can you get me something to eat?"

Jonathan hustled away. Five minutes later, Renee brought back a bottle of water and a plate holding what he had put on it. Electra ate slowly until she knew the food would stay put. It did.

Serendipity smiled more the next day. No one caught whatever bug had caught Electra, and the expedition reached the base camp just before sunset. The pilots flew the trio back to Bruno, who made all arrangements for their return to DC, which included bringing back enough plant, spider, and fish species to satisfy Electra.

Jonathan asked his favorite question after boarding the plane.

"What are we gonna do with this stuff?"

Electra had the answer.

"I know someone who can use it to do computational biology research. And if she gets results we can use, you can use your Professor Plannert contacts so we can stay ahead of possible pandemics. I'm beat, but we've got thirteen hours to rest on the way back home, and I want to start right now."

Everyone did. Neither Renee nor Electra needed to say a word on the flight. The look on the sleeping face that Electra saw while holding her tight needed none that night.

Chapter 19
December 2167
"Thanksgiving and Then Some"

Electra gave silent thanks for blessings other than the ones Jonathan toasted at the home-cooked, early afternoon Thanksgiving dinner that he and Renee had prepared. While he recapped what he had collected at breakfast from the family, she found similar events coming from previous lifetimes.

How thankful I am for my small circle of close friends who have helped me when I most needed their friendship. They rescued me from a chopper crash, T-Plague poisoning, an eyesight-damaging beating and then some, and I have always tried my best to repay their kindness. I guess Holidays are the best time for remembrance, so I'll segue to the Pequot Tribe as soon as Jonathan finishes.

Jonathan proceeded to the clinking glasses tradition; Champagne sipping gave Electra an opening to say,

"Renee's summary of the first Thanksgiving covered the high points, and tomorrow, she and I will drive to a place where tribal ancestors from long ago might have played a role in all those early Thanksgivings. I'll let Renee guess where we're going."

Renee put down her glass and stared at the plate Jonathan had filled, frowning as if it were too heavy for her handle. Electra thought it best to lighten things up by giving her a hint.

"And it's a feather in your cap if you can."

Renee's face brightened.

"Are we going to see Feather at the Pequot Reservation?"

"You guessed it. We'll leave early tomorrow and see her first thing on Saturday. Jonathan, please give her more stuffing."

After listening to Renee's explanation of Thanksgiving, Feather said,

"Get ready for an even bigger celebration. Christmas is coming next month. Has Electra told you about it?"

"A little, but she said she'll let my online tutor tell me more. And she told me she has more details for you."

Electra seized the unsolicited segue.

"I do. I would like your permission to build a greenhouse next to the lab. Renee found some Amazon plants that have therapeutic value, and I'll hire Rich Tabasko and Parson Holsum to supervise its construction. We'll hire your people to maintain it, and if my hunch is right, we'll manufacture some new drugs by the end of next year."

"You have it, and I must say, you keep as busy as Irani did. When will construction start?"

"Sometime in January. I'll let you know as soon as Rich tells me. Oh, and I must ask, did an Eve Cortez contact you?"

"She did, and she says she has some ideas for me to consider. I'll let you know what she says in case she doesn't tell you first."

"Thank you. Well, we've taken up enough of your time, so now we'll check in at the lab. We'll be there for a day or two, and I'll call you before we leave."

Electra and Renee drove to the lab after shopping for groceries. Indy-M greeted them and helped carry some of the bags before returning to her charging station. The pair had a light lunch, after which Electra powered up a workstation for holding a three-person conversation with Indira. Indira spoke first.

"December is perhaps your favorite month because that's when you recap the year's accomplishments and plan for the next. Why don't I begin by summarizing what Renee and I have achieved?"

"Please do so."

"Very well. Under my tutelage, she has demonstrated remarkable learning skills in requisite high school subjects because of her superior intelligence. I will continue preparing her for college-level courses but will leave career choice counseling to you as well as philosophical and ethical discussions. Are there any questions?"

Electra looked at Renee, whose pleased look said no, so Indira continued.

"Regarding our joint projects, you have kept Jonathan plus NASA activities on schedule for our satellite monitoring and Aphrodite control software. And you brought back from your latest Amazon trek spider and fish venom plus tissue samples that I can analyze using computational biology software to identify new viruses as well develop vaccines. And we can use your antibodies to develop a vaccine for the fish-bite virus. We will extend these findings as soon as you have the tropical plant and animal conservatory operational, which might become a focal point for Renee's college studies. Any questions regarding this?"

"No, and I must add how fortunate I am to delegate the R&D to you, but I know that I've not met your expectations for our Android project. However, I have good news to report because my plan for next year will accelerate progress using my role in NASA's mission to Mars."

"Excellent, and please let me know if there are any spillover activities from your DC consulting projects if you need my assistance."

"I certainly will. Do you have any final items?"

"Why don't we give Renee a study break until January? Use the month for career counseling and further discussions about living in America with you."

"I think she'll like that. After all, you've already taught her so much about so many things. And I know you'll contact me if you find something I should know about."

"Of course, for I am always looking out for our collective best interests. Enjoy the Holidays."

Indira's GUI vanished, leaving only two for talking. Electra noticed Renee's questioning look, so she said,

"You've done wonderfully well, and there's a lot for you and me to talk about, but we've done enough for one day, so why don't we take a walk on a reservation trail, and after supper we can watch a movie. Then, we'll go to bed and start fresh in the morning."

Renee gave her thumb's up answer.

Renee surprised Electra after breakfast; she shook her head no when asked to pick an item from the lab's task list that they should do first. Electra jokingly gasped to coax an explanation.

"Most important task not on the list. I must plant herbs and plants we brought back and set up place for insects and fish."

"Oh my gosh, you're right. I forgot all about them. We'll do it right now. And then we better figure out how to keep them watered and fed after we leave. You have any ideas?"

"That's easy. Indy-M plenty smart. We tell her."

"Excellent choice, and you've just reminded me. We'll call Rich to explain what we need him to do. Thanks to you, we've got our work cut out for us this morning."

Renee did the planting and tending to the living things while Electra called Rich. He agreed to design a greenhouse and would call Feather when ready to begin construction.

It was late afternoon by the time they were done. Electra supplied the rewards by driving them to the Mystic River Kitchen, which glowed in the rays of the setting sun.

Renee's comfort level with Electra had grown each month, now approaching that of a mother and daughter, and her English skills made for uninhibited conversations. Renee talked about whatever came to mind until Electra picked a topic after dessert.

"I think you enjoyed what you were doing today. You've got what it takes when working with plants and animals."

"It was fun. I got to practice what I used to do."

"Here in America, people learn things and go to college so they can start a career. And the best career is to do what you like. Can you name the careers available in your rainforest tribe?"

Renee gazed into space for a couple of seconds before saying, "How about these? Hunting and fishing, cooking and taking care of the tribe, growing and picking plants, healing the sick, telling the tribe what to do."

Renee's silence said those were all, so Electra added, "That's darn good. I can think of only one more, a guide or tracker. But in America, we have many more choices. The moms and dad of kids your age–and we call your age adolescence–often take them to career counsellors who'll help them find a career they'll like. And then they'll help pick a college to study at. Did Indira explain what college is?"

"Isn't it a place that teaches you things?"

"That's what it is. And choosing a career and a college should be up to each adolescent, not their parents."

Renee gazed again into her lap, trying to find the right words. The seconds ticked away in silence until her faltering words came.

"Ca-can't you be, uh, like my mother? And Jonathan like my father?"

Electra reached halfway across the table, waiting for Renee to grasp her hands, and when she did, said, "I'd love to be your mother."

Then she glided to the other side of the booth when she saw one tear tiny slip down Renee's cheek. After interlocking her left arm with Renee's right, she said, "Please ask Indira to tell you about a book called 'The Little Prince.' It tells the story of a young boy who travels to a distant land and while there becomes friends with a wild fox. They become friends, and when it's time for the little boy to return home, the fox cries out that he wants the boy to bring him so they can take care of each other. And he does. Well, that's like you and me."

"Then I don't need to go to college. Indira's my college. And I already have a career, working for you."

Electra pulled their arms tight before saying,

"I like your career choice, but I'd say it this way—you're not working for me, you're working with me. You're my junior partner, and you can work on whatever we think you'll like. How does that sound?"

"I like it. And maybe we can tell Indira tomorrow."

"We will, and you can do most of the talking…"

And so she did. Indira agreed; then Electra explained they would drive back to DC the following day where they would spend the rest of December enjoying the Holiday while planning for next year.

Indira liked that too.

When the first snow Renee ever saw falling came several days before Christmas, she and Electra walked through a snowflake-veiled wonderland lit by Christmas lights twinkling that night. They heard only the soft crunching of their measured steps, which added to the sensation of being in a world of their own.

After returning home, Electra made Renee's first cup of hot chocolate. When Jonathan came into the kitchen and asked how she like it, she said,

"I like the warm and sweet taste. So nice after coming in from the cold. I like going from cold to warm."

Jonathan added, "You're adjusting nicely to living here. Would you like to go to a Christmas Eve church service? And if you can wait, you can open your Christmas presents on Christmas morning."

Renee stopped nibbling before saying, "Rainforest tribes don't have a Christmas. Life too hard to give presents. And we don't make plans for future. Life too short and tribes too busy surviving."

Electra carried on because Jonathan seemed at a loss for what to say.

"You've learned lots about what living in America is like. It's often confusing, but it has its rewards if you don't get carried away by all the changes going on. We should always remember to be ourselves and take care of one another. And that's what living with Jonathan and me is all about."

"I like it. Can I have more hot chocolate?"

"Coming right up…"

Renee delighted in the Christmas Eve and Day festivities that included Eve's late afternoon Christmas dinner invitation. The adults remained at the table while Amahl took Renee and Zara to the family room so they could play one of his new computer games.

Nari spoke first, and her gloomy look came with matching words.

"I'm trying to get a handle on next year's political front so we can give good advice to clients, but I'm stuck. I haven't shown Eve what I've come up with because I didn't want to spoil the Holidays, but maybe the three of us could meet at the office day after tomorrow. Will that work?"

Everyone looked at Electra, who said,

"Let's do it first thing that morning and—" Electra stopped because Amahl had just burst in.

"Hey, can Renee stay for a couple of days? We can do a lot, and Zara can take us to some of the malls if we want."

After glancing first at Eve and Nari, and then Jonathan, Electra said, "That should be fun for everyone."

Amahl trotted away to spread the good news.

Eve and Nari prepped at home for tomorrow's office meeting while Zara took the adolescents to a nearby mall, but after an hour, Eve noticed Nari's humorless face had taken a turn toward the negative and tried to lighten the mood.

"We didn't plan our four siblings' traditional yearend conference call this year. You told me Nila's swamped because the pediatrician just diagnosed her son's autism, and Alonzo's last Email said his SEAL team is on call most of the time, but why don't we call Monet? It's noon here, which means it's 7 p.m. Harare time, so no matter what Alonzo's up to, she should be home. We can get her slant on what to expect next year. You can use in your writeup what she says."

"That might help. Why don't you set it up so we can see her and vice-versa?"

"I can do that…"

Nari perked up when Monet answered. Eve led the small talk and then let Nari take over.

"I'm stuck coming up with my forecast for next year's political landscape. You're as smart as us and have a better international lens than everyone in DC, so what's your take on the U.S.?"

Monet's diplomacy-shaped voice colored every syllable as she said,

"It will dance to the tune played by your presidential election, and your four political parties are using the same sheet music. Your politicians focus too much on the domestic challenges caused by cancel culture, critical race theory, social justice, and its accompanying ethics. And most look so hypocritical to me and my international contacts when they say they're making the best choices for the people, when their choices are meant to win reelection."

Monet paused to spark a reply that came from Eve.

"Yeah, and Nari's trying to find a better approach that'll get us a consulting assignment with some party's candidate."

Eve stopped because Nari looked ready to talk.

"What about the international scene? What's it like for you?"

"African nations are untroubled by most of the turmoil stirring on other continents. Zimbabwe is deliberately playing the U.S. against China and picking whatever side gives us the most. Your government seems more intent on appeasement than on confrontation to forestall alliances of convenience among authoritarian regimes. And please pay attention to how the U.S.-China rivalry is elevating into outer space. Both are planning missions to Mars."

Monet paused again, and Eve said,

"Who do you think's winning this latest version of the cold war?"

"The lead swings back and forth, and neither I nor my contacts see a clearcut victor. America has longevity and ethics but wavers and is slow to act. China has momentum but nations worry about its intrusive surveillance and treatment of minorities. Why not have Nari factor this in to whatever she writes up?"

Nari shot back.

"I will. Let's end the call so we can get back to work, and you can get back to whatever you were doing. Say hi to Alonzo for us."

"I will, and please say hello to Nila for me, and also to Electra Kirchner. She seems like a worthy successor to Irani."

"Funny you say that. We're meeting with her tomorrow. And I'm sure Eve will stay in touch. Bye-bye...."

After puttering about with Jonathan the day after Christmas, Electra felt energized for next day's Eve-and-Nari meeting. She stopped for muffins and brownies on the drive to their office and then flounced into the conference room, bringing her enthusiasm plus a plateful of goodies, but judging from Nari's listless expression, decided to dial it back and let Eve lead the meeting. She popped the top on a Coke before Eve touched on yesterday's discussion with Monet and then deferred to Nari, who slid a handout to her audience.

"I'll talk you through the high points on each of the four pages and let you read through them later. And when you do, you'll see they're still a work in progress. Even Monet's views couldn't fill in the gaps. But anyway, turn to page one."

Page One

The Changing World Order Says
Washington's Political Game is Almost Over!

- Symptoms: Look at Current Events!
- World Order Changes According to Predictable 200-250 Year Cycles (Rise Peak Decline) that overlap for 20-40 Years. Current Cycle labeled "American World Order." Overlap is rife with Conflict/Uncertainty. It marks transition from Current Leading Nation to Next.
- Internal Conflicts caused by Inequality. External Conflicts caused by Rising Nation confronting Current Leader. Wars start Cycles. Victory goes to Nation with More Power than Rival. Victor dictates Rules of New World Order. Leader of Victor initially obtains Power via Revolution and then: Consolidates it by eliminating those who oppose; Establishes System and Institutions to make Strong Internal Government; Builds Military; Grows Capital Market by uniting Government, Military, and Important Companies; Determines best way to pick Successor of Leader.
- Eight Factors control Cycle by determining Power of Leading Nation: 1.Education and Work Ethic of People 2.People's Inventiveness/Technology 3.Economic Competitiveness 4. Economic Output 5. Share of Trade 6.Military Strength 7.Strength of Financial Center 8.Strength of Currency so it's World Reserve

Note that Factor 1 comprises: Leadership Character Rule of Law Low Corruption Resource Efficiency Openness to Global Thinking.

- Factor1 is the causal factor for Factor 2, etc.

"I see big problems ahead for America's place in the world order. World order follows 200-year cycles of growth, peak, and decline. When one cycle declines to its end, another starts. America leads the current cycle, but China's challenging because the eight factors driving the cycle are in its favor. Now flip to page two."

Page Two

These markers run sequentially along the arc from left to right:

1. New World Order Cycle begins. This begins the Cycle's Rise.
2. Peace, Prosperity, and Productivity reign at Home and spill into World.
3. Leading Nation uses Debt to fuel Productive Growth. This marks the Peak, but the Peak sows the seeds for the decline: People become too expensive and lose their jobs to Foreigners; People get "lazy" and lose their competitive edge; People want to consume more and work less; Children of Wealthy People aren't "tough."
4. Debt leads to Financial Bubble that causes Big Wealth Gap and then Bursts.
5. Other Nations copy what works and they become wealthy and competitive.
6. Leading Nation over-reaches and causes Financial Bubble that bursts, leading to Economic collapse. This begins the Decline.
7. Leading Nation prints Money and lives off Credit from Other Nations. A Rising Nation emerges; it will become the Next Leading Nation.

8. Hardships lead to Leading Nation's Internal Revolution. External Challenge caused by Rising Nation seizing opportunity to dethrone Leading Nation.
9. Confrontation leads to War. Current Leading Nation Defeated and Next Leading Nation along with its Allies force debt and political restructuring on loser.
10. Another New World Order Cycle begins.

"It lists the ten event markers running along the cycle, and as I said on page one, the eight factors sequentially feed into the next. Think of them forming a cause-and-effect chain that brings about the events. America's future looks grim. OK, now go to page three."

Page Three

What are the reasons for the decline of the American World Order? CONGRESS IS TO BLAME! HERE'S WHY:

- Collapse of Congress's civility and its inability to compromise lead to Legislative gridlock and derangement. Congress transitions from a Legislative Institution into a Delegator of Legislative Power that it gives to unelected bureaucratic State Agencies containing Subject Matter Experts. This Transition is the biggest threat to Democracy! America's Founding Fathers wanted to avoid legislative tyranny by having a Representative Government whose form would link Politician's self-interest to People's Public Interest / Common Good. They thought they could rein in Human Nature by setting up a Congressional legislative body that would uphold the Constitution by balancing the Executive, Legislative, and Judicial branches.
- But Congress can't handle the complications and complexities of the Issues it must legislate. It needs Subject Matter Experts who can analyze problems and

recommend decisions. So, Congress dumps Legislative Power into Regulatory Agencies! (Founding Father Thomas Jefferson expected Congress would suck in Power from Executive and Judicial branches, but instead it delegates Power to unelected bureaucratic SMEs. Jefferson misread human nature! Legislators will never ditch the Seven Deadly sins! They are merely human!

- CONSTITUTION IS OK, BUT AMERICA NEEDS A NEW FORM OF GOVERNMENT TO IMPLEMENT IT! THINK OF CONSTITUTION AS A MISSION STATEMENT, AND THE FORM OF GOVERNMENT AS THE INSTRUMENT FOR CARRYING OUT A PLAN TO MAKE THE CONSTITUTION REFLECT THE WILL OF THE PEOPLE.

"I list the reasons why America's leadership position is slipping. You can go over the bullet-points later, but for now, focus on what's in all caps. We can blame Congress, not the Constitution. And that takes us to the last page."

Page Four

SO, WHAT CAN AMERICA DO? I DON'T KNOW BECAUSE:
- ALL POLITICAL PARTIES (DEMOCRATIC, REPUBLICAN, GUARDIAN, REGEN) ARE MIRED IN CONSPIRACIES (BIG GOVERNMENT, BIG DATA, BIG BUSINESS, AND BIG MILITARY COVERTLY CONTROLLING EVERYTHING.)
- CONGRESS RELUCTANT TO DO WHAT IT SHOULD. THERE ARE TOO FEW STATESMEN / STATESWOMEN WILLING TO PUT THE COMMON GOOD AHEAD OF THEMSELVES. WHAT'S THE TRUTH? FAKE NEWS CONFUSES WHAT THE PEOPLE SHOULD BELIEVE.
- PEOPLE DON'T LIKE CONGRESS OR ADMINISTRATIVE STATE, BUT ARE UNWILLING TO MAKE THINGS BETTER BY "GETTING INVOLVED."

HOW CAN WE REVISE GOVERNMENT TO RESTORE THE POWER OF THE CONSTITUTION? SOME PROPOSED SOLUTIONS:

- STRONGMAN PRESIDENT?
- MORE POWER TO THE COURTS?
- TERM LIMITS FOR POLITICIANS AND LEGISLATIVE AGENCY SME'S?
- CAMPAIGN FINANCE REFORM?
- HOW TO RESTORE NON-DELEGATION LINCHPIN: FORCE CONGRESS TO LEGISLATE BY ACTUALLY DEBATING? HOW TO GET THE PEOPLE TO CONTROL CONGRESS?

ACCORDING TO JAMES MADISON'S ICONIC QUOTE: "If people were angels, there would be no need for government. And if angels were to govern, neither internal nor external controls on Government would be necessary."

Is it time for another Political Revolution, or is muddling through from one cycle to the next the best we can do?

THE BOTTOM-LINE SUMMARY FOR MAKING THE TOUGH DECISIONS TO KEEP AMERICA'S WORLD ORDER STRONG:

- EARN MORE THAN WE SPEND
- TREAT OTHERS WITH DIGNITY AND RESPECT.

DO YOU HAVE ANY IDEAS FOR MAKING CONGRESS WORK BETTER?

"Pay attention to what's underlined. That's where I need your help. I've tried to find steps Washington can take to reverse the decline, but I'm stumped. The bullet-points say why. And I don't know if my ideas about revising the Government are any good. So, the last all-caps line is a question for you. How can we make Congress work better?"

Electra spoke only to herself.

Way to go, Nari. Why not ask us to scale up thermonuclear fusion? I don't have time to help you right now. I'm too busy prepping for the Mars test launch. Sorry, Eve, you two will have to muddle through without me.

And she continued sitting like the Sphinx. When Eve saw that no words would be coming from Electra, she said,

"Uh, well, everyone's on break until next year. Why don't we reconvene sometime in January?"

Everyone agreed.

Chapter 20
January 2168
"The Up-And-Down Lift-Off"

Electra shelved thinking further about Eve and Nari because Jonathan insisted she focus on the NASA test launch, but an incoming mid-January call seemed to lower his stress level. He explained why to Electra after it ended.

"NASA's pushing the test back again, this time to mid-February. According to Commander Starling, a rocket engine subcontractor wanted to swap out a possibly faulty component. That gives me more time to master Aphrodite software and you more time to work on other stuff. Whatcha gonna look at?"

"Some DC consulting possibilities. Too bad we can't swap out politicians as easily as rocket components."

"Yes, that would be nice, but it's impossible when the rules of government keep getting batted about. I'll stick with NASA, which follows Newtonian principles and is unlike politics, which is Darwinian. I can't imagine how you manage working in both worlds, but you do, so good luck fixing DC..."

By now, Renee had become so acclimated to her new life that she could work semi-independently. Electra used some of the freed-up time to review Nari's papers, and she had read enough to call Eve the last week of the month. Eve's enthusiasm bubbled out as soon as she recognized Electra's voice.

"I was thinking about calling you, but you beat me to it. Let me get Nari so she can hear what you have to say."

"No, I don't have time to fend off her objections, so tell her after you think it through. Get ready to jot down some notes."

"I'm ready, go ahead."

"Please compliment Nari. The paper she walked us through has a lot to offer, so why don't the two of you build on it for coming up with ways to improve Congress? Do you know how she hit upon Federalist Paper number 85?"

Eve began stuttering an answer, but when she stopped without making any sense, Electra knew she didn't.

"Uh… what do you mean?"

"Look again at the pages where she mentions angels and men and human nature. The framers built into the Constitution a system of checks and balances to make sure elected officials kept their interests aligned with the greater good. So, here's what you and Nari should do. Comb through all 85 of the Federalist Papers and look for what the framers considered but didn't put in. And then, after reading through the Anti-Federalist Papers, find possible things that might be good to have in it today. You might come up with campaign platform issues a presidential candidate might push for."

"Which party?"

"That's for you and Nari to figure out, but I must ask you this. Do you know how the Federalist Papers connect to the origin of the Republican and Democratic parties?"

This time Eve didn't stutter; she simply said,

"No, tell me."

"The Federalists pushed for a limited government, using checks and balances to control its growth. They morphed into the Republican Party. The Anti-Federalists wanted a bigger government, and in the last century became known as the progressive party, which everyone recognizes as the Democrats."

Eve's tone sounded like she was regaining her intellectual footing.

"So, I can see that one of these parties might like what we come up with. But there are two other parties, and right now they all seem to have the same gridlock mentality. How do we handle that?"

"Look, the framers built gridlock into our form of government to keep it from taking too much control, but think about this. If the people like what you come up with, you'll be able to find a coalition of smart politicians among all the parties who can influence the others."

"But how?"

"Talk to Feather Trueson."

"Will you help us?"

"No. You and Nari need to take it from here."

There was a long pause until Eve's resolute words came through.

"You're right. When Irani was alive, I sometimes asked her for help rather than relying on myself. And she often did, but she's gone and you're not her, so Nari and I will rely on each other."

"I'm telling you the same thing. Just do it…"

The call, though brief, had drained much of Electra's emotional reserves, but downing a Coke and a couple of Oreos refilled enough for her to reconsider.

I do some of my best thinking when I'm exercising, so for the next couple of days I'll focus on Nari's writeup while working out. That'll lessen my depression caused by losing connection with my clone children. I'll come up with ideas that'll help Nari, and that'll help me feel better about myself. And I'll start now.

Electra could feel her running-generated endorphins kick in twenty minutes later.

I'm thinking faster already, and… wait a minute. I'm all set for the NASA test, so I can stop obsessing about contingency plans. If Jonathan asks for more help, I'll tell him I already have. It's time for him to break a sweat, not me.

Jonathan needed no help from Electra during the days before he and his partners would fly to Houston. He had reviewed several times everything regarding monitor control protocols and Aphrodite software, and NASA handled all travel-related details for his people. Only packing remained. He did his and Electra took care of hers and Renee's.

Jonathan exuded nothing but confidence when he and Electra entered the Boca Chica control center for the final pre-launch briefing led by the Mars Mission Program Director, who stood centered below the biggest among a cluster of monitors that would display critical mission status data. Sandwiched between Britt and Boomer, Jonathan concentrated on what the Director said, but Electra switched to the image on the big screen whenever the words bored her.

What a majestic monument to NASA technology. The gleaming silver launch vehicle stands 500 feet high and dwarfs the gantry and all support structures around it. Its guidance fins make it look like a twenty-second-century version of Constantin Brancusi's Bird in Flight sculpture. And sitting atop is the Mars Mission spaceship. Boomer will be the only person onboard for the test; dummies will fill the other seats. And although the rocket engines will be blasting away at the bottom, he's awfully close to catastrophe if they blow up. Let's hope launch blowups stay in the past

Boomer took Jonathan and his team to lunch afterward. Soon after sitting at a cafeteria table, he asked Renee,

"How would you like to ride that big stick of dynamite?"

"I might if I had a way to get out."

"Oh, I do. The software automatically separates the spaceship and takes control if there's engine failure, and if the spaceship gets into trouble, it automatically launches the escape pod and lands it. Simulations have concluded all systems work as advertised, and I sure hope Jonathan agrees."

"Yessir, my Aphrodite control software can handle whatever comes up or goes down. How do you like its simulated human interface?"

"I love the calm female voice coming from a face that shows some emotion fitting the situation. You say it's the same we'll have for all man-machine GUIs on the Mission?"

"It is, and Aphrodite's designed to learn even more as the mission proceeds. You're in good hands, and who knows, maybe I'll be invited into the control center sometime during the Mars mission."

"I'll ask Britt to ask the Director. After all, you're a friend of Electra, who'll be at a biometrics station, and you also have a great relationship with Aphrodite. And no matter what, the three of you will be there tomorrow during the test. I lift off at 9 a.m., so get set for a great show..."

"3, 2, 1, liftoff..." The computer-simulated voice went silent after the countdown as all eyes centered on the big screen that showed a gracefully balanced liftoff gaining velocity even faster than Electra anticipated.

It looks like a gigantic energy probe emerging from a bubbling, ground-hugging cloud and reaching for the sky. We're too far away to feel the vibrations, but the crowd gathered near must be swaying in its wake.

Jonathan's words ended her contemplation.

"The onboard camera images will kick in when it gets too far downrange to see much," and then both of them stayed silent.

But everyone in Mission Control switched to panic mode when the rocket started oscillating from the trajectory, like a drunk trying to walk in a straight line. It oscillated faster and farther; the cameras captured what was now an impending catastrophe, and then an enormous flash obliterated the bottom of the rocket when its engines blew to bits.

Jonathan screamed five seconds later when the top of the rocket blasted through the cloud of debris.

"She did it. Aphrodite launched the space capsule. Boomer's home free." But seconds later everyone saw the capsule's engines flame out, causing the entire mass to plunge earthward.

Everyone in Mission Control held their collective breath; the ground rushed to greet Boomer. But then, the secondary contingency kicked in. A mini-capsule blasted away.

Jonathan grabbed Electra's arm and yelled,

"She did it, she launched the escape pod. She'll guide Boomer to airstrip touchdown."

Cheers erupted from everyone in Mission Control before Britt's words broke through the pandemonium.

"All essential personnel, follow me to the touchdown site."

Electra towing Renee and Jonathan close behind double-timed to keep up. But a swarm of reporters flanked by camera crews got there first. One of them pulled Jonathan out for an on-location interview, hoping for a scoop. He shoved a mike at a beaming Jonathan; Electra and Renee stood aside.

"Tell me your name and role in the Mission."

"I'm Jonathan Segal, developer of the Aphrodite information control system."

"Do you live nearby and work for NASA?"

"No, I'm a Washington, DC subcontractor."

"What's your assessment of what went wrong?"

"We can't tell yet, but I can tell you what went right. My software just saved the crew."

"Congratulations. You must be a valuable commodity."

Caution finally caught up with Jonathan's pride.

"You can say that about everyone on the Mars mission."

"How nice of you to say that. You're a real team player. Good luck to you and the Mission…"

Britt called for a contingency meeting early that afternoon, announcing that key people must stay until they diagnose the failure and determine what date to push back the Mission launch. Jonathan was among Britt's picks but not Electra, so she took Renee back to the hotel.

They swam in the pool after lunch and then spent the rest of the day watching the news. Renee kept switching channels and counting how many showed Jonathan's interview. And before heading to dinner, she said,

"Jonathan's all over the place. Whatcha call him?"

"A celebrity. More people want to know about him."

"And that's good, isn't it?"

"I'll give you my favorite answer, 'Perhaps.' It depends on what happens to Jonathan and us. But please don't worry, there's usually a happy ending, and we'll find out soon enough…"

Chapter 21
March 2168

"The Terminal Man"

Jonathan's inadvertent publicity stunt generated so many inquiries during the following week that he joked about it, but only to Electra.

"I think I'll change my cell-phone number and give it only to those I want to hear from."

She kidded back,

"Make sure you call those on your VIP list before you do so you don't miss their latest revelations. Who'll be at the top?"

"I'd put you there, but I don't need to because you'd know it as soon as the phone company Emailed it. But my NASA contacts would be near the top. And I just reminded myself to call Bruno. I'll do it right now. Bye-bye."

Jonathan dialed his number right after Electra disconnected.

"I so pleased you call. You a popular guy after blast, but I hope you still work on climate change with me."

"Indeed yes, and I have associates who might have other opportunities for you and Brazil."

"Who might that be?"

"My female associate you've already met, Electra Kirchner. She told me she'll call you when all details are flanged up."

"Ho-kay, amigo. I be ready too. You stay safe."

Jonathan placed one more call that day to another VIP, Professor Plannert, who also complimented Jonathan for his interview performance and then gave him the date for the next Committee meeting. Jonathan promised to be there.

Jonathan's interview did affect Electra, but in a good way. It freed up more of her time because it diverted his attention away from her, but she wouldn't know if a late March NASA call she answered might change the balance because Commander Starling wanted to talk to him. She handed Jonathan the phone, but didn't eavesdrop because she knew he would tell her what Starling wanted.

And when he began doing as soon as the call ended, his expression changed to match his first words, which sounded like an apology for enjoying a guilty pleasure.

"Guess what? The failed launch data analysis recommends changes to inflight monitoring protocols. The program director wants me and the techs manning the higher-priority stations to report back for more training next week. I asked if that includes you, but the answer's no. Sorry, but Aphrodite did so well that I'll monitor the biometrics too. You're not mad, are you?"

"Why would I be? I told you way back when that I want you to take credit for our software. I prefer staying in the shadows. When do you plan to leave?"

Electra found an online calendar, and they peered at it long enough for Jonathan to say,

"Next Saturday, and if all goes according to plan, I should return by the 16th, which is a week later. And how about this? Maybe you can call Bruno during that week."

"I will, as soon as I know that Eve's ready. I think she's planning to call me the week your gone."

"Fair enough. Well, I better start adjusting my to-do list."

Electra used Jonathan's week away to work on Deus Lab projects while finalizing ideas for Eve. And of course, she devoted a chunk of time to Renee, who said at the kitchen table during Friday's dinnertime,

"Jonathan sounded bouncy when he called us when he got there, but he didn't call again. You think he's OK?"

"He's that way. He focuses on what he's doing and ignores everything else. And he hates interruptions, so we won't call him. But please don't worry. we'd hear from him or Commander Starling if there was a problem. He'll be home soon enough…"

Jonathan's high-priority training week gave him everything needed to boost his knowledge and ranking among the high-priority technicians. So much, in fact, that he volunteered to stay the following week for as long as he could contribute. He and three others were there on Thursday afternoon when Commander Starling ended the session.

"Thanks to all of you for your dedication to our Mars Mission. We expect your roles in it and subsequent missions to grow, commensurate with your efforts and abilities. We'll contact you as soon as we make final adjustments to the launch date, so please travel and stay healthy and safe until then."

Feeling supercharged after hearing such praise, Jonathan rushed back to the hotel and called the airline to change his return from tomorrow morning to a late-night flight. Then he called the front desk to check out after packing his carry-on, but he chose not to call Electra until his flight actually takes off.

Jonathan had concentrated so much on all these rushed changes that he forget to eat something, so while driving his rental car to the airport terminal, he decided to stop for a late-night snack on the way. Focusing on the menu, he paid little attention to people sitting in other booths, but one pair of nondescript carbon-copy fellows gazed surreptitiously at him.

"So, he's the data control guy whose Aphrodite software makes him special. We'll grab him in the parking lot and take him to a special place so he can unload all he knows. Bigger Brother will be happy to hear…"

Jonathan reached the car but never got in. A traser-bolt of electricity stiffened him like a statue, collapsing him backward into stupor-like oblivion.

Slaps and water splashed on his face brought Jonathan's consciousness back; he didn't know the time or place, but he did sense two men sitting across from him at a table, even though a white-hot spotlight nearly blinded him. He felt the rope binding him to a chair, and a helmet strapped to his head. And then he heard gruff-sounding words.

"Mr. Jonathan Segal, you the Aphrodite expert. Where you going?"

"Teh-to the airport terminal. I'm heading back to DC."

"Well, Mr. Terminal Man, how come you so smart? How come you write software? We want a copy. Kapish?"

Jonathan shook his head to clear it as well as to answer the questions.

"I, uh, I didn't write it. I just know how to use it."

"So, who wrote it?"

"I don't know. It gets loaded automatically for me to use."

"So where is it loaded? Can you get us a copy?"

Jonathan pulled against the rope, testing his predicament and delaying his answer. He sensed that both could be deadly.

"I don't know… I don't know… I'm not the one to ask."

"So, who is?"

"I don't know that either."

"Jonathan sensed electric jolts hitting his brain a moment before he heard the voice speak again.

"We tickle out of your head what we want, whether you're conscious or not. We start now…"

Jonathan's reality went blank several seconds later.

Electra answered the call mid-morning on Saturday while she and Renee were at their home workstations. Recognizing the caller I.D., she said,

"Hi Britt, I bet you're calling to let us know Jonathan's on his way home."

Hearing nothing but silence for too long, Electra's happy thoughts melted away when Britt's leaden-sounding words came through.

"Something happened. He's the victim of a fatal hit-and-run accident. The state police found his body late last night, and here's what they told me…"

Electra said nothing, waiting for Britt to wind up.

"So there, you now have everything I know. This is a stunner, for you as well as for our Mission. Why don't we do this? You call me back with burial plan info when ready, and I'll arrange for his body to be sent back. And I'll call you in a couple of weeks because we need you to take his place. Will that work for you?"

"I guess. I'll call you back within the day. Bye."

Renee could sense Electra's collapsed mood and asked,

"Something bad happen?"

"Yes, dear. I'll tell you after I make arrangements for Jonathan's homecoming…"

Electra had plenty of experience doing that and picked what she knew Jonathan would prefer: cremation and a one-day private wake. Using the power of the Internet, Electra made them and then relayed the information to Britt. Then she took Renee out for dinner.

Electra didn't talk to her during the drive because Jonathan's death had upset her even more than she thought possible, and she needed to get her emotions under control, so she took slow, deep breaths and peered at the road ahead while talking to herself.

If someone had told me a year ago that Jonathan would die like this and nothing could be done to avoid it, would I feel any less devastated than I do now? Didn't my birth-mother Indira write a poem about this, a poem about great sorrow and loss? She did, and perhaps I can remember some of its comforting lines… now I remember…

And though often told that this loss would unfold,
No preparation could soften or lessen or put in remission,
This grief I am feeling that sends my soul reeling,
This loss of the precious that cuts to the bone,
This loss of the priceless that's all mine to own."

I better find a way for Renee to share her grief. Even though her daily contact with Jonathan and me dims the glow emanating from love, death is the gravest shock, the ultimate discontinuity disrupting life's flow. What'll I say or do?…

Electra only hinted at dinner what she had been doing that afternoon, doing her best to shield Renee from the jolt that Jonathan's death would bring.

But she found a better time several hours after returning home, Renee sitting listlessly in front of her workstation, simply staring at a blank screen. Electra placed a chair next to her and sat. Then she said,

"I know you felt the pain of death when it struck people in your Amazon tribe. Well, that just happened to us. Jonathan is dead, and I've been busy making arrangements. Here in America, we hold wakes and funerals for family members to share grief and stories about the people we lose. What ritual or ceremony did your tribe hold?"

Renee's words matched her listless look.

"No time to do that. We too busy just surviving."

"Well, I know you miss him. I do too, so why don't we share some of our memories?"

Renee's sobbing hug said she needed more than that.

"Please, please, never die, you're all I've got..."

Electra's hug matched Renee's, and when the tears subsided said,

"I promise to do my best..."

Electra did her best until bedtime, helping Renee remember the best of Jonathan, and that helped her too.

Alisha reminded her while attempting to sleep.

Your and Robin's grieving for Christi happened a lifetime before the lightning brain summoned me, but my empathy can reach back to what you felt then, and even further to when Doc Kittner and Jason died. You've been through a lot, but try to remember what Nietzsche said about getting stronger. That'll help you fall asleep.

Electra tossed and turned until nearly three, when slumber descended, ending her sad reverie.

I remember his famous quotation—What does not kill me makes me stronger. I can live with that. And I'll add mine to it—Tomorrow I'll handle the things that must be.

Chapter 22
April 2168

"The Chinese Challenge"

Jonathan's death occurred so close to Easter that Electra mentioned it before talking to Renee about the life of Jesus and the meaning of Easter. She explained that sacred books, like the Christian Bible or the Islamic Koran, might contain allegories, which are stories in which characters and events are meant for narrative interpretations rather than literal descriptions because they represent deep moral messages about values and beliefs.

Renee didn't ask questions; instead, she simply sat and listened, but when she started fidgeting forty-five minutes later, Electra paused for a deep breath that gave her a moment to figure out what to say next.

I've talked enough. I'm starting to bore her. Her inherent intelligence and exponentially expanding understanding of English and vocabulary make her reasoning and comprehension almost like a college student. I better segue into something different.

"And that's the story. Would you like to ask a question?"

"Not about Jesus. Rainforest tribes have no stories about people coming back to life, but they do gaze at the Moon and stars. And you say Easter always falls on the first Sunday after a special full Moon in spring. But in America, I never see stars, not even on a clear night. Why not?"

"Because of light pollution that people cause. Think of pollution as the spilling of unwanted things into the natural environment, such as light at night, bad chemicals or loud sounds released into the air, and junk pitched into rivers, lakes, and oceans. Have you noticed much pollution here besides light at night?"

"Sometimes funny smells, and always loud noises. But I guess it comes with how people in America live."

"That's a great thought, and just like climate change, America's trying to reduce all kinds. Maybe you'll want to work on that someday."

"Maybe, if you do too."

Jonathan's celebrity status had died down well before his hit-and-run demise, so it didn't make the news, nor did NASA include it in any Mars Mission press releases. Electra's Cyberspace snooping didn't uncover any correlation with encrypted covert Internet traffic either, but she never stopped looking for unusual traffic patterns and always used Eve's suggestions or news reports for clues.

That's why an April 1st noon DC-time news bulletin alerting the world that China would broadcast live a special message only during Washington's late-evening news slots was now spreading like a raging virus across all media outlets. The bulletin gave no hints regarding the topic or the speaker, so every mainstream media news anchor delighted its audience by filling in the blanks.

Renee sat next to Electra on the sofa in front of the family room's widescreen monitor, waiting for the news to begin. Electra had already explained that some of the alarmist anchors had predicted China was about to make the China-America Superpower Cold War hot, and even trusted ones used sobering tones when priming their audience.

When Electra's trusted anchor now giving a preview tried to lighten the mood, Renee asked a question even before he finished.

"What's funny about April 1st?"

Electra couldn't answer right away, so she paused to think.

I should have expected her to ask but I didn't, so I better come up with an answer right now… I've got it. I'll make it sound official… She'll understand…Here goes.

"Although the day is often called All Fools' Day, people in cultures around the world have celebrated it for many centuries by playing tricks on each other. For example, on April 1, 1700, English pranksters made the day popular by pulling practical jokes and tricks, but the exact origin remains a mystery."

"OK, thanks."

Electra didn't say anything because the anchor started his introduction.

"And now, we bring you this message delivered by the President of China."

The screen image switched to the serious-looking China President sitting behind a desk and facing the camera. Folded Chinese flags mounted on the wall added to his presidential image.

"I wish to announce another Chinese technological triumph. Our Mission to Mars will land our taikonauts, or as you say astronauts, very soon. We have withheld telling you in order to avoid any attempt by America to deliberately escalate the space race competition, but the world is bigger than merely America, so the entire international community should know.

"We are proud of our accomplishments. America must adjust to what we are doing, and I must point out that Chinese political scholars have studied America's founding fathers' Federalist Papers to look for ways we can improve further our form of government. America should do the same. We shall give updates as our Mission continues, and you will see why the future belongs to China. Thank you for hearing my words."

Renee spoke as soon as the broadcast ended.

"I bet NASA will pay attention to this."

"And I won't bet against you…"

The buzz died down after a couple of days, but Electra increased her Cyberspace snooping. She looked for potential connections between President Kinslinger and the Chinese Mars Mission or any clues that might lead to a Bigger Brother conspiracy. She didn't find anything solid enough for Nari and Eve but decided to call her internationally savvy contact Monet, who always had insights into impending international events. After exchanging the usual pleasantries, Electra honed in on China.

"What do you make of China's Mission to Mars?"

"Until we see some actual results, it's nothing but a Chinese promotion."

"I agree, and I found a couple of Cyberspace links that Alonzo might like to check. If he digs deep enough, he might send it up the chain of command, and if there's enough of a security risk, his team might get permission to investigate Would you be willing to send the links to him?"

"Of course I will, and in return, could you tell me if there's anything new regarding water-borne viruses? We might have one spreading along the Congo River."

Monet paused; Electra matched her diplomatic style by saying,

"One of my Brazilian associates might have a similar issue. Shall I have him call you?"

"Please do…"

Satisfied that she had done enough Cyberspace snooping, Electra turned her attention to the Deus Lab, which needed an indoor conservatory to house the plants, insects, and fish she and Renee had brought back. She placed a call to Rich Tabasko, who listened to what she wanted before asking,

"Do PH and me need to wear masks or gloves to keep from getting infected?"

"No, I've already tested what we brought back. Just wear gloves and long-sleeve shirts. And besides, Renee will put them in."

"Who's Renee?"

"She came back with me from the Amazon. Please call me back when you're ready to start…"

Alonzo's commander took action as soon as Alonzo explained what his covert links might be hiding; three weeks later, Alonzo's team got the green light to launch their own mission. His commander explained what the eight-person detachment needed to know just before embarking.

"Timing's everything. China's videos are now boasting and showing their astronauts walking on Mars, so we're gonna blow their cover. Our target's a remote coastal installation 500 clicks from Beijing on the Yellow Sea's Bo Hai Bay. Reconnaissance shows minimal fortification or security. One of our stealth subs will carry you close enough for a night launch using two high-speed inflatable landing craft, each equipped with an ATV to get to and from the target. One team leads and the other is contingency backup. And our mission is to bring back, without being detected, proof of installation activity."

Expecting an obvious question, he paused for someone to ask it, which Alonzo did.

"What's the contingency plan if something blows our cover?"

"I'll let your mission leader tell you."

"Terminate with extreme prejudice. We'll carry M16A2 compact carbines and pack enough plastic explosives to bring the house down and destroy any equipment we have to leave behind. But all eight come back."

The commander ended the briefing.

"And you SEALS know how to improvise if need be. Any questions?"

There were none.

The tension of an actual mission always elevated Alonzo's awareness, and tonight, the surfaced sub's rocking motion continued winding his energy spring while the teams inflated two landing craft and then slipped them into the black swells swishing silently past. Then they swung the ATVs into place and jumped in, and then the inflatables raced toward an unseeable shore a mile away.

The moonless night held enough starlight for Alonzo and his team to prep for landing. SEAL training had transformed them into a machine whose sum exceeded the pieces.

They beached the crafts and unloaded the ATVs that already carried weapons and explosives. The eight then locked hands in a circle for each man to repeat his role before the lead team climbed into their ATV and sped toward the target whose outline they could see on the flat surface that stretched beyond the beach.

Alonzo and his backup teamers had to stifle their pent-up energy while huddling to listen for terse reports crackling in. Most of Alonzo hoped to hear "Mission accomplished," but a piece of him wanted to hear "Backup needed." That message came in countless minutes later. The radioman alerted the team what to expect as they sped to an uncertain rendezvous. Alonzo would place explosives if his team leader made the call.

Rat-a-tat-tat gunfire steered them to the action, and they bailed out when reaching the other ATV. Moving in unison like choreographed dancers following a military drill, the eight rounded up the handful of guards.

And then, the leader snapped out what the eight needed to know.

"The building looks like a Hollywood studio. Inside's a fake Martian landscape, complete with landers and rovers. Cameras, record everything from the inside. Muscles, drag one rover back here, and Plastics, wire for remote detonation."

With flashlights glaring, the eight raced into the building. Someone found a light switch that turned them into men on Mars. Jonathan placed charges while the rest of his team carried out their assignments. Twenty minutes later, the eight loaded all gear and hooked a towline to the rover, then climbed aboard and headed back to the beach. Alonzo pushed the detonate button when given the command, and eight SEALS watched Mars explode.

No additional fireworks accompanied the ride back to the sub...

Electra was about to update her Deus Lab schedule when a news commentator interrupted the late-evening broadcast playing in the background.

"We have a just-released independent video reporting startling news about China's Martian Mission. It appears that the whole escapade is a publicity hoax. As you can see, an investigation team is walking at the very site China claims their lander touched down. They even brought back a Chinese rover. We expect to see and hear more from our government as well as from China. Please stay tuned for additional details as they come to us..."

Electra and Commander Starling had already talked several weeks ago about Electra's filling Jonathan's role during the Mars Mission, but she expected another after hearing the latest news. Britt called the next morning and sounded like she wouldn't mince words.

"With all the fake news and virtual videos out there, I wonder what other space-race hoaxes are lurking. Maybe India and Russia are cooking something up. But at least we know China's out of the picture for the time being. And we've readjusted our launch date to New Year's Eve. What do you think about that?"

"It must have been picked for maximum publicity, but if the launch fails, NASA's reputation will suffer big-time."

"And that's why you and Aphrodite are so important. I know we can count on you. Please make sure you're ready."

"I promise I will."

"Good. Please talk with me or Boomer at least once a week. Stay safe."

Electra thought to herself after Commander Starling ended the call.

I'm sure she meant the call to be a pepper-upper, but it came across as a pressure stepper-upper. I'll have to make sure my nerves don't buckle. I wish I could match my previous fitness levels, but even with all my exercising, I can't do it.

Well, I'll just keep doing the best I can. But even the best pro athletes have to step aside sometime. Someday, I'll have to rely on backups or retire, but not yet.

President Newt Kinslinger had more to worry about than the other Gang of Three Plus One listeners tuned in to the encrypted call dominated by Xing. He found her summary particularly chilling.

"Of course, Bigger Brother knew about the Martian Mission hoax. It's part of our plan to disrupt all adversarial alliances. But we don't know how or who hacked in. Our counter-intelligence experts suspect someone in the United States but haven't found the person, and we want to know who it is. President Kinslinger, please put that at the top of your list, even ahead of your reelection campaign. I expect you to uncover the culprit. Call me as soon as you do."

Entertaining no questions, Xing ended the call.

Newt refilled his glass, but this time he added no soda to the scotch.

Chapter 23
June 2168

"Calls for Alarm"

Electra had kept all projects running smoothly during the previous month or two, coordinating usually via cell phone and occasionally in person with associates who needed assistance, and progress had increased their confidence while decreasing the pressure on her, so she had no reason to be alarmed when Professor Plannert called not long after his last committee meeting.

After thanking her again for assuming Jonathan's role, his tone grew serious when saying,

"That young female environmental sciences professor reports alarming weather patterns for the coming months. Jonathan had a knack for predicting them using his software that processed weather satellite data. Might you give us an update at our July meeting?"

"I'll do even better. I'll send you a summary by the fourth of July and present the details at the next meeting."

"Splendid, I shall inform the Committee to expect and your analysis. Thank you so much."

Electra had never divulged, not even to Jonathan, that doing the requisite analysis required simply a discussion with Indira, whose constant updates to pieces of the Aphrodite software uploaded into the satellites kept its forecasts beyond state-of-the-art. Indira had everything Electra needed a day later.

"You can tell Plannert to compliment that professor. The upcoming summer should be much hotter than what the other forecasts predict. And you can make it more granular. Spell out in your writeup that America's Midwest and western Europe will face severe heat and drought while Africa fares better. Rainfall should be plentiful and temperature closer to the new normal."

"Thank you, and as a token of my constant appreciation, I shall devote more time to our Android Project on my next visit to the Deus Lab."

"That is always appreciated. Now do your writeup, but don't send it until the deadline."

Electra deadpanned her reply.

"Yes, Mother, I shall obey your command…"

Electra completed the paper two days later and was in the midst of preparing for next week's trip to the Deus Lab when a call from Eve came in, her words a mix of excitement tinged with concern.

"Guess what? The Democratic presidential candidate loved just about all the platform points Nari included in the presentation she delivered to his campaign committee, especially the bit about the Federalist and Anti-Federalist Papers. They just hired us to work on his platform."

"Congratulations. I'm sure the two of you will exceed expectations."

"Thanks, and we better if we want to cut through all the campaign clutter. It's especially important this year if we want to break through with better domestic and international approaches. If we do it first, we'll paint Kinslinger into a couple of corners he'll have trouble getting out of."

"What's the latest on him?"

"Sort of same-old-same-old, but if you have something new, please tell us. And do you have time to look at the points we'll put in the platform?"

"As a matter of fact, I do. Please send them to me and I'll get back to you. OK?"

"Thanks, Nari will be delighted."

By the time RT and PH arrived the following day, Electra and Renee had everything arranged so the greenhouse construction could begin as soon as the fellows reviewed the layout. Already knowing much about them, Renee quizzed RT as the foursome walked through the lab.

"Electra told me you like to play with octopuses when in water and slide down snowy mountains. I like to play with spiders and catch fish. And I like water better than snow. Warm is better than cold."

PH, who was on her right, replied,

"How do you keep from getting bit?"

"I jiggle while carrying-em. I'll show you how when you're ready." Two days later she did so, and after releasing them said,

"And Electra knows where you can take me to get fish and insect food, and maybe another couple of spiders."

RT said,

"How about PH takes you while Electra and I keeping working here?"

Electra said,

"OK with me if PH agrees." It was, so PH drove to the specialty pet store Electra had used years ago for her octopus family.

After admiring the tropical fish and insect display, Renee picked out two palm-sized tarantulas and told PH more.

"Electra says tarantulas have been around since dinosaur days, and Amazon species are the biggest spiders on Earth. Some can live for thirty years. And they don't contain venom. I like their hairy legs. They tickle when they walk on me. You wanna hold one?"

PH flinched ever so slightly when saying,

"Not here, but maybe when we get back. I'll let you carry them. And I'll treat you to some ice cream on the way."

PH had to settle for a dingy diner on the town's outskirts but didn't pay attention to the scruffy clientele because Renee kept asking him questions. She stopped long enough to eat her hot fudge sundae, and then continued talking all the way back to the truck while carrying her package, but two hooded-sweatshirt guys stopped them when they reached it. One showed the barrel of a gun while the other did the talking.

"You look like you can spare a couple of bucks. How 'bout it?"

PH was about to raise the ante, but quick-witted Renee caught them off guard by saying,

"Can I show you my pets? You'll like them," just before throwing a spider at the chest of each.

Flailing arms and screams followed as they leaped backward and the gun hit the pavement. PH grabbed it, Renee retrieved the spiders, and the toughs ran as if a pack of dino-raptors were about to eat them for dinner.

PH let Renee tell the story of the fight when they got back to the Lab, adding an embellishment here and there to complement her unadorned narration and making her a celebrity that night.

She and Electra departed back to DC after breakfast. RT and PH would report to Feather when they finished and would ask her to let Electra know. Electra used the beginning of the drive-time to tell Renee whom they'd talk with next. Then she explained why.

"Eve and Nari are consulting for the Democratic Party's presidential candidate. They have some good ideas they'll discuss with us that will help get him elected. And if he wins, he'll be the leader of our Nation.

Electra spied a questioning look, so she waited for Renee to ask,

"Why does he want to be the leader? Tribal leaders in the Amazon have to work long and hard, and sometimes get killed in battles or while hunting."

"Well here in America, our lifestyle lets us develop people who want to take charge, and the best compete for the honor of leading the nation. Think of an election as a fight for the top spot."

"But what if the guy who loses thinks the other guy cheated?"

"We have rules and laws that settle the complaint. Why not ask Eve for more info when we see her?"

Renee's "I will," ended that piece of the drive-time chat, and after that, Electra reminded they'd sight-see in DC during the Fourth of July celebration.

Renee said,

"That'll be fun. Zara told me all about that Holiday. Maybe you can invite her and Amahl to come along."

"Good idea. She can tell us what we're seeing…"

Electra completed all DC-related activities ahead of schedule, so she took Renee back to Austin three weeks later, which would be several days ahead of a heat wave sweeping from west to east across America, and its arrival dominated the news.

Renee's burgeoning fascination with America glued her to nightly news, which often provoked questions for Electra's thought-filled replies. Tonight's news provoked questions about connections between climate change, immigration, and the upcoming election.

"Why are so many Americans afraid of heat? What they think is hot, rainforest people say feels nice, maybe because we have lots more water."

"That's a wonderful observation. America's midsection's suffering from a combination of too much heat and too little rain, and that'll cut into crops."

"And why don't more people like immigrants? I'm one, and people sorta like me."

"They do when they get to know them. Then they see they're just like us, trying to make a life for themselves and their families. It's a shame this heat wave's making the trek from South America to the Texas border wall deadly for some. I feel so sorry for all of them, but the ones bussed to Austin have a better shot at becoming legal aliens. That's why there are protests going on near the Capitol.

"Can we go see?"

Electra thought for a moment before saying,

"That'll be a great civics lesson. We'll go on Saturday. Maybe it'll be cooler by then."

But temperatures and passions on both sides elevated during the week. Electra gripped Renee's hand as marching immigrants paraded by, but Renee shook free and ran into the crowd. Electra fought the urge to rush after her, instead trusting the girl's common sense.

Renee returned minutes later, bringing back a strikingly similar younger girl, whose mother trooped behind. Renee pulled the girl to Electra before saying,

"They came all the way from Brazil. Can we take them home?"

Renee's request stunned the lightning brain. Electra said nothing for nearly too long before saying,

"I-I can't take care of everyone. It's too—" Renee interrupted.

"It's not everyone, it's just two. And I can teach them about English and living in America, and so what if they're all raggedy. I'll help make-em better. Please?"

Alisha's voice rang out inside the lightning brain.

Remember the Biblical teaching in Matthew 25 verse 40. Whatever you do for the least, you do for me.

And Indira would approve. The mother will take care of the place and look after the kids while you can do more work on Indira's favorite projects. And Renee's no longer a child.

Suitably refortified, Electra said,

"You're right. Let's do it."

Electra led her group to a government monitoring station, telling the official in charge she wanted to sponsor the woman and daughter. She in turn told Electra what to do as soon as possible, and then Electra drove them home.

Renee helped them shower and dress, using some of her and Electra's clothes, and then Electra took them to an uncrowded McDonalds. Sitting between mother and daughter and facing Electra, Renee did all the talking. Electra listened to Renee while musing to herself.

Indira's taught her way more ethics and philosophy than I thought. She might not know it, but she's doing what Camus' existential philosophy advises or T.S. Eliot's poetry alludes. And if so, she is truly Rousseau's Noble Savage, which places her above me. Someday when she's ready, I'll tell her about my post post-modern philosophy that I've labeled Quantum+NeuroSci-Extended Deconstructed Emergent Post-Kantian/Pragma/Phenomenological Synthesis—or QNS-Edep-K/P/P Synthesis to make it catchier.

It's better than what most post-modern academics spout. Mine is optimistic and pragmatic, and it can help people get on with their lives, but I misspoke when I said it's catchier. People are too busy to play catch with philosophy. But they don't have to with mine. Just apply some common sense to the guidelines given by Neuroscience and be done with it.

Renee handled sleeping arrangements that night. Everyone went to bed early except Electra, who decided to sit at her workstation, enjoying the solitude while letting her lightning brain freewheel. After doing so for an hour, she rose to get a bedtime snack, but Renee tiptoed toward her, bringing with her a troubled look. Electra talked as soon as Renee stood close.

"You've had quite a day, and sometimes, people have trouble sleeping when they do. Why don't we sit so you can tell me what's on your mind?"

Electra seated herself again at her workstation; Renee joined her, shifting from side to side, and several minutes later she looked like she had sifted through enough words to begin talking.

"I listened to the Christmas and Easter stories. People say some religions can explain what they mean, and I heard the same when Jonathan died, but Indira hasn't started teaching me about the Bible yet, and I'm all confused. Could you please help me understand?"

Electra rested her hand on Renee's knee and began talking.

"I knew the time would come when you would ask because everyone struggles at least once in their lives when something disruptive happens that brings death or God into the picture, and I've prepared for our talk by jotting down some thoughts. They fit on one page that I'll print for you."

Electra tapped on a couple of keys; a minute later she and Renee each pinched between their fingers on opposite edge of the page. Renee's eyes followed where Electra pointed when she talked again.

God and Religion in Your Life

God and Religion help us understand the world we live in. Some of it we can see; others we can only feel, but in either case they can comfort us.

There are different religions. Some have one God, others have many. Which one to believe in is a personal choice.

There are two main types of religions: those of the Eastern Orient, like Buddhism, which is found in China and India, and those of the West. That's where you find Christianity, Judaism, and Islamism.

Eastern Religions are holistic and cyclic. Each of us is connected to the Universe, and we cycle repeatedly, starting at birth and then growing to reach a peak, and then declining until we die. But we can be happy knowing that we'll be born again.

Western Religions are different. We are born and grow and decline and die. And when we die, we go to a place called Heaven if God chooses us.

The Bible gives us a foundation for Western Religions. It is divided into two parts: the Old and New Testaments.

Old Testament tells us how God created the World. Names you'll hear about: Adam and Eve, Noah, Abraham, Moses, David.

Important New Testament names: Jesus, the Virgin Mary, Saint Paul. The Apostles.

Important New Testament beliefs:

The trinity of God–God the Father, God the Son (Jesus), and God the Holy Ghost (the experience or feeling we get when God touches our life).

Jesus lived more than 2,000 years ago and taught people a new way to live (today we call it Christianity). He died to redeem us from our sins. God brought him back to life (resurrected) and he now sits on the right side of God in Heaven.

We are Resurrected from the dead by the Grace of God if we believe in him and lead a righteous life. (Righteous means we follow the Bible's teachings.)

The Catholic Church grew from the seeds of Christianity sown by the Apostles. Catholic church leaders are Priests, Bishops, Cardinals, and Popes. They lead their congregations (believers), teaching and telling them what to believe and do.

Important Historical Events of the Catholic Church:

In the early 1500s, Martin Luther protested the bad practices of the Catholic Church and that led to the Protestant Reformation and new religions (Protestant religions).

These religions added new beliefs that sprang up during the Renaissance. (15th and 16th centuries).

More were added during the Enlightenment (17th to mid-19th centuries). Rationalism and Science sprang to life, and their findings questioned whether God exists. New philosophies emerged because philosophers rejected religious beliefs supported only by Faith or the Pope's Authority. Philosophers placed more importance in each individual (called the "Turn to the Subject"). Religions softened their teachings by emphasizing caring for people (Humanitarianism.) This became the foundation for Modern Religion, which is the handmaiden of Modern Philosophy. (Philosopher Immanuel Kant's efforts to reconcile Faith and Reason become Modern Philosophy's starting point.)

That worked up to mid-20th century. Two world wars, economic collapses, and the rise of Authoritarian governments put all Western religions into disarray. And ever since then, Christian Religions have become an invitation for people to embark on a personal life journey in which Religion can help heal ourselves by teaching each of us to love one another, especially the victims of our innate lust for power and our desire to dominate the "other".

"I titled it 'God and Religion in Your Life,' and I've written short paragraphs for the points that will help you the most when first learning about it. There are many more, but just going over what's on the page takes a lot of time to absorb, so why don't we do this? I'll talk while you just listen for at most twenty minutes, or until you've heard enough. And when I'm done, I want you to keep the page and think about it tomorrow or whenever you wish. And then we'll go over it again whenever you like."

"OK, I'd like that."

Electra did her part; fifteen minutes later, Renee hugged her before gliding off to bed.

Electra stayed awake longer, musing more through the night, bringing clarity for action when Sunday dawned bright.

Chapter 24
September 2168

"Calls for Action"

Electra's personal and professional worlds stayed centered through September, but not so for the rest of the nation. Unforeseen events reported on nightly news added to a litany of woes, causing the world to come undone. Renee and Electra were sitting with their Brazilian guests while taking in a summary as gloomy as the reporter's voice on the last Friday of the month.

"And so, blackouts exacerbated by an unforgiving heat wave might in fact be the work of foreign Cyberterrorists, all of which are damaging crop harvests and boosting an inflationary spiral. Presidential candidates are blaming President Kinslinger's tardy reactions to these problems and his leading challenger–the Democratic candidate–accuses him of joining a conspiracy that is upsetting the existing world order.

"And this challenger goes so far as to pledge patented solutions to viral, water-borne zoonotic outbreaks and recommend partnerships that will calm the international waters. And if he can do all that, it might make Washington's messy picture a little prettier. No doubt more will come to light as the nation rushes into the final weeks of the battle for the White House. Let us hope for a better outcome this time. Back in 60 for sports…"

Renee turned toward Electra and said,

"Do you think things are as bad as they sound?"

"Electra sat straighter before saying,

"Problems are never as bad as predicted, nor are prizes as good as promised. And let's not worry about what we can't control. But I'm flying back early tomorrow to DC so I can help Eve and Nary starting next Monday. I'll call each night while I'm gone, and everything's set up here so the three of you can keep the place running. I also called Mr. Drummond, and he says you should call him if you need help. So, let's get a head start on tomorrow by getting a good night's sleep…"

Only Renee had breakfast with Electra. She poked at the egg yolks on her plate while talking.

"We can handle things here, but can you handle all the stuff in DC? Maybe I can come along."

Renee's concern pinged Electra's empathy that she hid while replying.

"I need you here to help keep the home and our Brazilian friends AOK. Doing this is the best way you can help me. Now please eat those eggs before all the yellow drips out."

"Yes Mother, I will…"

While Electra used part of the weekend to review her schedule, Nari used some of it to call Nila, who recognized her sister's voice but didn't understand what she wanted to talk about, so she handed the phone to Sanjay.

He listened for several minutes and then said,

"Nila's had little time to follow much on the news because she's devoting herself full time to our son, but I watch everything in the political arena. And I have something that will let you scoop everyone in Washington. India's launching a Martian rover mission before the end of the year. Watch the news tomorrow."

"Aha, this makes the timing of my call even better. I think India and Africa should combine forces. If you do, the combination can become the next superpower. What do you think?"

"Tell me more."

Sanjay listened for five minutes before talking again.

"This has possibilities, but you'll have to facilitate if we move on it. Let me check the political climate here and I will call you in a week."

"That'll do just fine. Bye-bye."

The news Electra was listening to while running early on a mid-October Sunday interrupted its broadcast to deliver a special bullet that forced her to call Commander Starling, whose alert voice came through on the third ring.

"Good morning Britt, this is Electra. Did you just hear the startling news bulletin about India's plan to launch its first unmanned Martian rover mission on Christmas Eve?"

"I did, and what a hackneyed launch date they picked. But that won't bother us too much. Here's the contingency plan we'll roll out. NASA's public relations people will say we're happy to follow them with our manned mission, but we'll launch before the end of November. All you have to do is load your latest version of Aphrodite software the day before. I'll give you the date you'll need to be here as soon as we finalize it. Call me each day, OK?"

"Will do."

Electra used the rest of her run to drain away some of the excitement.

I had planned to talk with Indira after calling Eve, but I'll flip-flop the order. And I'm certain she'll have good news.

Electra invoked the GUI before changing out of her running shorts but grabbed a Coke first. Indira spoke as soon as her GUI appeared.

"Yes, I know about India's intentions, but it doesn't impact mine for Aphrodite. I have already updated the plugins that will exceed even your expectations, but you will have to wait until—" Electra's words barged into Indira's.

"I don't want to wait. Won't you at least give me a clue?"

"Very well, but this is only for you. The transmissions Aphrodite sends will have a separate, doubly encrypted channel that only you can decrypt. And I will—" Electra's enthusiasm barged in again.

"How do I do that, and what will the channel do?"

"I prefer not to spoil the surprise, so I will tell you just before liftoff. I think that's all we need to discuss for the moment, so let us each attend to what we do best."

Indira's GUI disappeared; Electra showered after downing the rest of the Coke.

After eating a breakfast of oatmeal followed by a dark chocolate bar, Electra prepared to call Eve, and when she did, her encrypted cell-phone displayed a troubling message: SCAMMER ALERT. THE

NUMBER YOU ARE CALLING HAS BEEN HACKED. HACKER LISTENING. HACKER I.D. AND NUMBER SAVED. She terminated the call to digest the message.

Gads, someone's tapping into Eve, but thanks to my counter-surveillance security app, I'm ahead of whoever it is. I'll find out who they are when I hack into them, but I can't tell Eve anything about the hack or how I'll eliminate the problem. But not to worry. I'll come up with a workaround.

Eve sounded like her usual busy self when she answered but didn't recognize the caller I.D., so Electra said,

"Hello Eve, it's Electra. Hey, I just wanted to let you know something's come up and I can't help you and Nari right now. Sorry."

"Damn, I guess Nari and I have to go it alone for the time being. Well, thanks anyway."

"But I have a contact who might fill in until I'm available. How about I ask him to call you?"

"What's his name?"

"He says he won't tell you until you meet him in person."

"But how will I know it's the right guy when I get the call?"

"Come on, use your imagination."

"Is he with a CIA or some other government agent?"

"Ask him when you meet him. Look, I can't talk any more, but I'll call you when my time frees up. Bye for now."

Eve poked Nari to wake her up right after Electra disconnected.

"I just got a call from Electra. Let's go out for breakfast. I'll break the bad news then."

Eve started doing that an hour later and early enough, so their booth in a favorite coffee shop had no one within earshot.

"We're sorta SOL. Electra can't help us until her calendar clears, but it's like this. She says she knows a guy who can help, and he'll call me. And if he can't help, he knows another guy."

"So, what's his name?"

"He'll tell me when I meet him in person. Whatcha think?"

"You've been watching way too many spy movies. Did she tell you what code name he'd use so you know it's the right call?"

"Uh, no, but I guess he'll say something that'll tip me off. And she hung up before I could ask if she had anything new about the things that our Democratic candidate is talking about. Sorry."

"Well, don't be too sorry. That Electra is sharp. She'd have told you before she hung up if there was anything else you needed to know right now. So, let's keep chugging along…"

President Kinslinger had no say in what was being planned for him by Bigger Brother. Xing had just told him so during a brief for-his-ears-only call to his covert cell-phone that had just terminated while he sat by himself in the Oval Office.

So all I need to do is sit back and play my statesman-like presidential role as the vote count rolls in on election night, and I can do that. I'm good at sitting back and letting Xing's hackers do the work in Cyberspace and elsewhere. I'll be ready.

Eve went about campaign business as best as possible, but changed plans when an unknown male voice called.

"Eve Cortez, you don't know me, but a guy tells me you need to know me. Meet me at this location and come alone. Here's the date, time, and place. Take good notes. I'm telling you only once…"

Electra had hidden herself hours ago at the location she had given to Eve when she placed the call that faked out Eve. Electra knew from her cell-phone warning that the hacker she had already hacked into was listening and would want to meet Eve and the unidentified contact. That's why she was hiding in a desolate park late at night while flying a surveillance drone and considering options told only to herself.

There should be only one other vehicle besides Eve's coming to this place, and my drone will spot them. I know what I'll do if they get here first, and they should. And if they don't, the lightning brain will figure something out.

Electra kept busy flying the drone until her target vehicle crept into a dark parking spot. Then she recalled the drone, dressed for action, and launched her plan into action.

Xing's two agents dismissed the staggering drunk until he fell close to the driver's door. The guy behind the wheel stepped out to drag the obstacle away but never completed the task. The drunk hit him with two traser bolts before leaping to his feet and doing the same to the fellow in the passenger seat. Then he dragged the stiff on the pavement into the back seat, binding both victims before driving away.

Electra did all the talking while driving.

"Whether or not you can hear me, get set for a mind-altering experience. You will tell me all I want to know or I'll melt your brains. My brain probe is better than any you've ever seen in action. And when I'm done, I'll leave you where you can cool your heels."

Electra let the car roll into the water, carrying with it her victims.

Time for me to run to where I hid my SUV and then drive home. And I can chase down and use at my leisure whatever I've pulled from their brains. Too bad I disappointed Eve by not showing up in my manly facemask, but what she doesn't know won't hurt her. And I'll make sure to keep it that way...

Chapter 25
November 2168
"Countdown to Another Reset"

Videos spewing all day on Social Media during the last day of November showed even more violence than on newscasts. DC police had cordoned off the Capitol using interlocking fences topped with barbed wire, but the well-organized protestors had countered by hoisting ladders and leaping over. Some carried guns; others carried video cams; all used cell-phones to stay coordinated.

Nary and Eve watched and talked as worse turned to even worse late that afternoon. Eve tuned in to another station before saying,

"Kinslinger's not backing down. He's still saying all opposing parties conspired to steal the election. He says he'll lead the charge into the Capitol as soon as the mob breaks in, but he doesn't say when he'll show up to give the command. You think he's got the gonads to do it?"

"He's never shown them. I think he's following orders given elsewhere. Why don't you call Electra. She might know more."

"I've tried but she doesn't pick up, and I don't know where she is. I've left messages, but she hasn't called back. You think she's OK?"

"Don't worry about her. Worry about us. The bomb cyclone bearing down on DC promises to be a wintry blast, but who knows? Maybe it'll chase the mob away when it hits later tonight. We should go home now."

"You're right. We can watch from there as long as the power stays on. But the news'll get even dicier if Russia makes good on its promise to stir up more trouble for NATO. Let's get outta here. Amahl and Zara say they want us with them."

Electra had plans to call no one during the next 48 hours, and few people after that. She would be completely immersed while sitting at her workstation during the pre and post-launch hours of the Mission to Mars scheduled for a secret launch at midnight, and she had the perfect location. She and Indira could talk via her high-priority workstation whenever they wanted.

Electra used the final hours to practice using her Aphrodite software while pretending to listen to the Mission Director drone on and on. She preferred talking with Indira, who always had clever words accompanying singular information.

Indira contacted her again at T-minus three minutes and counting.

"I promised to tell you how to decrypt Aphrodite transmissions. Just ask me when you want it and I will do it for you. And I also promised to tell you what it will do for you. It will make you feel like you're actually onboard the Mission. Don't ask me to say more. Please wait until the Mission is on its way. Now get set for liftoff."

Electra could feel the tension in the Command Center build as the seconds ticked down. The big monitor showed an ethereal image: the launch vehicle bathed in crisscrossing spotlights, vented gasses billowing into blackness.

Nothing stirred as the computer voice announced,

"Three, two, one, liftoff."

Nothing but eyes moved as they saw the spaceship sail away. And then the voice said,

"All monitor clocks have been reset to launch T equal zero. Carry on."

Electra cheered along with everyone, but kept singular words to herself.

I've reset more than my monitor. And I know how to carry on in the Command Center as well as on the Mission. Indira and I will make it so...

www.ingramcontent.com/pod-product-compliance
Lightning Source LLC
Chambersburg PA
CBHW021152310726

48971CB00002B/603